Praise for *Butcher, Baker, Candlestick Taker*, the first book in the Spokane Clock Tower Mysteries

"A vivid and intense historical thriller featuring murder and mystery, mayhem and madness in 1901 Spokane. Meredith can write!" — *New York Times* bestselling author William H. Keith

"From her ingenious title to the well-formed characters with quirks, Patricia Meredith has crafted a mystery that is unique and entertaining. I was never quite sure where this story was taking me, but I was glad to be along for the ride... Meredith's historical knowledge of Spokane shines, as does her mastery of blacksmithing and clocks.... Overall, a strong beginning to a new mystery series!" — Tonya Mitchell, author of *A Feigned Madness*

"A page-turner... The characters were compelling and likable, and the murder itself was something that made me fascinated to discover how everything would come together in the end." — Corin Faye, author of *The Beautiful Era*

"Fantastic historical fiction!" — Ginger Morticia, Bookstagram Reviewer

"Historical mystery with all the Agatha Christie vibes I could want. I think one of the great things that the author does is contain the energy and aura of the turn of the century. The new ideas, the mixing of different cultures, the inventions, and especially all the lovely literary references such as Sir Conan Doyle with Sherlock Holmes, Kipling, etc. The historical details in this are spot on.... This book is just perfect fall reading." — Bibliobrunette, Bookstagram Reviewer

"I was in suspense the whole time." — Alex Fergus, Spokane Historian

"Find a comfy spot to read this and don't be surprised if you can't put it down! The story and characters will have you locked in to find out what happens next and you will not be disappointed. The ending is so unpredictable and exciting you will be on the edge of your seat to solve this mystery! You will be addicted. I laughed so much as her characters have such a sense of humor. There's charm, wit, mystery, irony.... You will love these characters!" — Anne Fischer, Goodreads Reviewer

"I can't get the book out of my mind." — Kathy Buckmaster, Historical Fiction Reader

CUPBOARDS ALL BARED

CUPBOARDS ALL BARED

*Book Two of the
Spokane Clock Tower
Mysteries*

PATRICIA MEREDITH

Games Afoot, LLC

This book is dedicated to my grandmothers:

Patricia Hammond and Julia Rizzo,

faith-filled women of charm and wit

who have enlightened, encouraged, and inspired.

Prologue

Mr. London wished he was a dragon.

Then, instead of simply blowing out ferocious smoke clouds through his mouth and nose, he might also devour anyone who stood in the way of what he wanted.

He just couldn't catch a break. He should have known. He should have *known* things were going too smoothly. He'd made himself invaluable. Done everything required of him and more.

Now it was all gone. Poof.

He blew out more cigarette smoke from between his lips.

He'd lied to give himself a purpose, because that's what he'd been told to do. He'd come to Spokane for one reason, and had stayed in Spokane for another.

And now he found himself pacing the bluff that hung over Hangman Creek, the wind whistling in his ears and biting his red cheeks, threatening a spring rain shower as he looked out across the deep ravine carved over the years by what was now just a creek. A thin, rocky, very slippery path led down the slope to his left, but his feet wanted so desperately to take the shorter way down.

Hangman Creek, it was called, where Colonel Wright hanged a Yakama Indian chief in the 1850s without a trial. The city wanted to call it "Latah Creek" but that name could only be found on maps of the area.

He wondered what they'd call it if they found another body...

One

Friday, May 17, 1901

Spokane, Washington

Thomas Carew finally had something other than food on his mind. But somehow he wished it wasn't so.

When Marian Kenyon had run into the workshop a month ago in a whirl of red curls and flashing green eyes, his heart had stopped in his chest. The sun had blazed through the doorway behind her, silhouetting her petite form in an evergreen overcoat that had only enhanced the remarkable nature of her eyes. For days now he'd been unable to think about anything else but the beauty of her flushed face in that moment.

He knew what it was. Love at first sight. But to say such a thing aloud was to admit believing in such atrocious hyperbole.

It made him sick to his stomach.

No, maybe that was just Mrs. O'Flanagan's breakfast. She was the most recent in a long line of new cooks his sister-in-law had been trying out this month. This one was the first cook he'd met who could over-boil an egg.

Best not to think on it—Mrs. O'Flanagan's breakfast or the dryad of his dreams.

Instead he should focus on the task at hand. Which was more difficult than one would think seeing as it was just more mindless paperwork in preparation for the arrival of President William McKinley and his wife.

The President was due to arrive next week with an entourage that would fill a small country, let alone Spokane, Washington. A train had been arranged for his travels up and down the West Coast, complete with a private car for the President and his wife, two Pullman compartment cars as well as two Pullman sleepers, not to mention a dining and combination car. Traveling with them would be Mrs. McKinley's personal maid and physician, the general agent of the Southern railway, the passenger traffic manager of the Southern Pacific lines, two managers of telegraph companies, almost the entire cabinet, press representatives, stenographers, assistants, assistant stenographers...

And that was just those coming in the President's party. Chairman Black of the McKinley Reception Committee had said the city should expect upward of twenty-five thousand people to visit for the occasion. Public offices and labor of all sorts were to be suspended, the city declaring it a holiday.

It wasn't McKinley's fault he was a popular President, not that Thomas had voted for him. But that was just another long line of thoughts not worth delving into right now.

After the joys of catching a murderer—and probably the most inflammatory one of the century—Thomas was finding it extremely unlikely he would be able to focus on tedious matters like paperwork ever again.

Of course, if he wasn't doing paperwork, he was downstairs in the cells talking to Mrs. Sigmund, or as the newspapers called her, "the Baker."

He and Bernard were required to speak with her every day, to follow up on any questions they had while they closed up their investigation and prepared for the trial that probably would never happen.

But then, that wasn't really Thomas's problem now, was it? That was Bernard's. And he could have it, along with every-thing else that came with catching a murderer—especially the good stuff.

Unlike Thomas, who was right back at his desk with the pa-perwork piled high, Bernard was still enjoying pats on the back and "well done, chum" congratulations, thanks to the capture of the notorious person who claimed to have started the Great Spokane Fire back in 1889.

Bernard's five minutes of fame had stretched to a month. It felt like he'd continue forever in the spotlight, reaching a renown to rival the catching of Jack the Ripper, if he was ever caught, and Thomas had to admit, the Baker was almost as gruesome.

If his twin dared to say one more thing to him about the lauds and commendations he was receiving, he was going to—

"You'll never guess what I just received in the mail."

Speak of the devil.

Thomas turned his glare from level three down to level one—so as not to burn Bernard to a crisp—before looking up from his work.

"A congratulatory letter from the President himself?"

"You're not too far off the mark, actually." Bernard held out a piece of expensive-looking paper before Thomas's eyes.

The letterhead read "From the Office of the Washington Governor" and taking up half of the bottom of the page was a signature that would be difficult to mistake: John Rankin Rogers.

"He wrote to thank me for the enlightening dinner conversation we shared last night. Isn't that nice?" Bernard asked, his dark eyes alight.

Thomas couldn't stop the puff of air that escaped him. He shook his head. "I have to admit, that's pretty spiffing."

Bernard turned the letter back toward himself as though he didn't already have the thing memorized.

"It is, isn't it." His barrel chest was puffed up more than usual—almost as large as the gut he was gaining thanks to all the congratulatory dinners he'd been invited to enjoy.

* * *

"'Congratulations on catching the most intriguing deviant of our time,'" Bernard read from the letter. "'Intriguing deviant,'" Bernard repeated. "She is that, eh, Thomas?"

His brother just shrugged and turned back to his paperwork, making it clear he was too busy to offer further congratulations at the moment. Bernard had hoped for at least a handshake or a rough slap on the shoulder. But his twin had been growing oddly distant over the past month. Then again, Bernard had been oddly busy. It seemed everyone wanted to talk to the Great Detective Carew.

And why shouldn't they? To have solved such a twisted case in just four days? It was quite a feat.

Then again…he couldn't help but wonder… Sometimes he felt a little, what was it? Guilty? Because he hadn't actually solved the case, now, had he? The culprit had walked in, assumed he had all the pieces, and started defending herself with her story. And the Baker's part in all of it? Even the murderer hadn't been aware of her involvement!

He wished they could just send her to the Medical Lake asylum—all fresh and new, built just ten years ago, with a psychiatric wing perfectly designed for such a person. But no, they'd been struck with a smallpox epidemic in the north wing of the women's side, so as part of their precautions they were holding off on taking new patients. No matter how insane, apparently.

Bernard sighed and folded up the letter. He paused before returning to his desk, looking at what Thomas was currently working on, his neat handwriting filling the page.

"Writing to *The Spokesman-Review*?" he asked.

Thomas took a deep breath before lifting his head and blinking his eyes above the thin line of a smile. "As you're reading over my shoulder, I know you can see that yes, I am writing to *The Spokesman*. Was there anything the Great Detective Carew would like to add about the measures the police are taking to ensure President McKinley's visit will be not only entertaining but safe?"

Bernard rubbed his thick black mustache, choosing to ignore the heavy cloud of sarcasm emanating from his clean-shaven twin brother. "Well, considering the fact that Chairman Black received official word today from Secretary Cortelyou that the

President will no longer be coming, I'm not certain the information will be greatly received."

Thomas threw down his fountain pen, ink spattering across his words. "Well, that's just great! This morning's paper said Mrs. McKinley was rallying!"

"It appears she's not rallied enough to warrant a continuation of their journey. Word is they head straight back to the East Coast once she's well enough."

Thomas crossed his arms across his chest. "How come nobody deemed it worthy to tell me this somewhat important fact?"

Bernard shrugged. "I just did."

Thomas clamped his teeth shut with a click. "Thanks." He rolled his eyes and shook his head, then began cleaning the small mess he'd made.

If anyone else had spoken to him like that, Bernard would've quickly reminded him to show some respect to his superior. As a detective, he was above patrolmen like Thomas. But no one else *would* ever speak to him like that. Everyone else thought he was marvelous, even the other detectives who had always treated him like larva who needed to be kept in his place. Instead, he'd turned into a butterfly beyond their expectations, and even Detective Burns tipped his derby to him when he saw him, instead of hiding pins on his chair like a schoolboy.

Besides, Thomas should have known the news was coming. The First Lady had been reported as being at death's door for the better part of the week, and yesterday's front page headline had read "President Can Not Come North." So it wasn't *his* fault Thomas was choosing to be moody when Bernard was just trying to be helpful. Think how silly Thomas would have sounded turning this into *The Spokesman.* He should be grateful Bernard saved his hide.

Bernard decided to look beyond his brother's immature attitude for now and take the high road.

"Speaking of *The Spokesman,* I've finally found a new boarder to replace Prescot."

Thomas balled up his ruined paper and tossed it in the can at his side.

"He's a newspaper man," Bernard continued. "Came over from Tacoma to work with his cousin at the paper. When he interviewed me this morning about the Baker, he mentioned he'd love to get the 'inside scoop' as he called it."

Thomas pulled out a new piece of paper from a drawer.

"I figured since Prescot moved up to the House, and we still need a boarder, I'd offer him to stay with us for a week or two."

Bernard didn't have to clarify to which house he was referring. They'd taken to calling the late Miss Mitchell's house "the House" since it had become the house on the hill that continuously drew them to it. It was also where they'd discovered the wondrous and marvelous Mrs. Curry and her talents for cooking, though they'd originally gone there for a theft which had turned into a murder investigation.

Thomas dipped his fountain pen into the inkwell along the top of his desk, pressing the small crescent on the outside that allowed him to draw the ink into the pen, holding it for a couple seconds while it filled the small sac within. "It's your house, Bernard. You don't need to ask my permission."

"I'm not." Bernard shuffled his feet. "I'm telling you. Just thought you'd like to know so you weren't surprised when you came home for dinner tonight and found an investigative reporter seated beside you."

Thomas twisted the ring closed on his pen once it was full and wiped the outside with a pen wiper. "Can't wait to meet him."

Bernard gave up. He turned around and stalked back to his desk, letting his full weight fall on his heels just because he knew it irritated Thomas.

* * *

The Red Rogue was at it again.

And feeling like a deceptive nincompoop the whole time she did it.

Marian had told herself she was through.

But even though she'd inherited her grandmother's home free and clear, the interest from her grandfather's investments was not enough to live on in the booming economy and growing city of Spokane. She'd thought about returning to her job photographing people's homes, but as that had always been her way of casing a place before her nightly escapades, she'd worried that might be too close to temptation. So instead she'd found an occupation where she wouldn't even think about her alternate persona of the Red Rogue. What could be better than as a companion to a detective's wife?

Unfortunately, so far it hadn't made it any easier for her to quit. For the past month, she'd kept one foot firmly planted out the door and on the nearest rooftop, part of her ready to leave at the slightest hint that they distrusted her.

Detective Bernard Carew, the man who'd sniffed out her connection with Miss Mitchell's house—albeit not *her* connection exactly, but the Red Rogue's—was the very man for whom she now worked, which only heightened the risk of the whole venture. But that was what made it exciting.

If she didn't have that, she'd merely be a companion.

Nain would have approved of the Carew family, would have been filled with joy to know Marian had found a new loving home, and a respectable position.

Starting a new job, moving into a house with a detective and an officer of the law, not to mention her friend Archie Prescot knowing the truth, only emphasized the fact that she must give up the Red Rogue part of her life, no matter how difficult it might be.

So why couldn't she stop?

Maybe it was because the Maid Marian part of her felt she was still needed. Every time she passed a hungry street urchin, she couldn't stop the way her heart reached out to them, wanting to do more than hand them a loaf of bread or a couple coins.

And so, she snuck out at night, hitting the houses mostly located on the South Hill, where the rich lived in their swell mansions, feasting on food they never finished and throwing parties that cost as much as a week's wages. They lived in safety, while the men in the mines they owned toiled and died on a less-than-average day's wage.

And if they suddenly found themselves short a couple candlesticks, a few expensive baubles and trinkets from their travels abroad? They probably wouldn't even notice.

But those candlesticks and baubles and trinkets would mean the world to that hungry street urchin.

As Thomas Love Peacock had written in her favorite book,

Maid Marian, "William took from the poor and gave to the rich, and Robin takes from the rich and gives to the poor: and therein is Robin illegitimate; though in all else he is a true prince."

Marian closed the back door of Nain's house and removed the burgundy overcoat and driver's cap that were the apparel of the Red Rogue.

"For the last time," she said aloud, standing before Nain's chair in the living room.

The armless daisy-printed chair stood before Nain's fireplace in quiet acceptance of Marian's claim.

"*You cannot make an omelet without breaking eggs,*" she heard Nain's voice say.

So perhaps not entirely quiet.

"I know it'll be difficult to give it up, but I mean it. I'm done," she said, this time with more emphasis, wrapping the coat and cap together into a small ball.

Then she turned on her heel and marched down the hall to her old bedroom. The bedroom that had been hers since she'd come to live with Nain at a young age.

She barely remembered her parents. Just the faint glimmer of a smile, but that was mostly because it was the same smile that had crossed Nain's face whenever she looked at her. Her father's smile.

In her bedroom, Marian shoved the heavy dresser over two feet before carefully lifting the loose floorboards hidden beneath it. When she'd discovered them, Marian had hidden her diary inside, even though it had only been filled with the musings of a child unaware of the complexities of the real world.

But since her return from Seattle, she'd been using it for quite a different purpose. Beneath those floorboards was hidden her treasure trove, to her more precious than that of Jim Hawkins in *Treasure Island*.

She'd sold most of the larger pieces in order to finance a personal mourning wardrobe, so she wouldn't have to continue borrowing from Nain's closet, an act that had felt uncomfortable to say the least.

What remained now were her favorite priceless first editions and her first pair of stolen candlesticks. She'd taken to stealing a set at every house after reading *Les Misérables*, in a sort of ironic tribute to the fact that a set of stolen candlesticks had launched her into a new life, just like Jean Valjean.

She gently set down the rolled up cap and coat amongst the collection.

"'Parting is such sweet sorrow.'"

With a heavy sigh, she buried the Red Rogue in her bedroom.

Then she stood and returned the dresser to its place before moving on to the next hardest thing.

One by one, she wrapped Nain's things in newspaper and covered the furniture in sheets, shutting the door on each room as she completed it, until all that was left was Nain's chair.

"'I have too grieved a heart to take a tedious leave,'" Marian quoted, even as she stood there, holding the folded sheet to her chest, vacillating over whether to cover the chair or leave it as it had always been.

Everything you have in this world is just borrowed for a short time, the chair said softly. *This is the beginning of anything you want.*

Marian knelt before the chair, placing one hand on its soft cushion.

"Perhaps," Marian said, finding herself once more arguing with a memory. "But as you used to say, 'You know it's love when you have been saying goodbye how many times but still you're not ready to leave.'"

There was no escaping death. Perhaps it was part of what gave life its meaning.

* * *

Peter Bach had been blessed with a gift: an ability to draw people in with his chiseled cheekbones and striking, full beard, coupled with his unassuming nature which made him likable and charming. When people spoke with him, they found themselves saying things they wouldn't normally have shared with anyone outside immediate family. So naturally, when he'd decided he needed to try a new career on for size, he'd picked being a reporter.

Picking a name had been a bit more difficult.

His friends had called him "Peter Piper" after the Pied Piper of Hamlin, who could whistle the rats out of every corner. Given the alliterative nature of the name, however, he'd felt he couldn't claim Piper, and instead had opted for Bach as a surname, given its musical connotations.

Of course, attracting rats did mean one was bitten occasionally. He hadn't *meant* to unmask one of the leading lumber magnates in Tacoma as an adulterer with three mistresses on the side on his third day on the job. But, really, was it his fault? Shouldn't the man have been more careful, more prudent, since he was from a family of such high standing?

Peter understood how important a man's background was

to his reputation. A year ago, he'd moved out of his family's inglorious home near Commencement Bay, refusing to live and die a fisherman like his old man. And so, through a variety of jobs and names, he'd moved up in the world both physically and mentally, from Old Tacoma around North 30th Street with its modest shops and homes up to New Tacoma and an apartment above a grocer on Pacific Avenue.

But that was his old life. At first, Peter had thought being exiled to the wilder eastern side of the state meant the end of his newest career path. Fortunately, it had turned out that Spokane was a lot like Tacoma: a small town that wanted to be a big city. And that meant plenty of social-climbers with skeletons in their carriage houses.

His cousin even had quite a nice setup at *The Spokesman-Review*, and best luck of all, the Baker's recent arrest was turning heads and pages, perfect for a go-getter like himself willing to do anything to learn the truth.

Unfortunately, no one had been allowed to speak with her yet—no one but police, at any rate. They'd kept her confined to a jail cell in the bowels of City Hall. Peter wondered what they were hiding...

But luck had still been in his favor—it usually was—and at his interview this morning with Detective Carew, he'd landed an inside informer position by acquiring an invitation to stay at his home as a boarder. His cousin Daniel had cursed his good luck. He hoped that perhaps the next step would be a chance to speak with the Baker herself.

Now he sat in the front room of the Carew residence, overly decorated with Swiss bear furniture, drinking tea with the lady of the house. Mrs. Carew's flaxen hair was as blonde as his beard, her eyes an intelligent blue, but she was trapped in a wheelchair, causing Peter to question why a man as broad and strong as Bernard Carew had allowed himself to be tied down by an invalid.

The quiet, polite young lady who sat beside her in somber black was of good form and moderate breeding. And yet she, too, had bound herself to this incapacitated woman. It was a shame to waste such beauty.

"I'll not beat around the bush, Mr. Bach," said Mrs. Carew. "I hear the reason for your stay with us is to acquire further information on the subject of Eleanor Sigmund."

"Elean—yes, the Baker." Peter nodded and sipped his tea, hiding his surprise that Mrs. Carew had referred to the Baker by her given name, rather than her infamous title.

"You must understand, then, that my companion, Miss Kenyon, was a friend of Mrs. Sigmund's, so we only refer to her by her true name in this home."

Perhaps Peter hadn't hidden his surprise, after all. He glanced at Miss Kenyon, whose eyes over the rim of her teacup dared him to contradict this statement.

"Of course, Mrs. Carew. And I shall naturally do the same as long as I am in your charming company. I had not realized there would be so many people attached to the case under one roof. I seem to have struck gold."

Mrs. Carew merely tightened her lips and reached for her scone. She was going to be a difficult one to warm up to. He attempted to change the topic of conversation. "I understand Detective Carew's brother was also involved with the case?"

Miss Kenyon and Mrs. Carew exchanged a glance.

"It might be best, Mr. Bach, not to speak of the case with both brothers at the same time," Mrs. Carew said delicately. "Speaking with them individually will provide you with two unique yet cohesive points of view."

Peter nodded and sipped politely, smiling over the rim of his cup at the wooden bear crawling up the leg of Miss Kenyon's chair. He had struck gold all right. And maybe a few rats.

* * *

Some days Roslyn Carew felt like she was nothing more than a talking carriage. Only, her carriage couldn't take her anywhere. Instead it inhibited her movement, like putting a saddle on a horse only to have it go in a constant circle on a lead. She wanted to gallop. To run. To be free.

But she was limited to stretching muscles only in her mind, making her a voracious reader. She had long since given up on reading novels and moved on to the wonders of discovery to be found in books of learning. Philosophy, psychoanalysis, astronomy, physics—new and old sciences, they all appealed to her.

Unlike other women who usually turned to the small women's column found in *The Spokesman-Review* alongside recipes and gossip of the week, she read the paper cover to cover, and then when *The Chronicle* arrived in the evenings, she did the same. The blatant, gory details of murders and hangings intrigued her, but she found herself even more fascinated by the anatomy behind the event: Why exactly *would* a man's body require dismemberment before being cooked in a blacksmith's forge? How might one go about doing such a thing?

And when the local papers had nothing new to offer, her magazines from across the nation and some from overseas kept her active mind engaged. She'd taught herself Italian, Spanish, and French, finding them to be similar enough in their Romantic style that she could pass between the three with relative ease. She'd even become fluent enough in French to read the papers directly from Paris, though she preferred the scientific journals to the fashion mags.

So much knowledge in the head of someone considered an "invalid" was often overlooked, and she'd thought so many times that she'd make a decent detective for that reason. Who better than someone taken for granted to manipulate the unwitting into revealing all their secrets? Of course, the police would never hire a woman, much less one in a wheelchair, no matter how intelligent she might be.

She'd been blessed in finding the Carew brothers—both of them were well-read and remarkably intelligent—but it was Bernard's kindness that had won her to him, and his persistent love overtures.

No one else would think it to look at him, as he was quite a bear of a man, but he was soft inside like pudding when it came to Roslyn. She knew he'd do anything for her, and she for him.

And for that reason, among others, she'd taken it upon herself to find an exceptional cook for the house. She'd allowed Mrs. Hill to stay on for far too long, but as she fired the fourth cook in a month, she remembered why she'd eventually settled on her. At least she could boil an egg—sometimes. She was starting to worry she'd never find someone the equal of Mrs. Curry up at the House, whom both brothers claimed was the best cook they'd ever met—and she had to admit, after sampling the meals she'd sent home, that Mrs. Curry would indeed be quite the catch. But the good cook refused to leave the inventor who had inherited the Mitchell estate, so there was no way of persuading her to come to them.

Once again, her poor companion, Marian, would have to take over in the kitchen. She filled in the gap quite willingly, saying always that cooking reminded her of her Nain, but then again, *everything* reminded her of her Nain. The girl was grieving, Roslyn knew, but sometimes she wished the conversation didn't always turn back to her dead grandmother.

Other than the constant Nainisms, Marian was proving to be quite a remarkable find. She was sweet, helpful, and surprisingly intelligent and well-read. She could hold her own in a conversation, even when Roslyn didn't agree with her take on something.

In fact, Roslyn was beginning to think she wasn't the only one who'd taken a shine to her. Thomas, who always had something to say, had been unusually silent of late whenever Marian was in the room. Of course, he was also often giving the cold shoulder to his brother ever since *The Spokesman-Review* completely ignored his involvement in the catching of the Baker.

She understood his jealousy—she had certainly been the one overlooked on several occasions—but she was waiting for Bernard to ask her for her opinion or figure it out for himself. It had been a month, however, and she was beginning to consider how she might subtly bring up the topic.

After the departure of the new boarder to collect his things, she now sat with Marian in the kitchen, chopping vegetables on a wooden board in her lap to be of assistance.

"Really, Mrs. Carew, I don't mind doing that," said Marian for the third time.

"If you try to take this knife from me I might 'slip' and slice your finger off and then every time you look at the stub you'll be reminded what happens to those who think I cannot do something for myself." She focused on her cutting as she spoke and then looked up with a smile.

Marian smiled in return from where she dressed the roast that would accompany the vegetables in a long day's stew for supper. "Oh, Mrs. Carew, you know I would never think such a thing. I merely meant I did not think the lady of the house should have to find herself working as a cook's assistant."

"I suppose it is somewhat uncouth, but then I've never been one to stand on ceremony." Roslyn studied the young woman with her sleeves forced up above her elbows, an apron protecting the black mourning gown that emphasized her fashionably pale skin. "And how, pray tell, did you come to have such fine cooking skills yourself? I know you had a maid growing up, didn't you have a cook, as well?"

"My Nain"—there she was—"insisted on doing all the cooking herself in our home. Said no one else could bake apple pie the way my grandfather liked it. The only hired help she'd allow was a maid...like...Eleanor..."

And of course, naturally the conversation had turned to Eleanor, the ghost that occupied Marian's other shoulder opposite Nain, though she was not dead. Yet.

Roslyn ignored the specter. "And how did the closing up of your grandmother's house go this morning?"

It took a moment for the depressing cloud to roll away from her brow. Finally, Marian jingled the key to Nain's house, which hung from her chatelaine along with the key to the Carews'.

"It's done," she said with a sigh. "But I intend to stop by every now and then to make sure everything's all right. Wouldn't want thieves to think it's the perfect unguarded location."

"At least if they did, you'd know who to call," Roslyn said with a smile. After all, even though Bernard had solved a murder case, that didn't mean he was removed from the more normal jobs of the Spokane Police detectives: that of thieves, drunkards, and ruffians.

"Thank you again, Mrs. Carew."

Roslyn set down her knife. "For what?"

Marian wiped the back of her hand across her cheek distractedly as she looked up from her work. "For inviting me into your home and life. I was feeling quite lost and I...really needed it."

Rosslyn smiled. "I do wish you'd call me Roslyn, my dear. As my companion, I hope you'll look upon me as a friend rather than a mistress."

"I suppose it has been almost a month since I moved in, though I can hardly believe so many days have passed by already."

"Yes, somehow we've survived Mrs. Harwell's 'world-famous blood sausage,' Mrs. Dougherty's corned beef—or foot, it was hard to tell—as well as Mrs. Malone's British tea cakes—or rocks."

"And Mrs. O'Flanagan's dreadful boiled eggs this morning." Marian wrinkled her nose.

"Ah, yes. I never thought someone with such credentials might never have cooked an egg before. I still cannot believe that she tried to tell me all boiled eggs are green on the inside." Roslyn laughed, and Marian joined in.

* * *

Marian missed laughing. These days it seemed the only times she did so was when she was with Archie Prescot. She wished he hadn't decided to move out of the Carews when she moved in, but she'd gotten the distinct impression he'd felt it improper for him to remain, and he could certainly accomplish so much more living up at the House with his colleague, Mr. Matsumoto, with whom he did his sound theory research.

She wondered what they were working on today.

Marian sliced through another carrot, focusing on the even back and forth of her knife. Nain had taught her knife skills from an early age.

"Never look away from your knife while it's in motion," she'd said. "Keep your fingers curled, so should you nick anything, it's only a knuckle and not an entire finger tip. Always wash and dry your knives immediately after use, to ensure they remain clean and free of rust."

Marian had run her fingers along the cuts in the cutting board in her kitchen before she'd closed up the house that morning. It was good for her to be out of Nain's house officially. Perhaps by doing so the dream-memories wouldn't be so terrible. She'd been plagued by them almost every night since her return, though now they tended to be about Eleanor, not Nain.

Eleanor hadn't known she'd been living a double life, with a secondary personality that sometimes took over to defend her against abusive husbands. Or she had known, but she'd hidden it? Or...something like that. It didn't make much sense to her, but Roslyn had promised to look into it, to do some research, which was her strength and certainly not Marian's. Marian was a woman of action, while Roslyn was a woman of the mind. She actually understood the psychology of the problem in a way Marian just couldn't. And it was going to take all the best doctors to figure out what exactly was wrong with Eleanor.

But the whole double personality thing wasn't what haunted Marian. It was the look on Eleanor's face when she'd walked through that workshop door and her eyes had connected with Marian's... She'd known Marian had figured it out.

Marian hadn't even bothered speaking with Eleanor about it first. Instead, she'd rushed right to the police.

Why? That was what bothered Marian, had tormented her for a month now. *Why* had she done that? Why, upon making that connection, had she felt the need to run to the Carews to tell them she knew what Eleanor had done? Why hadn't she, instead, taken Eleanor aside and given her a chance to explain herself?

If she had, if Eleanor had still told her the truth, and the Baker had still revealed herself as Eleanor's whatever she was...would Marian have reacted differently in a private setting? Would she have forgiven Eleanor for murdering abusive husbands who deserved it anyway? Would she have shared about her own secondary personality and her temptation to steal? Would she have connected with Eleanor, or even the Baker?

"If ifs and ands were pots and pans, there'd be no work for tinkers' hands," Nain's voice calmly reminded her.

She shook her head and turned her focus back to the meal at hand, wishing her doubts and worries were as easy to trim as a cut of beef.

* * *

Archie Prescot was knocking down walls with sound.

Walls of glass, that is.

One of his favorite stories growing up had been the story of Joshua and the battle of Jericho. He'd been very young when he'd first suggested to his father that one day, he would bring down walls with sound, just like Joshua.

His father had laughed and said, "These days, men are more interested in building walls between people and countries, rather than breaking them down."

His father had misunderstood.

Of course, as he stood next to the Japanese inventor, Matsumoto, he wondered if maybe both of them had been correct.

Through experiments with sound theory, he and Matsumoto planned to break down walls in many different ways, but for today, they were starting with glass.

Matsumoto set up the thin pane of plate glass between two vices from his workshop and then took a step back.

Bang. Bang. Bang.

The glass wall shattered.

Fifty feet away, Archie stood, banging one of Mrs. Curry's old cooking pots with a metal spoon in front of a large, conical funnel aimed at the wall.

"It seems it does not matter whether we use a brass, tin, or steel pot," he called out.

Matsumoto pushed his white shirt sleeves higher up his arms, though they were already rolled above his elbows, and pulled out a pad of paper and a pencil from his blacksmith's apron pocket. Although blind, and therefore unable to read his own handwriting, he was still capable of reading and writing. He and Archie had taken to using a thick pencil that pressed into paper with something firm behind it, in a way that engraved the words onto the page, allowing Matsumoto to feel the words while Archie could still see them.

"I count five attempts with each," Matsumoto called back. "Shall we try the cast iron next?"

Archie nodded as he approached to assist in sweeping the broken glass bits safely to the ground, and then realized he should probably say his yes aloud, even though Matsumoto had the uncanny ability of using his hearing to "see" far more than one would expect of a blind man. It was this ability which had allowed him to continue in his trade as a blacksmith, even though most people would think blindness the end of his career.

Matsumoto replaced the notepad and headed to the workshop to grab another glass pane from the collection set neatly inside, well away from the funnel so as to ensure they were kept whole until it was time.

Archie was pretty certain he was living the dream. Getting to work alongside an absolutely brilliant mind on something that he'd thought only interested him, while also working on his clockwork masterpiece for which he'd traveled from Connecticut? That was pretty extraordinary. Even though Matsumoto had offered him free room and board in exchange for his assistance with his research, Archie had insisted on paying him the stipend the Seth Thomas Company had sent along with him for lodging. It was the least he could do.

Matsumoto needed the money, he knew, to hire new staff, seeing as the butler had disappeared after faking his references, the chauffeur had been murdered, and the maid was currently in jail. They didn't need a new butler—it wasn't like anyone was going to come out here to visit them—but they would need a new maid. The chauffeur question was still up in the air, though, as they'd considered selling the automobile that had only recently been acquired by the previous owner. Archie realized that for either of them to be able to keep the thing in working order, they'd have to learn a whole new set of skills, but for now he thought they should hold onto it. If anything, it might have parts that would be useful to their experiments.

Especially his Big Idea.

The sound engine. In his head and on paper he'd been working on a theory that used vibrations in water to turn gears, thereby creating movement with sound as the force—a rather inexpensive resource when compared to the electric and gas combustion engines on which automobiles currently ran. But so far, it wasn't an actual thing. That was where Hayate Matsumoto came in.

Matsumoto had designed a sound gun that combined his ironwork skills with something he called "echolocation." It had the possibility for multiple uses: from assisting others afflicted in their ability to see, to a weapon that could maim rather than kill, which might even end wars before they could begin. Like Archie, however, he didn't have a prototype that *worked* as yet. They hoped that through the combination of Matsumoto's experiments with sound and Archie's familiarity with complex small machines as a clockmaker, they might be able to begin making prototypes of their ideas.

Thus far, they'd managed to work together amicably, but Archie had worked with others before on projects and things had not ended well. At least, not for him.

Then again, if they could survive both of them being suspected of murder they could probably survive anything.

The events of last month had rattled him a bit, what with being considered as a possible "butcher" by his previous landlords, but in the end, the Carews had also become good friends.

And then there was Marian. He sighed. He could almost smell her seated beside him, laughing at his words, and joking about the trials they'd survived together since their chance meeting not so long ago. Discussing books and desperately trying to avoid the subject he knew she wanted to talk about: her secret past as a thief.

He sighed again and tried to turn his thoughts back to their experiment.

Once Matsumoto had the new glass pane in place, Archie hit the cast iron pot, and a low, reverberating tone like a gong rang out and through the funnel toward the glass pane. But this time, the glass did nothing. He tried again, trying different parts of the pan and hitting them repeatedly in quick succession, but nothing worked.

"I suppose that explains why the Crystal Palace of the Great Exhibition was made of cast iron and glass," Archie said as he crossed to where Matsumoto stood.

Matsumoto nodded and ran a finger over his chin, considering their next move, giving Archie a chance to catch his reflection in the glass. Like the dog in Aesop's fables, he studied his reflection and didn't like what he saw.

He'd given up his attempt at a fashionable mustache after realizing it would never look like anything more than a caterpillar, but that unfortunately left his face bare for all to see, other than his frog-eyed glasses. He was cursed with cherub's cheeks and two chins—four if he tilted his head down just right—that would have been adorable on a baby but were less than admirable on a man who'd be thirty this year. The roundness of his features didn't stop at his neck, either, but continued in curves upon curves all the way down to his toes—or at least he imagined so, for he hadn't seen them in years.

He wished he'd been born into a time when the girth of a man symbolized great wealth and power. If he'd been born a redhead he might have been able to pull off a worthy impression of King Henry VIII in his later years.

But he wasn't redheaded—dull black curls instead—and this wasn't the 15th century—or whenever it was the king had made his name as a wife-killer.

His thoughts returned to the beautiful redhead that was a part of his life and he sighed once more. There was nothing for it. He was doomed never to be his Maid Marian's Robin Hood, but only ever her Friar Tuck.

* * *

Bernard leaned back at his desk with his hands folded beneath his chin. He tried not to look at the letter from the governor, but his eyes kept flicking to it. Finally, he threw open a drawer, tossed the letter in, and slammed the drawer closed again.

What did he care what Thomas thought. He was acting just like when they were younger and their father had complimented Bernard on his memorization of the entirety of Hamlet's "to be or not to be" speech. Thomas had been upset because he'd helped Bernard memorize it, had offered him ways of remembering which line was next by acting out the lines in a sort of sign language. Yet when Bernard tried to tell their father this, he'd merely smiled toward Thomas and then continued in his congratulations to Bernard since *he* was "the one who'd performed it so eloquently."

Was it really Bernard's fault Thomas wasn't getting any credit? Perhaps he could say more when the interviews came, but he felt he did try. The papers just weren't interested, really, in the solving of the crime. For now, they wanted to know all the juicy details about the Baker, since Chief Witherspoon wasn't letting anyone speak to her outside of the Carews as yet.

Bernard wasn't sure if this was a decision of protection or promotion, as by hiding her away he was creating a great hubbub of interest, which would undoubtedly be good publicity for the police department as they fought the politics of possible cutbacks.

"Detective Carew."

Bernard looked up to see Sergeant Hollway's mustache headed his way—for it was impossible not to notice the immense thing on his face before realizing there was a small, thin man behind it. The facial hair demanded Bernard's focus before Hollway stepped aside with a wave of his hand.

"This man would like to speak with a detective," was all Hollway said by way of introduction as a hobo plopped into a chair beside Bernard's desk, and Hollway disappeared back to his place as the gatekeeper of the station.

It was like the man had been soaking in gin in the bottom of an oil can packed with horse manure. Bernard politely breathed through his mouth as he pulled out a piece of paper and his fountain pen.

"How may I help you?" he asked, turning to the hobo, his red-rimmed eyes studying Bernard's feet warily, as though he found something familiar in the dirt on their soles.

He sniffled and brought his fingertip up toward his nose, but that was all Bernard saw, for he averted his eyes to study his pen for a minute before returning his gaze. The hobo's eyes were red and watery and his large, Roman nose hovered above a mouth full of blackened and yellowed smoker's teeth, the lines around his mouth and chin caked in dirt. Had the man been eating out of the sewer as well as living in it?

Bernard cleared his throat and tried again, louder this time. "Sergeant Hollway said you wanted to speak to a detective?"

It was difficult to guess the man's age under all that filth and rags, but he might've been a soldier once upon a time. Maybe he'd returned from the Spanish-American war without all he'd left with. It had happened to many.

The hobo looked at Bernard's elbow and then back at his feet. Bernard began to wonder if the man had lied. Maybe he'd just wanted a place to sit down for a few moments in a real chair.

"I..." He paused, as though searching for his voice.

The hobo rubbed his hands together—the fingernails bit to the quick and caked with grime, which probably explained how the dirt had gotten on his mouth, too.

Bernard was not a patient man, but he took a deep breath and tapped his pen to signify he was ready to take the man's statement, no matter what it ended up being.

Finally, the hobo started again and this time slurred out seven words: "I saw a body in Hangman Creek."

* * *

Thomas licked his sticky fingers one by one. There was nothing quite like Millie Lawson's cinnamon rolls. Walter Lawson was a lucky man who willingly shared his weekly bounty with Thomas—perhaps only after Thomas irritated him to the point of offering one, but nonetheless, he was a good Christian man all for it.

He'd just decided he was going to grab a cup of coffee to wash down the crumbs when his twin stomped up to his desk. A smell followed him, and it wasn't a pleasant one.

"Good heavens, Bernard." He swiped the air in front of his nose. "Whatever soap Roslyn has been making you use, she needs to find a spice blend that's less...manure-y."

Bernard frowned and thumbed over his broad shoulder to a stooped figure behind him. "We've got another case."

Thomas tilted back in his chair to get a better look at the hobo. This one was particularly mournful and maintained a fixed gaze on Bernard's knees.

"'We' you say? Since when does the Great Detective need assistance?"

"Move your behind or I'll tell Captain Coverly you enjoy walking the beat at night."

Thomas shoved back his chair. "As usual, you know best, Detective," Thomas said with a small bow.

Bernard spun on his heel and stalked away, taking the hobo with him. Thomas pulled on his helmet and coat with a sigh and followed them out of City Hall and into the streets, heading west.

He kept his thoughts to himself until they had let the streetcar pass them twice without flagging it down and still they were walking due west.

"May I ask where we're headed?"

"Hangman Creek," Bernard said gruffly, keeping his eyes forward, his long strides moving at a pace not much slower than a streetcar, anyway.

Thomas almost asked why they hadn't caught a streetcar if that was true, seeing as it was a good mile and a half walk, but then considered the hobo who must have brought them the case. No streetcar would pick them up with him in tow. A backward glance revealed the hobo had vanished from their company, though.

Rather than point this out to Bernard, Thomas tried a different tack.

"What happened at the creek? Someone steal his sleeping spot?" Thomas asked.

"Something like that. He found a body."

Thomas whistled.

Bernard looked over his shoulder but then stopped, raising his heavy eyebrows in surprise when he realized the hobo had left them.

"He told me he was sleeping in his patch last night when

he heard something heavy roll down the bluff from Browne's Addition and hit the creek-bed with a splash. When he went to investigate, he found a body."

Thomas winced. He imagined the body was not in the best condition after such a tumble. The bluff was covered in sharp rocks, and only a steep, narrow path led down to the creek, no more than a deer path somewhat widened by the use of tramps like the hobo.

Bernard gestured toward a coming streetcar. Once aboard, they couldn't very well speak about the case, so it wasn't until they'd disembarked on Pacific Avenue, as close to the bluff as possible, that he could resume his questions. But as soon as their feet hit the pavement, Bernard started his marching pace west again, the houses steadily growing larger by the block as they traversed the neighborhood that boasted the mansions of the monied elite: lawyers, doctors, and investors who'd scored big in the mines of Idaho and Montana.

"Male or female?" Thomas asked.

"What?"

"You were telling me about the body the hobo found. Male or female?"

Bernard shrugged. "Don't know."

"Why didn't he come straight to the police last night?"

"Don't know."

"You didn't ask him or he didn't tell you?"

Bernard came to a sudden stop again, and Thomas nearly collided with him. He took a deep breath. "I know you're frustrated with me right now, Thomas, but I do know how to do my job."

Thomas bit back a quippy reply and simply nodded.

"He didn't look closely at the body last night, he just ran, no doubt thinking we'd consider him a suspect. I'm sure that's the same reason he didn't report it till now, after he'd worked up the courage to inform us."

Thomas nodded and started the march this time, but he didn't get far before he heard their names being yelled and they turned to see a young man hailing them.

* * *

Peter had gone to the police station after moving his things into the Carews' home, only to learn he'd just missed the brothers as they headed out for a new case. He'd followed the desk sergeant's instructions to get to Hangman Creek via streetcar and was pleased to find they hadn't begun without him.

He ran up to them on the sidewalk, and he had to look twice as he finally saw the two brothers for the first time together.

"You're twins!" he exclaimed.

From his interview with Bernard, he'd assumed he was the older of the two, which he still might have thought initially given Bernard's heavy eyebrows, mustache, and larger structure. Thomas was shorter by just a few inches, slighter in build, and clean-shaven, but their noses, eyes, chins, even cheekbones were too similar to belong to mere brothers. And the way they stood beside each other made it clear in a second Peter had stepped into the middle of a beautifully tense moment.

If he was gonna make it as a reporter, he couldn't be afraid to notch it up a bit...

Bernard grunted. "Yes. Now, can we move on? We're nearly there."

Peter smiled and walked up to Thomas first, offering his hand. "Peter Bach, Detective Carew." He let the slip fall lightly, as though he hadn't noticed Thomas's uniform and Bernard's plainclothes and derby. His breath caught slightly as he tipped his bowler saying, "Pleased to make your acquaintance."

Thomas's jaw tightened as he shook Peter's hand. "Please, call me Thomas." He jutted his chin toward Bernard. "He's the detective. I'm just a patrolman." He tipped his helmet. "I understand you're to be our new boarder, Mr. Bach."

"Yes, I hope you don't mind."

"It's not up to me, Mr. Bach." He shook his head. "Nothing is these days."

The brothers started walking in tandem, Peter following. "Where are we headed?"

"Hangman Creek," said Bernard, pointing up ahead to where the street ended in a row of newly planted trees.

Beyond the trees was just air, air and a breathtaking view of rolling hills beyond a hundred-foot drop down the side of a deep ravine to a small creek.

Peter stepped carefully to the edge and looked down.

"That'd be quite a fall," he said, his breath catching without his meaning to.

"And it seems that's precisely what happened," said Bernard, pointing down to a pile that lay in the creek directly below.

The Carews led the way down a slippery little path, Peter in the rear.

"Who is it?" Peter asked as they neared what was obviously a body.

"We'll find out in a minute," said Bernard.

He squatted beside the ragged pile, his eyes studying the mess before him.

Peter's stomach tightened. He wished he hadn't taken that last scone with Mrs. Carew.

Where the face should have been there was only a mess of red and bone and bits of rock, the rest of the body twisted this way and that in unnatural angles and contortions.

He turned away and looked up the little path they'd just descended, up at the great bluff with no barrier, past the trees marking the end of a residential lane.

How simple it would be. To feel the wind upon your face and wonder what it would be like just to let go and fly out into the bosom of Mother Nature herself. All it would take was one small step and...

Peter shivered. It reminded him too much of the wreck in Tacoma last year, the one that had caused him to wake up and realize if he was gonna do something with his life, he better start now or forever hold his peace.

He pulled out his notebook.

Hangman Creek they'd called it? Surprisingly apt today.

* * *

Thomas squatted in the muddy bank across from Bernard, who was still studying the bits and pieces like he could put the puzzle back together by simply staring hard enough.

"That face is awfully bashed up. More than you'd think could happen naturally, wouldn't you say?"

Bernard didn't answer.

Thomas adjusted his position as his boots squelched in the

soft mud. "Especially considering the condition of the rest of him. It's almost like someone took a rock and disfigured it more, as though to hide his features."

Bernard grunted this time.

Thomas stood and realized the reporter had turned away, no doubt to stop the bile rising in his stomach. Thomas didn't have that problem—he'd seen worse.

"Maybe your missing informer did it after all?"

Bernard stood and glared at Thomas. "I know it's not as complicated as our last murder—but then, what can be? But just because it's not convoluted enough for you doesn't mean you need to start bringing conspiracies into this, or poor, helpless hobos."

Thomas's eyes widened. "Why are you jumping to his defense? I don't care who he is or where he's from: he ran off. Doesn't that usually mean something?"

"Yeah, that he's done his duty and felt now he could move on. If I'd seen this in the middle of the night, I wouldn't want to stick around to see it a second time, either."

Thomas shook his head. "Aren't you the one who's always quoting Holmes? The simplest solution is usually the right one and all that?"

"You're right, Thomas. And the simplest solution is that this man took a flying leap into God's arms and ended up here. It's happened a million times before."

Thomas scoffed and shook his head again, noticing the reporter had gone very quiet and was writing furiously in his little notebook. Bach glanced up and smiled at him.

Thomas didn't return it. He reached over the body and

grabbed Bernard's elbow, leading him farther away from listening ears.

"What's going on with you, Bernard?"

Bernard pulled his arm free. "All I'm saying is that 'when you have eliminated the impossible, whatever remains, however improbable, must be the truth.'"

Thomas rolled his eyes. "Don't you ever read other books?"

"Haven't the time," Bernard growled. "Too busy solving murders in real life."

"You've solved one, Bernard. One." Thomas pointed his index finger angrily toward the sky. "That doesn't make you Sherlock."

Bernard's eyebrows furrowed. "What's wrong, Thomas? You've been so grumpy lately. More than me, even."

Thomas shook his head. "It's nothing. It's just that all this notoriety has gone to your head."

"Is that all you think about? Who's more popular? Who cares! We solved a murder! We caught a murderer so insane in a murder so crazy I still have difficulty believing it all happened!"

That wasn't the issue here.

"It's not that I don't think you deserve it, Bernard, really. I know it's been a whole month and it's all beginning to get a little hazy, but...wasn't I there too? Didn't I help, even a little?"

Bernard took a deep breath. "Of course you did, Thomas."

"Well, then, why aren't I being invited out for dinner and being sent thank you letters from the governor?"

Bernard got very quiet. He rubbed his mustache. "I don't know, Thomas. I really don't."

"Do I even come up in your grand recounts of our exploits?"

"You know you do, Thomas. You've heard me give them."

"Sure, in the police station, to the men, when I'm standing right there. But at the fancy dinners? At the parties? At the after-theater 'drinks are on me?'" He waved his hands for emphasis.

Bernard's cheeks turned a little red and he rubbed his mustache again.

"Never mind. You don't have to answer. I know." Thomas turned to go.

"No, wait." Bernard put a hand on his shoulder and turned him back to face him. "Listen. I'm sorry, all right? I'm sorry I'm the one getting all the recognition. I told the chief how helpful you were—I thought for sure he'd make you a detective. But he just mumbled something about cutbacks. Said he couldn't afford another detective. But if there *are* cutbacks, at least he won't let you go, right?"

"You mean, so long as I keep playing Watson to your Holmes, they won't fire Watson?"

Bernard shook his head. "No, I mean at least you get to keep your job, you whiner. For heaven's sakes, you sound like a child."

"I do not."

Bernard waved his hand. "Never mind. Just don't forget I'm looking out for you as best I can."

"Bernard. I am not your little brother. I am the same age as you and I am just as intelligent as you and in some ways more so. There were parts of that case you never would have solved without my help and you know it. All I'm asking for is some gratitude. Some recognition of the part I played. Is that really too much to ask?"

"No. It's not. But it is too much to ask of me when I've already given it to you. If you need more, talk to the chief yourself."

And with that, Bernard turned on his heel and stomped away.

* * *

Bernard could growl, he was so frustrated. No, more than frustrated. He was angry. He wanted to just—just—punch something—

"Detective?"

The grizzly bear whirled around on his unsuspecting prey ready to take a bite out of him.

"What?" he bellowed. Then he realized he'd just yelled into his new boarder's face—and a reporter no less.

The bear slunk back into its lair.

Bernard took a deep, calming breath. "Sorry. What can I do for you, Mr. Bach? Do you have some questions? I don't have any answers yet. Still getting my bearings."

The reporter took a quiet breath before smiling and saying softly, "Ah, yes, of course, naturally. Is that why you sent Thomas off? To find out who the dead man is?"

Bernard turned to see Thomas halfway up the steep path already.

"Bah!" he said aloud. He didn't need him.

He turned back to Bach's inquisitive face and raised eyebrows, pencil poised over his notebook. If he didn't know better, he'd think the little bearded imp *wanted* him to voice the tension between him and his brother. What had he been thinking inviting a reporter to stay in his house? Never trust a newspaperman, his father had always told him, and even though *The Spokesman* liked him now, he knew that could change in a heartbeat. Bach's heartbeat, to be exact.

Bernard quickly tried to rearrange his face behind his mustache. "Would you be so kind as to head back to the station to notify the coroner and request the paddy wagon? I can't leave the body unattended now we've discovered it."

"Thomas—"

"Was sent on a more important errand."

He could tell immediately that Bach wasn't falling for that. But thankfully, with a tip of his hat, he tucked his notebook and pencil away and followed in Thomas's footsteps up the path.

Bernard pushed all distractions away and knelt beside the body. Time to get to work.

Cause of death was clear, and outside of the hobo's testimony of when the death had occurred—"sometime in the middle of the night"—it would be difficult to tell how long he'd been dead resting in the cold, wet creek-bed all night.

The mud had risen a little as the weight pressed into the soft earth, and Bernard knew once they moved the body a small imprint of the broken form would remain.

The face couldn't tell him much of anything, the hair a mess of mud making it difficult to tell if it was dark blonde, brown, or somewhere in between, so he turned his attention to the clothes. Leather dress gloves protected the hands, so he couldn't tell whether the man bit his nails or wore a wedding ring or anything useful without removing them, which the coroner wouldn't like before his examination. The cloth was ripped and mangled, but had once been a rather expensive suit, navy blue, almost black in color. The coat was open over a once-white waistcoat that was now more reddish brown, with a vibrant red tie still about the neck. This gave Bernard pause for a moment as he looked to the man's feet. Yes, he was wearing evening dress shoes.

Why would a man of his class, dressed as though he'd just come from a fancy dinner, throw himself off a cliff in the middle of the night?

Not that rich people didn't have cause for suicide, for they certainly did. In some ways they had more to lose than most people. His father used to say something like that, about "the higher you climb, the farther you have to fall," but he usually was talking about falling at Jesus' feet. He'd been a devout Baptist and had brought his boys up in the ways of the Lord. He'd often said the only hope a man could have—especially when he constantly saw the most depraved side of humanity like he did on the force—was in God.

Again Bernard thought about the hobo. He wondered what his name had been. He'd never asked.

Speaking of names, he patted the pockets of the coat and waistcoat on the body, trying not to disturb anything but hoping for—yes, there it was: a calling card case.

And inside—yes. The poor soul who lay shattered before him now was a Mr. James London.

* * *

Thomas stalked halfway back to the station before changing his mind and turning resolutely homeward.

He'd been trying to get up the gumption to ask Miss Kenyon to go walking with him since she moved in to be his sister-in-law's new companion. But he just hadn't found the right moment. In a month. He'd been busy...

Well, no time like the present. He rode the burst of energy fueled by his frustration right up to the front door, but stopped short when said door flew open as he reached for the handle.

"Oh!" cried Miss Kenyon, her hand to her chest. "You startled me! How are you, Mr. Carew?"

Mr. Carew couldn't speak at the moment, lost as he was. His tongue was suddenly stuck like it had been that morning whilst making a go at the uneatable concoction the cook had called "jam." He searched for words other than "breathtaking nymph."

A fortnight later, he cleared his throat and tipped his helmet. "Thomas, Miss Kenyon, if you please."

Her eyes flashed with pleasure and a blush crept up her cheeks as he stared.

"Then you must call me Marian. We are living together, after all." The blush crept to her sparkling eyes, his own face no doubt mirroring her flush of color at the unintended suggestion. "Well, we mustn't stand here exchanging names in the doorway. Were you coming home for luncheon?"

Thomas tried to recall his original purpose and simply nodded.

"I'm headed up to the House just now," Marian said. "Mrs. Curry heard about our predicament finding a good cook and has been busy all morning making pies for us. I offered to pick them up myself..." She drifted off as though waiting for him to say something.

He thought of meat pies and cherry pies and apple pies all made with Mrs. Curry's personally seasoned meat and canned fruit...

"Would it be an imposition for me to accompany you?" he found himself saying, as a smile spread across her face.

"Not at all." She closed the door behind her and suddenly she was standing very close. He could smell thyme and sage and rosemary. She must have been doing a little cooking herself. A soft pink blush was creeping up her cheeks again, and had almost reached a bit of flour hidden in the cleft of her nose.

"You've got a little...um..." He touched the side of his own nose with a finger.

Her blush deepened to scarlet as she raised a gloved hand to wipe the bit of white away.

He smiled. "All good. Just some flour, I think."

She laughed softly to herself. "Thought I'd attempt some rolls to go with stew for dinner since there's a fully stocked kitchen and no one to use it. I am so pleased Mrs. Curry thought of us, however, as I'm useless without a cookbook, no matter how many varieties of fruit or flour we have available. I'm afraid I've never had my Nain's touch when it comes to bread, so we shall see if you're allowed to taste the rolls."

"I'm certain they'll be divine." He was so close he could count the freckles sprinkled across her nose.

He cleared his throat and took a step back, bowing slightly as he offered his elbow to her.

Her touch was gentle yet firm as he led her to the stop for the streetcar that would take them down Monroe, through downtown, then up the South Hill and out to the edge of town, to the home of the late Miss Mitchell, where they'd first met that sunny spring day.

Marian laughed suddenly and he quirked a brow toward her as they walked.

"I was just remembering the first time I saw you, you had a little something on your nose, as well."

"Ah," he stuttered, "yes, probably ash." They'd been digging through the remains of the blacksmith's forge in search of bone fragments, in the hopes of proving their theory that a second body had been consumed by the flames, hidden from notice. He cleared his throat. "May I ask you how you're faring as my sister-in-law's companion? Roz can be quite a surprising handful."

Marian's smile grew as the streetcar neared. "Mrs. Carew is truly remarkable. I am ever so grateful to everyone for taking me in and providing distraction from...well, you know. Your family has been so welcoming...as has Mr. Prescot."

Thomas helped Marian aboard and they found seats quite luckily in the back. As it was nearing the luncheon hour, many of the working class that could afford such a luxury would be rushing home for a quick bite with their families before returning to work.

With a *clang-clang* the streetcar was on its way, rolling smoothly into downtown.

"Mr. Prescot?" Thomas asked. He knew who the man was, of course, as he'd been lodging with them until recently, but he'd forgotten Marian also knew the quirky clockmaker.

"Yes. He and I met in passing at Montrose Park the day of the—well, the day Eleanor became the Baker, I suppose."

"Ah," he said.

"He's been quite a dear friend ever since. We've often met in Montrose Park—I take photographs while he records sounds for his experiments. We both arrived around the same time in town, so perhaps we connected mostly out of that similarity. But he's also very well-read, and funny in his own way." She chuckled and turned to look out the window, so she didn't see Thomas's face frown involuntarily at this news.

"You enjoy reading?" Thomas asked instead, turning the conversation back to his advantage.

"Quite a lot. My favorite discovery so far has been a wonderful detective story called *The Leavenworth Case*, written by a woman."

"Ah, yes, Anna Katharine Green." He enjoyed the way her eyes lit up with pleasure at his familiarity with the book. "You know Miss Mitchell owned a first edition copy? It was on display when we first came to the House to investigate." Thomas almost said that if they asked Prescot, he was certain to let them borrow some of the great works shelved there, but he didn't want the clockmaker to re-enter the conversation. "Did you know Anna Katharine Green is credited by some as the creator of the American detective?"

"I thought Poe's Dupin was the original?"

Thomas held up a finger toward the roof of the streetcar. "Ah, but Dupin is French, Sherlock is British, and then there's Collins's Sergeant Cuff and Dickens's Inspector Bucket and Gaboriau's Lecoq and—"

"My, my, you certainly do know an awful lot of detectives." Marian shook her head. "Literary and real-life, for that matter."

Thomas smiled. "True. And no matter who was first, I'd argue Detective Gryce is a far more human detective than either

Sherlock or Dupin, which is why I prefer him to the brilliant, can-do-no-wrong detectives."

"I did quite enjoy the way Detective Gryce bumbled about, seeming to be distracted by the things around him, all the while collecting clues and noticing things others thought immaterial. Some of her descriptions of him talking to a lamp stand or door-knob, or having a secret conference with his fingers, made me laugh aloud!"

Thomas laughed at the memory of his doing the same. "Perhaps we might visit the library before we depart? I could show you that first edition."

"I'd love that."

Before he knew it, they were making the long walk up the drive to the House, she laughing in great spirits and clinging to his elbow, and he wishing the House was just a little bit farther out of town.

* * *

Archie's stomach tried to travel in two directions at once as his eye caught sight of Thomas and Marian walking up the drive together. He had just been leaving the house when Marian's laughter flew across the air in rivulets he could almost feel, so connected were they to his heartstrings.

But her arm was hooked in Thomas Carew's, and not because she needed assistance to walk.

He turned away for a moment to force his face into a proper form before pivoting and hailing them.

"Oh, Archie, how good it is to see you!" proclaimed Marian, reaching out long, gloved fingers to give his hand a small squeeze.

He glanced at Thomas and saw something like jealousy cross his face an instant before it vanished. Then Thomas politely nodded in greeting. "Prescot," he said deeply.

"Thomas," Archie replied, with a similarly stiff bob of his head. "What brings you to our humble abode?"

"Mrs. Curry sent a telegram suggesting we stop by to pick up some pies," said Marian.

"Ah, yes, she mentioned at breakfast she planned to provide you with subsidence."

Marian and Thomas both quirked their mouths and exchanged a glance.

"I did it again, didn't I?" he asked, before they could say anything. What was it about Marian's presence that always made him so flustered he couldn't get the right words to travel from his brain to his mouth?

"I think you meant 'sustenance,' old chum," said Thomas, hitting Archie's shoulder. "Speaking of which." Thomas flipped open his pocket watch to check the time. It was a beautiful Elgin, obviously loved and cared for by its owner.

He held it just long enough for Archie to notice Marian admiring it. There was something about clockworks that seemed to fascinate her, and he wished it was just them so he could tell her about his latest idea for his personal timepiece.

"If we head to the kitchen now we'll be just in time for luncheon," Archie said, hoping this would encourage Thomas to close his watch and move on.

Thomas rubbed his stomach. "I knew my inner belly clock was telling me something." Thomas pressed the cover closed on his pocket watch with a *snap*, causing Archie to wince slightly.

That watch cover wouldn't last long if he continued to close it without holding the button as he did so, but most people enjoyed hearing the satisfying *click*. "I'm famished. Let's see what delicious concoctions Mrs. Curry has in mind for us."

"We'll be right behind you, Thomas," said Marian, releasing his arm and taking Archie's. His joy spread from his heart to his head so swiftly he nearly fainted with delight. "I'd like to catch up with Archie, if you don't mind. Tell Mrs. Curry we're on our way."

Thomas nodded. "As you wish, m'lady." He tipped his helmet to them and turned on his heel, striding quickly toward his home away from home.

"Such a gentleman," Marian sighed happily, and suddenly Archie was afraid she might pour out her heart about how she was falling in love with the man.

He quickly changed the subject. "And what have you been reading of late, Maid Marian?" he asked, using the name he often teased her with, as he knew her favorite story of all time was that of Robin Hood and his lady love.

"Well, let's see. When last we spoke I'd just picked up Poe's first Dupin mystery, but I'm afraid I was terribly disappointed by the ending."

"Ah, yes," Archie nodded sagely. "The orangutan?"

"Yes, an orangutan!" she cried angrily. "Of all the silly—here I was, reading along thinking, 'This is one of the first detective mysteries so it must be something inspirational,' and then *splat* like a cow pat: violent death by crazed monkey. I mean, really."

Archie tilted his head back and laughed a genuine laugh. "'Splat like a cow pat'? Now, that's a good one."

The other day, they'd met in Montrose Park and had begun a silly rhyming game while he worked on some sketches for the job that had brought him to Spokane in the first place: namely designing and assisting in the building of the clock and tower that would live at the new Great Northern Railroad Depot being built downtown.

Marian shook her head. "I think the man should stick to poetry, personally."

"You mean Poe should write mysteries 'Nevermore'?" Archie croaked and winked.

She laughed and the sun shone all the brighter for it. "He did write a couple more mysteries before he died, though, didn't he?"

"Yes, I think there's just two others with Dupin. The others, as I recall and you'll be happy to find, are not nearly so farcical in their deniability." Or was the word "plausibility?" His neck warmed and he pushed his glasses up his nose with his free hand, keeping his gaze forward as they meandered the long way around the house to the kitchen entrance at the other side, his steps slower the closer they came.

"I admit, I've learned I love a good mystery. I even find myself wishing I had discovered the genre earlier on. Perhaps I might have become a detective, rather than a...," she lowered her voice, "...thief."

"A female detective. Now there's something you'd be hard-pressed to find."

"Nonsense. Kate Warne was a detective under Allan Pinkerton out in Chicago."

"True, true. I had heard that. Though if you enjoyed *The*

Leavenworth Case, you'll want to try *That Affair Next Door*. It's Amelia Butterworth's first case."

"Oh, I did enjoy *The Leavenworth Case*. Thank you so much for recommending it to me. Thomas mentioned you have a first edition in your library here. We were wondering if we might take a look at it before we head back."

Archie stiffened and she misread his reaction, unhooking her arm from his so she could face him, leaving the crook of his arm drafty and cool.

"We won't take it back with us, don't worry. Even though you know I have a soft spot for first editions." She winked merrily at him again and he recalled how she'd admitted to him that of the stolen objects she'd held onto were several first editions worth thousands.

Why did he have to fall for a thief? *Former* thief, he corrected himself.

Archie attempted to press his heart back into its correct position but he didn't want to stop speaking with her. Once they rounded the corner they'd be outside the kitchen doorway. He searched his brain for some other subject that would keep her standing there talking with him.

"Before we go in, I wanted to ask you privately how you're doing with the whole Eleanor thing," he leaned in and whispered.

Marian's smile fell into the collar of her evergreen jacket and she didn't answer right away. The last time they'd met in Montrose, she'd revealed her misgivings about her actions. He'd hoped he'd encouraged her, but it appeared she was still wrestling with demons.

"I do think I did the right thing. I acted without thinking, though." She twisted her grandmother's ring on her right pinky. "I turned my friend in to the police as a murderer before even speaking to her or asking for her side of the story. If I had... I wonder if I would've still told them what I'd figured out."

"The poor woman needed help. She'd killed two husbands."

"Yes...but...," Marian faltered, "didn't they both deserve it?"

Archie pushed his glasses up his nose. In Archie's opinion, she was getting dangerously close to becoming both judge and jury for the world. And why wouldn't she? How big of a leap was it, really, from a Robin Hood thief who finds it morally excusable to "rob from the rich to give to the poor," to someone who spent the night saving beaten women from abusive husbands with a quick vial of something untraceable?

"Yes," he finally said, "I suppose. But you must admit, she needed help in other ways, too."

"Of course, I know the Baker had to be stopped." She sighed. "But the Baker is also my Eleanor. And I just wish Eleanor might have been spared."

Archie still didn't quite understand that part—how one person could have two completely unique personalities, one of them trapped inside the other. It was like something out of a Jules Verne novel. Or Wells. Not something one expected to encounter in, well, real life. Like an orange orangutan haunting the streets.

"Dear me," she said, glancing toward the corner, "we've spoken for much longer than I'd intended. I'm certain lunch is getting cold, and I don't want to disrespect Mrs. Curry. Shall we join the others?"

Archie simply nodded. He'd borrowed her long enough. Time to return her to Thomas.

* * *

Peter walked to the nearest streetcar and climbed aboard, dropping in a nickel to pay for a ride back to the police station, located on the first floor of City Hall at Howard and Front.

He'd obliged happily to Bernard's request, thinking he'd use this opportunity to get into the police station not as a reporter, but as a detective's friend, which might open more doors for interviews that would normally be slammed shut in his face.

His cousin had once said the best thing about being a reporter in America was the lack of rules. "You can do whatever you like, however you like, to get the story. All readers care about is the story."

He leapt from the streetcar with a spring in his step, taking a moment to brush off his overcoat, straighten his tie and bowler, and run his fingers over his mustache before walking into City Hall like he belonged there.

He marched up to the front desk sergeant, a man Bernard had called Hollway, but who Peter thought could play the part of the Walrus from *Through the Looking Glass* quite nicely.

"Sergeant Hollway? Peter Bach again, friend of Bernard Carew. I came by a little while ago and you sent me to Hangman Creek? Well, he sent me back to acquire the coroner and the paddy wagon for his use."

"Hobo did find a body, then, eh?" Hollway asked in a low, ponderous voice that was equally walrus-like, scratching one of his elephantine ears beneath his police cap. "All right, then.

Lewis is out today. I'll just go get Lawson." He plodded back through the maze of desks.

Peter leaned against the front desk and glanced casually at the book Hollway had left lying open. It was lined with metered writing recording every visit of the day. Next to 10:17 he had written: *Hobo, unnamed. Claims found body at Hangman Creek. —B. Carew.*

Peter returned to standing and wrote down the information in his own notebook.

After tucking it away in his chest pocket, he ran a hand over his mustache and beard, a habit he'd recently acquired to ensure all the hairs were lying in their proper place. A perfectly coiffed beard didn't come naturally, after all.

Finally, Hollway returned, his pace still slow and steady, though he was now accompanied by a short, broad policeman.

"This is Officer Lawson," said Hollway. "I'll go get the coroner from next door and then he'll take you both back to Detective Carew."

But Peter was already shaking his head. "No, thanks, I'll stay here if you don't mind. Needed to speak with Captain Coverly, anyway. Is he in?"

"I can check after I get the coroner," Hollway said, his eyes glancing to the right as he spoke.

"It's all right. I'll just go on back." Peter waved him off and walked purposefully toward the office doors on the right.

Hollway didn't stop him, so Peter found the door labeled *Captain James R. Coverly* and knocked.

"Come in," came the reply, so Peter did so. He was greeted with, "Who the hell are you?"

Coverly sat behind his desk, his fountain pen poised above a paper before him covered in—unfortunately for Peter, who'd been blessed with a gift for reading upside down—illegible scribbles.

Coverly's nose beat out Hollway's narrow one in size. His mustache followed the same curve, but was far smoother than Hollway's bushy one, as though Coverly spent time grooming it every morning, like Peter. His heavy eyebrows protruded slightly over his eyes, which were piercing and angry at the moment as the captain glared at the intruder.

"Captain Coverly," Peter began, "Bernard Carew said I should speak with you in regards to getting a chance to speak face-to-face with the Baker."

Coverly snorted. "Right. Who're you with? *The Spokesman? Chronicle?* Doesn't matter if you're with the *New York Times,* the answer's the same."

"And that is?"

"No!" Coverly shouted, returning to his scribbles.

"But I'm a friend of—"

Coverly pointed to the door with a rather forceful finger.

Peter shrugged. "All right. But I have to ask: What are you hiding, Captain?"

Coverly looked up long enough to give him a firm glare and to belt, "Out," before impressively ignoring his presence once again.

"Have a good day, Captain," Peter said politely, tipping his bowler as he escaped through the door back out into the main lobby.

Peter ran a hand over his beard again and scratched at one of the sideburns that were coming in nicely. At least he hadn't been physically booted from the police station. A quick look around revealed Thomas hadn't returned, as Peter had suspected, and he knew Bernard was still a mile away, so he decided to help himself to their desks.

The lunch hour had left him practically alone, with just a few men too focused on their own work to notice a well-dressed gentleman helping himself.

He wandered through the maze until he found a desk marked "Detective Bernard A. Carew." A copy of *A Study in Scarlet* sat on the corner under a framed photograph of his infirm wife.

The first drawer revealed a letter from Governor Rogers himself. Peter was impressed. The remaining drawers didn't reveal much of anything, however, and certainly not a memorandum book filled with remarks on the Baker case or something helpful like that.

Perhaps Thomas's drawers would be more accommodating. His desk was only a few seats away, and rather disorganized by the looks of it. Half-written papers here, partially filled out forms there—

"*Ahem.*"

Peter looked up and met the dim eyes of Sergeant Hollway.

"Bernard asked me to look for his pen," Peter said quickly. "A blue one. Refillable. You wouldn't happen to know where he keeps it, would you?"

Hollway twitched his gigantic mustache.

"I'll just take him this one, then." Peter grabbed a very new-looking Conklin crescent from the drawer he currently had open. "Thanks for your help." And with that, he scurried out of the police station before he made any permanent enemies, already reaching into his pocket for a cigarette.

* * *

Bernard's patience was almost completely worn through when Coroner Baker finally arrived with Lawson and the wagon. It was unfortunate their current coroner shared a name with the most recent big news murderess, but it wasn't like he could change it.

The little man made his way boldly down the steep path, his black bag in one hand and the other stretched out for balance.

Once he reached his side, he gave Bernard a quick nod in greeting, and then got straight to work, perching his pince-nez upon his pointed nose above a graying mustache.

Bernard gave the man room to work and joined Lawson, who'd also descended and was now looking back up the steep path with a worried expression.

"Guess I'll have to haul the body up to the street, Detective Carew. No way to get the wagon down here safely, I think." His deep voice had a resonance that seemed to reach inside Bernard's chest.

"I agree. I'll help, of course. Shouldn't be too difficult with us on either end. It's good there's plenty of light for Dr. Baker to do his work before we have to move it."

Lawson nodded.

The man smelled like cinnamon, which was a nice change from the stench of the hobo and the body. Bernard wondered if the smell had begun to cling to him and made a plan for a lavender cleanse with the bowl and pitcher that evening, as he wasn't one to enjoy their modern claw-footed tub.

It didn't take long for Coroner Baker to rise and close his bag, removing his pince-nez as he turned to tell Bernard his thoughts.

"Looks to me like the man took a bad fall."

It was difficult to tell if the Minnesotan was joking or serious, as he was also a Presbyterian.

"His face looks rather the worse for wear compared to the rest of him, wouldn't you say?" Bernard asked.

"Yes." Baker looked back up the hill. "But I'm certain you'll find a large rock with the rest of his face somewhere between here and there." This time the man's mouth twitched at the corners.

"Can we move him to the wagon now, Dr. Baker?" Lawson asked, eager to be about his business. He had no doubt entertained plans of going home for lunch, now dashed.

Baker nodded. "I'll do an autopsy this evening and let you know if anything turns up. But I think you landed a simple one this time, Detective."

"Yes, sir, thank God for that."

But the little man shook his head. "It's the simple ones you have to watch out for. There's always more to them than first appears. Often the difficulty lies within their simplicity."

And with that, he tipped his hat, briefly revealing his balding head, before telling Lawson he'd make his own way back.

"Well, let's get to it," Bernard said, and clapped his hands together as though he anticipated rather than dreaded the coming task.

* * *

"So, my dear, I see you've settled in rather nicely with the Carews?" Mrs. Curry's eyes twinkled at Marian, who felt herself blush for the hundredth time that day even though Mrs. Curry hadn't said a thing about the young man accompanying her.

She despised her inability to keep her face from flushing scarlet whenever it felt like doing so. It was so very un-Victorian to allow her feelings to show so plainly. Nain would have been shocked. She'd been quite capable of keeping her emotions just under her high-necked collar. No pink cheeks were ever to be seen on her stern but loving face.

"Speech is silver, but silence is golden," seemed to be her life's motto.

If Marian couldn't get her blush under control she was going to have to start biting the inside of her cheek or pinching herself to stop.

"Mrs. Carew is quite wonderful," Marian said, reaching for another pie to wrap in the numerous waxed handkerchiefs Mrs. Curry had prepared for their journey downtown. "She's the most intelligent woman I've ever met and we have the most interesting discussions. Not about fashion or recipes or anything like that. She has me read her articles from *The Scientific American* and we learn about the newest inventions coming out of England and France and all over the world."

"Sounds like our Mr. Prescot should join you sometime," Mrs. Curry said.

After lunch, Archie and Matsumoto had taken Thomas to the workshop, to show him their latest experiments. Although

Marian had longed to join them, she'd felt like someone needed to help Mrs. Curry prepare the food she'd so lovingly offered to them.

As her Nain would say, "You don't get something for nothing."

"And Detective and Officer Carew? How are they treating you?" Mrs. Curry asked.

Marian bit the inside of her lip. "They're both perfect gentlemen."

She thought of Thomas leaning in to point out the flour on her face. She'd almost expected him to reach out and brush it away himself.

She'd almost wanted him to.

Marian turned her mind to safer memories, like her conversation with Thomas on the streetcar. He'd been quite knowledgeable when it came to novels. She'd always felt one could tell a lot about a person from their bookshelves. He was handsome and charming, funny and intelligent, and he made her feel...a *thrill.* Like she was full of wit and daring, capable of anything.

It was almost like the thrill of stealing.

If she was honest with herself, that was the reason why she'd taken the job with the Carews in the first place. For the thrill. The ever-present question of whether they'd uncover her secret and find out who she was and what she'd done...

Perhaps the thrill of Thomas's interest in her would be enough to stifle the urge to return to thieving?

Wait. What on earth was she thinking?

Here she was, a thief—all right, an ex-thief—flirting with a policeman! Yes, she was living with two policemen, which had seemed insane in and of itself, but to encourage a relationship with one? She must have lost her mind.

The last thing she needed was a relationship. She had to figure herself out first. She'd been attracted to the idea of starting over with a clean slate: a new home, new friends, new job. She'd been all ready to settle into this new role as companion, to finally make a new female friend—who wasn't a murderer.

And now this.

She really didn't need this. She was a modern woman. She supported the suffragettes and their work in enabling women to be who they wanted to be, whether that was a mother or a lawyer. In Idaho, women had held the vote for five years now, since '96. She just had the unfortunate circumstance of living almost twenty miles west of the border. It made her wish she could just pick up the border line of Idaho, like an embroidery stitch, and move it west of Spokane rather than east.

Often it felt like that would be simpler than Washington state giving women the right to vote.

She was not looking to be tied down.

And yet, Nain had never felt "tied down." And Roslyn and Bernard—they seemed so happy. Marriage didn't have to be a bad thing, she supposed. In fact, there were lots of women she could think of who were happily married, and yet still found ways to work in a man's world.

Anna Katharine Green sprang to mind. She'd become a famous author in her own right, published over twenty books thus far, and all while being a wife and mother!

Her thoughts returned to her discussion of the author with Thomas. From Green they'd turned to Wilkie Collins, Émile

Gaboriau, Poe, Conan Doyle, then back to Green, but this time to comment on her poetry, some of which was quite beautiful.

She soon found herself lost in the memories of the twists and turns that accompany a heartfelt discussion of the best books, and soon her mind was overtaken by her heart.

* * *

"They've decided to build a temporary depot just east of the Washington Street bridge," Archie said, leading the way around the house toward the workshop, Matsumoto in the lead, and Thomas in tow.

Thomas had been kind enough to show interest in their work, and as Archie didn't care to turn down a chance of showing off his skills before his rival in Marian's affections, he'd eagerly offered a quick tour.

But now he was getting cold feet since they hadn't made much progress in the month since he'd moved up to the House. So he'd thought he'd switch the conversation over to his other job—the depot—since there was more to share on that front.

"Wait, they're going to build another depot while they work on building the new depot?" Thomas asked.

Archie nodded.

"How much is that going to cost?"

"They estimate no more than a thousand dollars, and it's only temporary."

"Right. So why spend a thousand on something temporary instead of putting that money toward the final building?"

"I'm just a clockmaker." Archie shrugged. "They don't tell me everything." So much for sounding like he was well-infused...infiltrated...*informed*. "There've been some minor delays in beginning construction, so I suppose they figure they better get something put in, just in case more problems come up."

"If there's one thing you can count on with construction, it's that there'll be delays," said Thomas with a grunt reminiscent of his brother.

"True," Matsumoto put in, reminding Archie that he was listening to their conversation.

"Apparently, the original contract was let to some other builder out of St. Paul," Archie continued, "but when he failed to do anything for the past six months, they relet the contract and gave it to the second lowest bidder, G.A. Johnson and Sons, whom I've been working with. So far, they've been great. They even sent a representative of the firm out here, like Seth Thomas did with me, to get the work started."

"And has it?" Thomas asked as the workshop came into view.

Archie pushed his glasses up his nose. "We broke ground on the depot last Wednesday, and they're starting the rock excavation in preliminary of the stone foundation this weekend."

Matsumoto went through the workshop door, leaving Archie and Thomas outside while he grabbed their latest prototype sound gun. It was still difficult to believe how easily the blind inventor moved about his workshop, but when everything was kept clean and orderly, he always seemed capable of finding exactly what he was looking for. So long as Archie didn't mess things up and put things in the wrong place.

"And this Mr. Johnson didn't come in and make changes to your plans?" Thomas asked. "Isn't that what a new lead tends to do?"

Archie shuffled his feet. It was exactly what Mr. Johnson had done, but he hadn't made changes to Archie's clock tower, and for that, he was grateful. "Sure, but nothing major. He changed the arrangement of the steel and iron work, and eliminated the terra cotta. But that was an expensive addition that added nothing to the facade of the building."

"Uh huh," Thomas said, though he didn't sound like he agreed.

"Mr. Johnson said he hopes to visit Spokane once a month over the course of the construction, which I suppose I could have done, as well…"

Archie trailed off. In fact, Seth Thomas had suggested exactly that, but he'd been the one to point out that it would be cheaper for him to take one train out and one train back at the end of the summer, and then not return again until the final spring installation once the tower was completed.

He'd wanted to get away, to see the country. He'd never left the East Coast before, and the Spokane clock tower had sounded like an opportunity to see the wild west in all its glory. Instead, he'd found Spokane, a town that boasted more real roads than any city west of Denver, complete with paved streets, electric arc lights, and enough public parks, schools, churches, colleges, and theaters to keep anyone happy.

And, Archie realized as Matsumoto returned and held out their prototype to Thomas, if he hadn't made plans to stay in Spokane for longer, he wouldn't have been able to join Matsumoto in working on sound theory. In the end, everything had worked out perfectly, even with the death of their patroness—except for Marian.

Archie watched Thomas hold up the sound gun and turn it this way and that, asking Matsumoto questions.

He pushed his glasses up his nose. He still had a chance with Marian. The summer wasn't over yet.

* * *

Roslyn was craving cornbread. She hadn't had a good slice of cornbread in...she couldn't think how long. She daydreamed about biting that slightly crisp outer crust into soft, moist, crumbly cake soaked in melted butter and honey...

But no one around here made a decent cornbread—too far north and west. For sure, there were other Southern belles who'd traveled west with their families, but she didn't know any personally who also had a recipe for cornbread.

There was nothing for it but to hire a cook who could make good cornbread. She briefly considered placing an ad in the paper for just that. *Wanted: Cook with skills in cornbread. Only the best need apply.*

She chuckled to herself and went back to reading the ads that were listed. There were very few and all for housework rather than cooks. She realized she just might have to place an ad after all, as she'd done with Marian's position.

She glanced up at the clock on the mantel. The ornately carved wooden Swiss bears who held the clock in place smiled back at her. Marian had mentioned she'd most likely stay up at the House for lunch, so Roslyn expected she'd be back around three o'clock.

Until then, Roslyn was alone. Well, other than the new maid, Mary—they were always named Mary or Maria, or Marian, she realized. It seemed there was a great shortage in unique names these days, and she was forever grateful her dear mother, God rest her soul, had named her something beautiful and personal. Roslyn.

Bernard often referred to her as his "rose" which she'd always loved. His rose. As though he'd plucked her from a garden after considering all the other flowers and decided only *she* would do.

She glowed at the thought until she looked down at her still feet.

Why had he chosen her? He'd known she'd be confined to a wheelchair for life, that it might be a shorter life, and that she might not be able to birth life. They'd never had the pleasure of finding out if that was so, though. And now that she was almost thirty it was too late.

She sighed. It was probably for the best.

Mary knocked on the door behind her and Roslyn called out, "Come in," as she set down the paper. The maid was a slight girl with gray eyes and brown hair of perhaps eighteen, though Roslyn understood her to be married with one or two nippers at home already.

Mary bobbed politely before her. "Is there anything I can get you, ma'am? I'm headed out now and I just wanted to check."

"Thank you, Mary, that's very kind of you. I don't believe I desire anything at the moment, though I did want to thank you again for being so kind as to clear lunch earlier while my companion was out. Being without a cook is quite distressing to one's schedule."

"Yes, ma'am. I do wish I could be of more help in that area, ma'am, but I'm afraid I've no skills in the kitchen. Mum does all the cooking."

"Does your mum need work?" Roslyn asked, for if her mother was anything near as polite or helpful or efficient as Mary had turned out to be, she felt she might be an answer to prayer.

"I'm afraid not, ma'am. She's at home with the little 'uns; without her there I couldn't be here, you see." Mary shrugged apologetically.

"Of course. Well, do let me know if you hear of anyone seeking work as a cook. I'm willing to try anyone with or without previous employment experience. I believe often the best cooks are the ones who cook out of love for their family, rather than a desire for money."

Mary bobbed again. "I will, ma'am. Thank you, ma'am."

"Thank you, Mary. I'll see you next Friday."

As she left, Roslyn was reminded of her last companion. Liza Gillen had been only a few years older than Mary, and unmarried, yet had found herself "in the family way." She'd attempted to hide it from Roslyn until she no longer could, the morning sickness keeping her from her duties.

Roslyn had felt it best that Liza return to her family. It was her mother and father's decision what happened to her next, but Roslyn did continue to pray for the girl and her child, and whoever the father turned out to be, that God would bless them all the same.

When searching for a new companion, she'd decided she'd be looking for someone with more experience in the ways of the world, and although Marian was only a few years older than Liza, she certainly seemed to carry the weight of life on her shoulders.

Besides, Marian was the sort that Roslyn imagined might never marry, which made her all the more suitable as a companion.

Thomas's mooning face said otherwise, however, and she revised her thought: Marian might also make a suitable sister-in-law.

But, she mustn't start counting those chickens before they hatched. Better to let things grow naturally between them. After all, it was Bernard's friendship that had been the basis for her love for him, as through it he'd shown he had fallen in love with *her*, all of her, and therefore had something of an idea of what he was in for.

* * *

Bernard had no idea what he was looking for. He only knew that Coroner Baker's comment about a rock with the rest of the dead man's face on it was not just a sad attempt at humor. He'd been right that there should be a steady, bloody path from the body back up to where Mr. London had taken his last step.

From there, Bernard hoped it might be possible to determine whether the man had jumped, fallen, or been pushed. And like he'd found to be true on their last case: "There was nothing like first-hand evidence."

Bernard crouched down, balancing on the balls of his feet, to reach out over the mud from dry earth. Where the body had settled, he could still see a rather depressing six-foot-long outline in the mud.

Immediately, he discovered two items of interest, which must have fallen out of the dead man's pockets: a pair of smashed spectacles and a key. Carefully, he reached out and collected the items.

He turned on the balls of his feet while still squatting in the muddy bank and searched the ground for more. Then he began crawling slowly, slowly up the cliffside, his eyes scrutinizing every rock for blood spatter. He only slipped once or twice, and was pleased to find there were indeed signs that led almost directly up the bluff. He also found quite a few coins, a small pencil, and a matchbook. He couldn't know for certain that they had fallen out of the dead man's pockets as he bounced down, but he held onto them nonetheless. One never knew what might end up being the final, necessary piece of the puzzle.

Finally, Bernard pulled himself up to the top of the bluff, where a sidewalk lined the residential street. He stood and dusted off his trousers before turning around to look back down the hundred-foot drop he'd just climbed. For a moment his eyes swam before him and he felt quite light-headed. How could anyone walk this bluff without worrying about how simple it would be to misstep and take a plunge down, down, down into the creek-bed?

Bernard took several steps back, but then stopped, squatting down. His foot had rolled over something on the ground—a cigarette. And not far from it, another. The first had been smoked longer than the second, and at first glance appeared to be of a different brand. Unlike Sherlock, Bernard had not yet memorized 140 varieties of tobacco, but he collected them to analyze later or to ask someone who would have a better idea.

He looked around for anything else worth noting and then stood, brushing his hands off as he did so. He took a few steps up and down the sidewalk, thinking this would make a nice spot for a park, if you didn't look down so much as out and across the ravine.

No more than a decade ago, he might have seen teepees set up on the west bank, belonging to the people who had given the creek its official name: Latah. Sometimes you'd still see Indians fishing the creek for salmon where it met the Spokane River farther north. In the opposite direction, there were hills upon hills of tall evergreens stretching to the sky, the creek winding through on its leisurely way south.

Bernard sighed and turned from the view to the line of houses behind him. Browne's Addition was known as Spokane's first neighborhood, and it was a sign of the town's exponential growth that so many additions had followed since its establishment.

If Thomas were here, he'd have told Thomas to walk door to door asking if anyone knew a James London right after they first learned the dead man's name.

But he wasn't.

So, Bernard stretched his back and cracked his neck. Time to hit the pavement like the good old days.

* * *

Thomas's arms were almost as full as his belly as he and Marian left Mrs. Curry, too laden with her gifts to even spare a hand for waving farewell. Since there was a telephone in the house, Prescot had taken the liberty of calling them a cab to take them back home, seeing as otherwise they would have to carry five enormous baskets full of every bit of food Mrs. Curry had found "just lying around in want of a home."

"There's just the three of us at the moment and seeing as the inventors only eat when I force them to take a seat, there's plenty to share."

"Mrs. Curry, I have to say, I'd never treat you with such disrespect if you came to cook for us," he'd said, dabbing at his mouth before reaching for another soft roll.

Mrs. Curry had waved away the comment. "Oh, nonsense, it's not disrespect. They're busy changing the world, and I'm just glad to be a part of it."

The thought crossed Thomas's mind once again that if Mrs. Curry were nearer to thirty than sixty he'd have married her the moment he first tasted her homemade lemon muffins. He smiled to himself, knowing that a batch of those muffins was currently tucked safely away in one of the baskets he now carried.

After settling their load into the back of the horse-drawn carriage on one of the seats, he reached down to help Marian in, only to find Prescot already at her elbow.

"Thank you again, Archie, for calling the cab for us," she said, stepping up into the carriage and taking a seat. "How handy it must be to have a telephone!"

Prescot shrugged. "I imagine in the future every home will have one. Out east they're particularly standard now, so it won't be long before it's the same in Spokane."

"Well, we'd better be off," Thomas said, taking his seat beside Marian but leaving a respectful bit of space between them.

Prescot closed the carriage door and nodded. "Come by anytime," he said to Marian, and Thomas wondered if he'd only meant it for her. "You're always welcome."

"I will," said Marian with a smile and a wave. "Goodbye!"

The cabbie driver flicked the reins and they were off down the long drive.

Marian sighed. "I could live out here," she said wistfully. "Couldn't you? It would be so nice to step outside and smell fresh air and see trees."

Thomas nodded, though he actually preferred to live in town, in the center of things.

"I've always loved the color green," Marian continued. "It's such a natural color, whereas it feels man is only capable of creating browns and blacks."

"You are wearing a green coat, you know, made by a man, or a woman," Thomas pointed out.

"Yes, yes, but it's not *green*, like the green you see in nature." She looked down at the dark color of her coat, which Thomas thought looked quite becoming on her, and then back up to the trees they were riding past. She laughed then and waved a gloved hand across her coat. "Of course, I believe this color is often referred to as 'evergreen' or 'forest green' so perhaps I'm just being silly."

Thomas bit back the "perhaps" that had almost slipped out. He'd never want Marian to think he thought she was silly, even though he did feel a little lost in the conversation. In an attempt to change the subject, he asked the first thing that popped into his mind and he almost wished he'd gone with the "perhaps" comment instead.

"So what did you and Prescot speak about when I went on ahead to the kitchen?"

She looked up quickly, as though surprised by the question, and then looked away, out over the front of the carriage.

"Eleanor." She sighed.

Thomas nodded and relaxed his shoulders. "Ah, yes, of course. You know, she's doing quite well down there—as well as can be, at least."

"You mean in the jail cells?" Marian shook her head and looked at him. "I just have a difficult time imagining anyone being comfortable in the same place you throw drunkards and thieves."

And murderers, Thomas thought. And Eleanor was a double murderer and crazy to boot. She was where she belonged, as far as he was concerned.

"Perhaps you could come visit her sometime. It might ease your mind a bit."

Marian's face lit up at the same time his stomach tightened as he realized he'd just offered her something he probably shouldn't have.

"Really?"

Shoot. She was too happy to go back on it now.

"Sure. I could take you there now, if you'd like." Before Bernard came back from Hangman Creek and found out what he'd done.

"Can Mr. Prescot come too?"

Uh, no. No. Why would he need to come, too?

"Sure, why not?" Thomas would've kicked himself if she wasn't so close to him.

"Oh, thank you!" she said, reaching over and giving his arm a squeeze. "Thank you so much, really. It means so much to me." And before he could get his heart out of his mouth she was telling the driver to turn around and head back to the House—they needed to pick up one more person.

* * *

As Archie took a seat next to the now more-precariously balanced baskets of food, Marian reached over and touched Thomas's arm one more time.

"Thank you," she said, hoping her eyes showed the gratitude bubbling up out of her.

Then she turned her focus out of the carriage, away from the two men, and tried to compose her face to reflect serious thoughts rather than her real ones.

She worried that she'd encouraged Thomas only to gain access to Eleanor. If she admitted it to herself, though, she was even more worried about the warm feelings she was having toward Thomas all of a sudden, a man she'd only met a month ago, and had never engaged in actual conversation—thanks to his busy work schedule—until today.

At least Marian was finally going to see Eleanor. It had been a whole month since that day she'd never forget, watching her dear friend being led away by the Carews after having admitted all the terrible things she'd done.

Marian had woken from a nightmare just that morning where she and Eleanor had been playing as they'd done when she was young. Eleanor was chasing her around the yard of Nain's house, her longer, older legs keeping up with Marian's shorter sprints. They were laughing and having a grand old time. Then Marian hid behind a tree, and when she poked her head out and looked about, she couldn't find Eleanor. She turned back around and jumped, for Eleanor was right there, looking at her. Only it wasn't Eleanor. It was the Baker, her face contorted and strange as she tilted it side to side like a hawk eyeing its prey. In her hands was Marian's favorite doll, which she squeezed, and squeezed, until suddenly Marian couldn't breathe—

And that was when she woke. It had taken her several minutes to catch her breath, and after a splash of cold water on her face she had decided she needed a Red Rogue romp about the neighborhood to clear her head.

But that was over now. She'd given it up for real this time. It always surprised her when Archie said something about it, because he obviously assumed she'd given it up after their conversation a month ago when he'd made the connection.

But she hadn't then. And now she had, though she had to continually remind herself of it. And that was that.

She shook her head at her own thoughts, which Archie must have noticed, for he suddenly asked, "Are you all right, Marian?"

He was leaning forward in concern.

She reached up and touched her warm cheeks as she attempted a comforting smile toward him. "I'm fine. Just a little anxious, I suppose, about seeing Eleanor."

Archie nodded. "I would imagine so. I'm quite anxious myself."

"You have nothing to fear," Thomas said. She turned to look at him and his charming smile. "I'll be there with you."

He reached out and touched her hand, his fingers sending an electric shock through her lace glove. "Ooo, sorry about that." His eyes were so bright. She knew if she looked too long she might get pulled in.

She wasn't comfortable sharing this moment with Thomas

in front of Archie. She turned away and focused on her hands, clasping them and un-clasping them until the carriage finally rolled up outside the Carew house, where Thomas and Archie unloaded the baskets and delivered the food to the kitchen. Marian went in to tell Roslyn where they were headed.

Roslyn gave Marian a quizzical look but simply said, "All right. I look forward to hearing about it when you return."

Once they were back in the carriage, it was just a short ride to City Hall.

Thomas led the way. Outside the door leading to the cells was a thin officer with deep-set eyes and a thick mustache over-hanging his lips, whom Thomas addressed before turning and beckoning Marian and Archie to follow. Marian couldn't keep her hands still. She felt a light touch on her elbow and nearly jumped out of her skin.

"Sorry," said Archie quietly. "I merely wondered if you'd like to take my arm. I've never seen you so nervous."

She exhaled. "I'd be grateful for the support, thank you."

What was wrong with her? She'd never been like this before, crying and shaking and needing a man's support. It was like by giving up the Red Rogue she'd lost her shield, her protective outer armor that kept her from feeling emotions like this.

She clutched his arm firmly with both hands, and he put one hand atop hers comfortingly. "It'll be all right. For all intensive purposes, she's still Eleanor."

Marian breathed out slowly. That was just it: Would she be?

* * *

Six houses down from the place Mr. London had stepped out into Hangman Creek, Bernard was finally answered with something other than, "Never heard of him."

"Mr. London? Ain't 'e the nervous fella' 'oo was workin' next door for Mr. Campbell?" The gardener stood with an oil rag in one hand and a bottle in the other just outside Mr. Finch's garden gate.

Everyone in Spokane knew which houses belonged to John Finch, William Wakefield, and Amasa Campbell, as they were three of the grandest homes built by Kirtland Cutter in Browne's Addition.

Bernard took a moment to admire the three houses, for even though they were all designed by Cutter, they were each built in a completely different style. Finch's three-story residence was completely white with columns like a Greek temple in the Neoclassical Revival style. Wakefield's was Mission Revival with a white-washed stucco exterior and an orange-tiled roof.

Meanwhile, Campbell's three-story feat of timber and brick brought to mind the English Tudors. There was a main house, a clearly defined service wing to the right, and a carriage house tucked behind them both.

Bernard gauged each of the entrances: the impressive, assertive front door that said, "Here lives a Great Man," or the more modest side door that led to the wing. He decided to try the humble door first, as he didn't want to disturb the entire household if Mr. Finch's gardener had been wrong.

Squaring his shoulders and straightening his derby, he strode toward the door determinedly. After ringing the bell and knocking, he was greeted kindly by a housemaid. She was small and blonde, probably in her late 20s, with a nose and mouth that suggested to Bernard a Swedish background.

Bernard introduced himself and handed over his card. The maid immediately invited him in.

"Are you here to speak with Mr. Campbell? I'm afraid he's not in at the moment, but he should be returning shortly."

"I'm not certain yet, to be honest," replied Bernard, looking around the small entryway.

Across from him were several doors and the bottom of a winding staircase in the corner. On the wall to his left hung an annunciator call bell system with a collection of labeled brass arrows pointing to whomever had rung for the servants. The maid reached up and pushed a small button hidden under the device, resetting the "Side Door" arrow that had apparently moved when Bernard rang the bell.

"I'm looking for someone who knows a Mr. London."

"Mr. London?" The maid turned from the arrows, her blonde eyebrows raised. "Mr. Campbell's assistant is a Mr. London, but he didn't show up for work today."

Perfect.

"Could you describe him to me, perhaps?"

The maid's eyebrows moved farther up, followed by her blue eyes as she tried to recall him. "Tall, over six feet, I should think. Dark hair and eyes, clean-shaven. He wore round spectacles. And very nice suits for a personal assistant, but then he'd been sent 'specially to help with preparations for the President."

Bernard nodded. Sounded like a match to him. He reached

into his pocket and pulled out the broken pair of spectacles he'd found beneath the body. "Do these look familiar?"

The maid flushed and put a hand to her pale cheek. "Those look like his. Oh dear, oh dear. What's happened?"

Bernard thought it best to avoid telling anyone the man was dead until he'd spoken with the head of the household, especially as the maid seemed to be nearing a fainting spell simply over spectacles. "I think I had better talk with Mr. Campbell after all. Is there anyone else who worked with Mr. London? Who might be able to answer a few questions?"

The maid moved her hand to her chest and took a deep breath as if to steady herself. "I suppose you might talk with Mrs. Campbell. Is Mr. London all right?"

Ignoring the maid's question, Bernard asked, "Might I see Mrs. Campbell?"

The maid asked him to wait in the reception room while she checked to see if Mrs. Campbell was available.

She led him through a side door into the main house and he noticed immediately the darker stained oak paneling in contrast to the lighter pine that had marked the servant's side, something he'd also seen done in Miss Mitchell's home. Down a short hallway, he passed a large, open dining room dominated by an ornately blue-and-white tiled fireplace at one end of a long, shining table. They rounded a magnificent grand staircase that took a sharp corner on a midway landing so Bernard could not see what lay at the top, passing a beautiful grandfather clock that told of the time, as well as the day, month, and location of the sun, something he knew Prescot would love to get his hands on.

Turning back from the clock, he almost hit his head on a low-hanging ornate electric chandelier at the bottom of the grand staircase. Clearly the designer had not planned on men taller than Mr. Campbell passing through.

The maid led Bernard down a small set of stairs into a foyer reminiscent of a castle, with thick, dark oak beams criss-crossing the ceiling, and even an ornate tapestry lining the walls, depicting windmills and castle ruins amongst a forest of trees. It made him wish he'd entered via the front door, rather than the back. From this vantage point, however, he could see an impressive suit of armor hanging above the front door—an odd collection considering it looked to comprise a Spanish breastplate and helmet, Chinese swords, Turkish axes, and standard gauntlets.

Off either side of the foyer were two large pocket doorways. One led into the largest room in the house, a living room, filled with tables, chairs, a grand piano, and a cozy inglenook fireplace. The other led to a sitting room, a very unique sitting room.

To begin with, it was pink. The couches were pink. The chairs were pink. The walls were lined in pink silk. Heavy rose-colored velvet draperies embroidered with gold filigree hung across the leaded windows. The ceiling was white in contrast, sculpted with acanthus leaves interlaced with twisting vines in an elaborate design. The pink was broken by gold filigree lining the cornices, the chandelier, the rococo curlicued molding, and the ostentatious white marble fireplace inlaid with rose gold scrollwork, above which hung a gigantic mirror that reflected all the pink and gold back upon him again.

Now, he knew some might think that Roslyn had gone a little overboard with the Swiss bear furniture in their own front parlor, but this right here was a woman's reception room worthy of Versailles.

The maid bobbed and left him there, but thankfully for no more than ten or fifteen minutes before returning to say the lady of the house would see him now. She led him back the way they'd come, and not up the grand staircase, which implied to Bernard that it led to private bedrooms. Instead, they crossed back onto the servants' side, and went up the set of narrow twisted corner stairs he'd glimpsed before, causing him to wonder why he hadn't simply been asked to wait by the annunciator. At least this way he'd gotten a chance to glimpse more of the house.

On the second floor, the door to the right opened into a corner room lined with built-in linen cabinets and filled with all the accoutrements of a sewing room: a model figure, a sewing machine, and more bolts of fabric than Bernard had ever laid eyes on.

The sunlight was streaming in through the large leaded-windowed walls, caressing the bent shoulders of a woman in her early forties, with graying sandy brown hair in a pompadour. She lifted her gracefully long neck as they entered, revealing a round face with a thin nose above thin lips. She was quite beautiful for her age, and had that delicate radiance of one who'd been breathtaking when she was younger, reminding Bernard of Roslyn's quiet beauty in some ways. She wore a high-necked soft yellow dress that was modestly covering her neck and shoulders and displaying a rather impressive pendant necklace. A large sky blue bow hung at the bottom of a Chantilly lace v-neck that draped from her shoulders down across her chest as she leaned over an array of papers spread out before her on an oak table.

Her gray-blue eyes rose to meet his, though it was clear she was still distracted by the thoughts tied to the papers before her.

"Mrs. Campbell, ma'am," bobbed the maid, "this is Detective Carew."

"Detective," Grace Campbell said with a nod of her head, then looked to the maid. "You may return to your duties, Carrie."

The girl bobbed again and left quietly.

"How can I help you?" Mrs. Campbell asked.

Bernard removed his derby as he said, "Just a few questions, ma'am, in regards to a Mr. London, whom I understand has been working with Mr. Campbell."

Mrs. Campbell straightened. "Yes. He joined us last month to assist in final preparations for the President's stay."

Bernard turned his hat in his hands. "I suppose you must have heard, ma'am, that the President is no longer visiting?"

"As the President and his wife are dear friends of ours, we, of course, were the first to be notified."

Bernard nodded politely. "I, myself, only just heard confirmed word today. I was greatly grieved to hear of Mrs. McKinley's waning health."

"Indeed. I just wrote to her again this morning. As to the other matter, Detective," Mrs. Campbell said softly, coming around to Bernard and shutting the door behind him so that they were alone together. "I would not like the staff to hear it, but I am worried about Mr. London. He has not reported to work today, which is very odd, very odd indeed."

"The maid said he had not come in, ma'am. She was also quite distressed when I showed her these." Again he displayed the smashed spectacles.

Mrs. Campbell's mouth pressed into a thin line. "I had feared as much. Is he dead?"

She was so blunt, it might have surprised Bernard, if it hadn't been for her quite straightforward manner and appearance. It was clear she was a woman who had no time for dilly-dallying.

"Yes," Bernard said.

Again she nodded. Then she sighed and went back around the table. She waved a hand at the papers. "All this work for nothing. And now a man is dead because of it."

"Because of it?" Bernard repeated.

"Yes." Mrs. Campbell sank into a simple wooden chair, resting her head in her hand as she bent her elbow upon the table. "I have no doubt Mr. London is dead because of President McKinley."

* * *

Archie was glad he'd been able to offer his arm to Marian before Thomas. Not necessarily for her sake so much as for his own need to hold onto someone as they stepped across the threshold and entered the cells.

It was dark, and it took a moment for his eyes to adjust to the low lantern light that only added to the eerie ambience of the place. Once they did, he saw that before them was a line of barred cages, all empty but the very last one. As they walked toward it, Archie could see a huddled figure seated on a cot in the corner.

It was trembling, and soft cries reached his ears as they neared.

Thomas walked ahead of Marian and Archie and knocked on the bars as though on a proper door.

"Mrs. Sigmund?" he called out gently, and Archie wondered if he always referred to her by that name or if he alternated, to see if it changed the reaction of the woman in the cage and affected which personality would come forward first. It was what he would have done.

Marian's jaw was clenched tightly, her mouth a firm line, her eyes wide and fearful. Her hand clutched tighter to his arm.

The prisoner continued to tremble, her hands over her face, her shoulders hunched forward.

Then one piercing blue eye peeked out through the fingers.

Archie tried not to tremble, himself, it was so unnerving. He had to force his feet to keep taking steps forward.

The eye connected with his, and for an instant he could hear her voice creaking in the workshop, *"It was slow work, baking him a piece at a time. But the meat sloughs off rather quickly, you know, when Fire is given his head..."*

He gulped.

Then the eye moved from him to Marian. He squeezed her hand to reassure her. Her eyes were steadily focused on the woman, and he realized he could hear her murmuring over and over, "Let it be Eleanor, let it be Eleanor, let it be Eleanor..."

"Marian?" And like that, the spell was broken.

"Eleanor?" she cried as tears spilled from her eyes. Marian released Archie's arm and ran to the bars as Eleanor did the same on the other side, the two women grasping hands. "Oh, Eleanor!"

In Marian's voice, Archie could hear all the guilt that had been clutching at her grab hold firmly, and he worried that perhaps this hadn't been such a good idea after all.

Thomas caught his eye and seemed to be thinking the same thing.

"Please, can you give us a moment?" Marian asked, turning a tear-streaked face to Thomas and Archie.

They glanced at one another again, but it was clear they were of one mind.

Thomas shook his head. "I don't think that's such a—"

"Please, give me just five minutes with my friend," Marian interrupted. "Please," she repeated softly. "She's my friend."

Thomas avoided Archie's eye this time. He sighed. "All right, five minutes. We'll be right outside. Just yell if you need me and I'll be right here."

Marian looked like she wanted to kiss Thomas. Archie turned away.

The two men shuffled down the hallway slowly, but Marian and Eleanor still hadn't said anything as they let the heavy door fall shut behind them.

On the other side, the officer who had let them in—whom Thomas called Smith—took the opportunity of Thomas's appearance to take a bathroom break, so it was just the two of them. Archie found a seat and sat down.

"Well, that could've gone worse, I suppose." He pushed his glasses up his nose and rested his head against the wall behind the uncomfortable wood chair.

"Worse? Yes, I suppose," Thomas muttered distractedly. He took two steps, then shook his head and walked back to the door, pulling it open just enough so that he could fit his boot in the crack to keep it open.

"Don't trust her, eh?" Archie asked, watching the policeman war with the lover.

"Who, Marian? Oh, no, you mean the Baker...of course, I don't."

It surprised Archie that Thomas had even considered that he'd meant Marian. He, personally, trusted Marian completely, even knowing her past. What had Thomas on edge? Did he think she might sneak the Baker a hatpin? Somehow he doubted she'd thought of that. No, it was much more likely that she was baring her soul to her friend, asking for forgiveness.

* * *

"Eleanor...I...I'm so sorry...," Marian cried. She avoided looking at Eleanor's eyes.

It was worse than she'd expected. The room was cold with a chill that wasn't just from lack of heat. As she clasped Eleanor's hands through the bars, the metal pressed into her wrists in a way that reminded her of the one time she'd been in handcuffs. That was the closest she'd ever come to being in Eleanor's place, and she was grateful that was all.

The cell was merely a few feet long and wide, with enough room for a cot on which to lie and that was it. Eleanor wore a plain brown dress and boots—prisoner's garb. Marian noticed her skin was red and irritated where the collar rubbed at her neck, and she imagined her friend must be immensely uncomfortable.

"I'm so sorry...," she repeated.

"Why, my darling Marian?"

The way she said it, suddenly Marian was a little girl again.

As her grandmother's maid-of-all-work, one of Eleanor's many tasks had been to wrangle Marian as a child, as she'd been too old for a governess and too full of energy to sit still for much outside of a really engrossing book. Marian had spent so much of her time with Eleanor that she'd become part mother and part older sister to her. The memories made her feel even worse.

"Why ever are *you* sorry?" Eleanor was saying. "*I* put my-self here."

"Oh, but you didn't. You might have gotten away. They might have never figured it out if I hadn't... If I..." Marian couldn't bring herself to say it. The guilt was choking her words and stopping up her throat. She gripped the thin, cold hands between her own and looked down. "I'm so sorry..."

"Stop that," Eleanor said in her governess voice, the one she'd used whenever Marian had broken into tears over the silliest things, like tripping on the edge of a rug or losing her spot in the book she'd been reading.

Marian glanced up and smiled. Eleanor smiled back. Marian wiped the tears from her eyes with the back of her hand and took a deep breath.

"You mustn't worry about all that," Eleanor said. "It's not like you could have ever understood why I did it."

Marian thought of her own hands in handcuffs again; she wasn't so sure about that.

Eleanor swept a hand back along her blonde hair pulled into a bun. "Even I don't understand it completely. I have no idea what I'm doing when...*she* takes over. I just wake up and time has passed and there's blood on my hands and all I can do is clean.

But in this case, I was glad it had happened. I was happy She defended me. I needed someone to defend me against him."

Marian wondered if that was true. Couldn't Eleanor have spoken with Miss Mitchell about it, at least? Eleanor's late employer had been a spokeswoman for women's rights. Wouldn't she have wanted to do something about a husband beating his wife?

But then Marian remembered. Eleanor had been convinced Miss Mitchell was having an affair with her husband. Seeing them in the workshop together had simply been the last straw. When she'd witnessed her husband strangling Miss Mitchell, all Eleanor could do was defend herself before he killed her, too. It was self-defense. Surely that was enough for her to escape hanging?

Eleanor must have seen the doubt entering Marian's eyes again for she snapped, "Now, listen, child." Her voice reminded Marian that Eleanor was nearly twice her age. She'd lived an entire life before Marian had even been born. The thought was difficult to comprehend. Even more so when it meant that when Marian first met her, she'd just murdered her first husband, which had caused the Great Spokane Fire.

Marian felt a chill run down her spine. It wasn't just self-defense for Eleanor. Because there was Someone Else in Eleanor. Someone Else that made Eleanor need a lot more help than a cold jail cell could offer.

She looked up into the blue eyes of Eleanor, but something had changed. There was something...different...

"My sweet, child," the voice said, the intonation higher, and more sing-song. "Did you really think *you* could save *me*?" The woman in the cage was tipping her head to the side, and Marian had the distinct impression that Someone Else was sliding into place. "To be perfectly honest, I was rather glad when you caught us—well, Eleanor. After all, I'd been simply *dying* to tell someone about my *marvelous* scheme." She began slowly tipping her head the other way, the blue eyes flashing with delight. "If you hadn't caught on, I might have been forced to bake someone else. That silly butler, for instance. He was just crazy about Eleanor. Determined to save her from her wretched husband. But he never would have done. No, there was nothing for it. As usual, *I* had to do the messy work." She grinned, her lips spreading wider than normal. "And I do so love to bake..."

Marian fell away from the bars with a gasp. She turned and flew down the hall, her heart racing, her head thumping. She didn't even notice someone was coming until she nearly collided with the black-clad figure.

* * *

Thomas wasn't quite sure what to say to Prescot while they waited, so he kept himself busy by pressing his ear to the cracked door trying to hear the conversation that was occurring at the other end of the cells.

He nearly jumped out of his skin when he realized someone else had joined them.

"Jee—cheese and crackers!" He stopped himself from blaspheming when he realized it was a nun.

The nun nodded. She had heavy-lidded eyes and her arms were crossed beneath her scapular. She was tall, probably equal to his six feet. A silver cross hung from her neck, and her only other defining feature was her prominent aquiline nose, which protruded like the beak of a crow.

She took a small breath before declaring, "I have come to speak with the Baker." Her voice was sonorous, which surprised him yet again, for didn't all nuns have the high, soprano voice required for singing hymns day in and day out?

"And you are?" Thomas asked, for he'd already let one person in to speak with the Baker that he shouldn't have, and he wasn't about to make that mistake again, especially with a nun. He didn't need a bad report going up to the Big Guy Upstairs—and he didn't mean Commissioner Lilienthal.

"Sister Mary Grace," the nun said with a bow of her head. She took a soft breath in again, as though preparing to sing. "I was sent by Sacred Heart Hospital to speak with the prisoner, as I am told she is unable to move to Medical Lake until the smallpox epidemic is cleared."

Thomas nodded. That made sense.

But the nun wasn't finished. "Sister Mary Clarence wished me to offer prayers of comfort and healing, in the hopes that through God alone the prisoner might be saved. For with God's help all things are possible." She studied Thomas, but he looked away quickly.

He went to church every Sunday at his sister-in-law's request, but it seemed to him there were some things beyond God's assistance. The Baker being one of them.

"I'm sorry, but...have I seen you before?" Prescot asked, coming up behind the nun.

"Perhaps you have seen me on the street corner, passing out

bread and soup to the homeless," said the nun with a bow of her head.

She'd probably just come from doing so, if the smell of cigarette smoke was anything to go by. If Thomas didn't let her in soon, she'd probably start praying for all of their souls right then and there. He wished Officer Smith hadn't taken off, or he'd have left the decision to him.

He almost said as much when he heard the sound of running feet coming from beyond the heavy wooden door, which had slid almost shut again without his foot to prop it open.

His heart stopped in his chest. Marian.

He reached for the door as Prescot leapt forward, obviously having heard the sound, as well. Thomas flung the door open, but the nun said deeply, "Allow me," and slid right past him. In the same instant, Marian ran through the door and straight into his arms.

He gathered her to him as the door shut firmly behind her, cutting off the echoes of the nun's footsteps. All he could think was how well Marian's slim body seemed to fit into his chest.

She buried her head in his shoulder, trembling from head to foot.

Finally, she lifted eyes sparkling with tears and said quietly, "She's still there. The Baker. I had hoped that perhaps…it had all been a dream—or a nightmare…" She shook her head and pulled back, reaching for a handkerchief from her chatelaine.

Thomas cleared his throat. He wasn't quite sure what to say, was too busy wishing she'd stayed where she was.

After she'd wiped her eyes and nose, she blushed and looked

up at him. "I'm terribly sorry for that. I was just so—over-whelmed. Please pardon me."

He cleared his throat again, getting his voice to work. "Not at all." He smiled. "Anytime."

She blushed deeper. He liked making her blush.

Someone cleared his throat behind them and Thomas was reminded they were not alone.

"Thomas," the clockmaker said, coming up to them, "that nun—"

"I know, I know. I'll go in after her and tell her she needs to come back another time."

But Prescot was shaking his head. "No, it's not that, though I suppose you'd better. I just...she looked familiar in some way. Didn't she?"

Thomas furrowed his brow. "Like she said, you must have seen her on a street corner."

"No, no. I don't think she was a nun the last time I saw her..."

"What do you mean?" Marian asked.

"I can't quite put my finger on it...but she greatly resembled someone." Prescot shook his head. "I don't know. Maybe she just reminded me of someone from Connecticut."

Marian nodded and Thomas nodded, too, even though he was also starting to wonder if he'd seen the nun before, but in a different black outfit. He'd been so distracted by her sudden appearance, and then Marian...

Smith returned at that moment and Thomas was grateful to pass the nun off to someone else. Marian's pale white face made it clear she'd had enough for one day.

"Let's get you home," he said, wrapping a comforting arm around her shoulders and leading her out.

* * *

Bernard stood in the sunlit sewing room with Mrs. Campbell, repeating her last statement over again in his mind.

Mrs. Campbell let her hand fall from her face and she clasped her hands together, her elbow still resting on the table full of papers and plans.

"Mr. London came to us by recommendation of one of the McKinley Reception Committee members. I assume you're familiar with the committee?"

"Yes. The police have had to become acquainted with all the members, especially Chairman Black. No shortcuts have been taken in preparing for the President's safety."

"I'm glad to hear it." The thin line of her pressed lips did not show any sign of gratitude, however. "So you see, from the beginning, Mr. London was connected with the President's visit. He was a...quiet man. Nervous, you might say. Always fiddling with his glasses and avoiding your eyes, never answering a direct question. I don't trust men who won't look me in the eye when I speak with them."

As if to show proof of this, she looked at Bernard, daring him to avoid her piercing stare. He did not, even though it did make him a bit uncomfortable. She had the look of a woman who could see into his very soul if she stared long enough, and he was grateful when she broke it off and turned to gaze out the window.

"And then there were his...political leanings," Mrs. Campbell continued. "When he did speak, it was to berate the conditions of the working man, and the class structure that he said kept him confined there, unable to break out. Of course, he never said such things before Mr. Campbell. He told Mr. Campbell he'd voted for McKinley, and greatly respected his efforts to unite the country through capitalism. He was quite meek and respectful, like a worm attempting to make a home in a large red apple."

She shrugged slightly. "But Mr. Campbell seemed to like him well enough. And I do admit, Mr. London was very good at his job."

"And what was that exactly?"

"He was Mr. Campbell's personal secretary."

"And what did that entail?"

Mrs. Campbell sighed. "You'll have to ask Mr. Campbell. All I know is, they were never apart, not since that first day they began working together. I suppose when two men find a partnership that works, they won't let anyone come between them and the road to progress. Not even a wife."

Bernard heard a note of bitterness in her voice. He glanced at the papers before her. "No doubt you, too, have put in a lot of work in preparation for the President's visit," he said, hoping he was reading her correctly.

Mrs. Campbell sniffed. "More than anyone could ever dream." One of her hands drifted out to pick up one of the pages. "We've known since the beginning of April that President McKinley and his wife would be stopping in Spokane. We knew them from our Ohio days, you know."

Bernard nodded, though he hadn't known that. He knew the President was from Ohio, naturally, and the Campbells, but it was a big state, so to assume the two *knew* each other was a pretty big leap.

"Mr. Campbell wanted our home to be a place of peace and quiet during their visit. He did not want to make a big deal out of the McKinleys staying with us, which was why he kept the information from the newspapers as long as possible."

Again Bernard nodded. He could still recall the article from the beginning of May where Mr. Campbell had stated, "Yes, President and Mrs. McKinley are to be our guests. That has been understood for some time and the arrangements are being made with that in view. I did not want any publicity about the matter, but as far as that is concerned, I don't know that it makes any difference."

"It was to be quite the experience, to showcase the very best of Spokane with parades and carriage rides around town," Mrs. Campbell went on. "But we also hoped that by having them stay with us we could offer some much-needed rest for them both." Mrs. Campbell pushed some of the papers about on the table before her, then pulled out a news clipping headlined "On McKinley Day". She handed it to Bernard, who took it and skimmed it quickly, as he'd already read the article but didn't want to appear rude.

In it, *The Spokesman-Review* had outlined the basic timeline of the President's thirty-seven hour visit to Spokane. He'd arrive at one o'clock in the morning on Sunday, May 26 and head straight to the Campbells' to stay the night. The next morning, he and his wife would breakfast with the Campbells before heading to the First Methodist church with them for a ten thirty sermon. The remainder of the day would be spent with rest and relaxation at the Campbells'. Monday's festivities would then begin at nine thirty a.m. with a drive through the streets of the city followed by a parade and a speech by the President. He would then depart at two o'clock in the afternoon after sharing one more meal with the Campbells.

Bernard had remarked to the chief that he thought it a bad idea to clearly delineate the entirety of McKinley's trip in the press. He feared that anarchists might use it to plan an attack on the President. Chief Witherspoon had merely clapped him on the shoulder and pointed to the subheading in the article that read, "Police to Preserve Quiet" and said, "Isn't that why you'll be there?"

He handed the article back to Mrs. Campbell to stop his current train of thought. The President was no longer coming, so he needn't continue worrying about what might have happened during his visit.

"It was only to be Mr. and Mrs. McKinley, and her personal maid and physician, who would stay in the house, as everyone else beds on the train car. Nonetheless, it's not every day one has the President and First Lady residing under one's roof."

Bernard nodded sympathetically.

A small knock at the door was followed by the creak announcing its opening. A very pretty child of perhaps eight or nine peeked into the room.

"Mother?" she asked.

Bernard stepped out of her line of sight so she could see Mrs. Campbell, who stood up from her chair behind the table.

"Yes, Helen?"

"Father has returned and you said you wanted to see him when he did."

"Thank you, dear. That was very kind of you. This is Detective Carew," she said, waving a hand in his direction. "Detective, this is my daughter, Miss Helen Campbell."

Bernard nodded to the little girl. She had thin eyebrows and her mother's nose, which looked a little large on her young face above full lips. Her small ears peeked out from long, thick brown hair pulled back loosely into a large bow and draped upon her shoulder. Her brown eyes sparkled inquisitively at him. She wore a blue dress that was all frills, which shimmered in the sun-strewn room.

"It's a pleasure to meet you, Miss Campbell," said Bernard, with a tip of his derby.

"The pleasure's all mine," said Helen sweetly, bobbing a small curtsy. "Are you here to help my father find Mr. London?"

Bright child, must have been listening at keyholes. "In a way, yes."

He glanced at Mrs. Campbell, who came around the table as she said, "I'll take him to your father now. Is he in his study?"

"He said he'll be up shortly." Helen smiled. "I hope you find Mr. London, Detective Carew. Goodbye." She bobbed again, then ran from the room.

Mrs. Campbell shook her head and pressed her lips together. "If I've told that child once, I've told her a thousand times not to run in the house." But her eyes did not show too much distress at the matter. She turned to Bernard. "The study is just here." She led the way out of the room and to the door of the next room over.

It was closed and so she knocked. There was no answer, so Mrs. Campbell opened it, revealing a dark red, manly study. In one corner sat a large roll-top desk, while in the other were two overstuffed armchairs before a tiled fireplace.

"I'll just tell Amasa you're here," said Mrs. Campbell, and she turned to go, leaving Bernard to shuffle his feet as he awaited his first encounter with a man whose name was familiar to all in Spokane.

* * *

"Peter!" a voice yelled across the smoky room.

Peter waved in return, though he didn't recognize the voice. Obviously one of the other reporters he'd met since starting at *The Spokesman-Review*, or as the locals called it, simply *The Spokesman*. He crossed the room, weaving his way around table after table with blocky, feverish typewriters and matching reporters. Practically every reporter he passed held a cigarette or cigar between his lips as he worked.

"What d'ya got for me?" the young reporter asked without introduction.

He was tall, brown-haired, and barely old enough to shave. He knew Peter's name, so at some point they must have met, but that left Peter in the awkward position of not knowing someone's name who knew his own. Peter didn't like being at a disadvantage.

"What do you mean 'what you got for me'?" Peter asked with a sneer. "I'm not about to let you in on the gold I've just uncovered."

The kid's eyes rose. "You found gold?"

Peter gave a half-laugh. "I don't mean actual gold, *mamlaz*. I mean story." Jiminy crickets, where did they find these guys?

"The name's Richard," the kid said, as though Peter had mistakenly thought his name was "*mamlaz*." It was one of the few words Peter had kept in his vocabulary from his childhood amongst the Croatian fishermen of Tacoma, meaning "idiot." No matter, now they were on even footing.

And he'd keep calling him *mamlaz* just for fun.

"I knew that." Peter swung his coat off and onto the back of the chair next to Richard's desk before taking a seat with a confident grin.

"So, tell me: are you in?"

Again, Peter was thrown off by the amount of information this kid seemed to possess about him. He ran a hand over his beard. "In where?"

"The Carews', of course. Heard you'd finagled a nice set up for an inside look at the Baker case."

"Oh, that. Of course. I also got to be the first reporter on a new case." He removed his bowler and gave it a twirl between his hands.

Richard's eyes widened. "Do tell." He whipped out his notepad and licked the tip of his pencil.

Peter leaned forward and wagged his finger. "Nah uh. What did I say?" Peter rested an arm on the back of the chair and threw the hat down. "I'm not sharing. I find the story, I get to write it. That's how it works."

Richard slumped back in his seat. The kid was obviously desperate for a chance. Probably stuck writing the obituaries and marriages every week.

Finally, Peter leaned in and lowered his voice, inviting Richard to bring his head closer in confidence. "I'll tell you what, *mamlaz*: you tell me what *you* know about a Mr. James London and I will tell you what *I* know about him."

Richard's blue eyes narrowed for only a moment. "Deal." He reached into a drawer and pulled out another notepad, this one red. "I know Mr. London. He came by yesterday for something for Mr. Campbell... Yes, this, here." He stopped on a page covered in thin, slanting writing including a long list of names. "These are the names of representatives coming to meet the President from Washington, Idaho, and Canada. London made a copy for Mr. Campbell's records."

"Mr. Campbell? Is he someone of import here in Spokane?"

"Yeah, he comes from mining money in Idaho. Owns several mines over there—the Gem, Standard, Hecla—and made millions."

"Millions?" Peter repeated, his eyes wide, encouraging Richard to tell him more.

Richard nodded. "Yeah, many millionaires in Spokane come from that kind of luck." He shook his head as though he was in the wrong industry. "But there've been lots of labor disputes, so the owners of the mines come live in the safety of Spokane, rather than in the mining towns closer to their investments."

"Labor disputes?"

"Bombs, shootings, riots. Two years ago this April, the Western Federation of Miners blew up the largest concentrator in the world up at Wardner. Federal troops were called in and the entire Silver Valley was put under martial law. The miners were all imprisoned in barracks and only released once they proved they were not associated with the anarchists." It was clear from the way his hands were waving every which way as he spoke that Richard was enjoying the knowledge he shared.

"I suppose it's not only in Tacoma that anarchists are to blame for most every problem these days."

Richard shrugged again. "They are known for bombs, shootings, and riots. Anarchists reject authority in any form while claiming to be for the people."

"Sounds like the French Revolution to me."

"Which was inspired by the American Revolution," said Richard confidently, as only a kid fresh out of the schoolhouse could say.

Peter pursed his lips. He'd never thought of it that way.

"President McKinley's staff is urging him to limit his exposure," Richard went on, "but he refuses."

"I thought he canceled the rest of his trip, that he isn't coming to Spokane as planned."

"Yeah, but that's because of his wife's health."

Peter leaned back in his chair and pulled out his cigarette holder, but he didn't light one. Not yet. "At least, that's what he's claiming."

Richard nodded.

Peter flipped his cigarette holder in his hand. "What if he really canceled because he's finally admitting the anarchist threat is real?"

"It's possible. President McKinley and former Governor Steunenberg have both been rumored to receive threats for declaring that martial law two years ago." Richard leaned in closer and whispered. "We could go grab a drink, and I could tell you more, while you tell me about the new story you just landed."

"Not tonight, *mamlaz*." Peter returned his cigarette holder to his pocket and stood. "I got to go." He pulled on his coat. "I've got a story to write, and it would not do to be late for my first home-cooked meal at my new lodgings."

"Wait," Richard called out, "you didn't tell me what you know about London!"

"Oh, that," Peter said, tugging on the brim of his bowler and tossing his words over his shoulder as he left. "He's dead."

* * *

Bernard was examining some Dutch engravings on the stone mosaic mantel in the study when Mr. Campbell stomped through the doorway and up to Bernard, his hand extended.

"Detective Carew, I understand you're here about Mr. London." His voice filled the room and bounced off the walls, as boisterous as his manner. "Terrible news, terrible news. Mrs. Campbell just informed me he's dead."

Bernard shook his hand firmly, hiding the fact that he would have preferred to deliver the news himself and observe the man's reaction. But then, he hadn't asked Mrs. Campbell not to tell her husband.

"May I offer you a drink?" Mr. Campbell asked.

He closed the door to the study behind him before taking his seat at the broad oak desk in the corner. Then he reached between his desk and the wall to pull out a thin bottle of something that matched the burgundy-red wallpaper.

He smiled sheepishly. "The wife is temperance but she doesn't understand a man's needs when he's working. Especially with such terrible news as this."

Bernard wondered if the man realized he'd just said the phrase "terrible news" three times now, and felt it meant one of two things: either Mr. Campbell truly was saddened by the death of his personal assistant, or he was trying to hide the fact that he'd known he was dead already.

If the second was true, there seemed only one way he could have known.

Bernard straightened up to his full height, which was a good few inches over Campbell, and declined the proffered drink. Campbell did not replace the bottle without first filling himself a glass and downing it. After hiding the bottle again, he reached up to a jar full of cigars. Again he offered one to Bernard, who declined, though it was much harder for him to do so. He could see they were of a fine brand.

Campbell cut and lit the cigar, puffing on it a few times so the end burned red before he sat back in his chair and breathed out the residual smoke. His tightly wound body finally relaxed.

Amasa B. Campbell was an indomitable man, even seated and smoking. His presence filled the room with a pervasive energy that made you want to get up and do something, anything, to achieve this man's greatness.

Some were intimidated by that greatness, by the wealth he'd amassed. But the Campbells were just another American dream, starting from nothing. Was it their fault they'd made good decisions and moved up in the world? Bernard could have invested in mines as well, instead of becoming a police officer like his father. He'd made his choice and Campbell had made a different one. And Campbell had this beautiful house as proof of his good decision-making capabilities.

Did that make Bernard's decision any less right? Not for him. He'd known he'd wanted to be a policeman long before his father had told him he should be one. Thomas had felt differently. He still wasn't sure why Thomas clung to his job when he'd probably be just as happy if not happier running a bakery or something. Or maybe that was disparaging Thomas in a way he didn't deserve. After all, he supposed he had been helpful in the Baker case.

Bernard scratched his mustache. Finally, he cleared his throat and began, "Mr. Campbell, when was the last time you saw Mr. London?"

Campbell nodded his head. "A worthy first question, Detective. I may well have been the very last to see him alive, after all."

Bernard reached for his notepad and pencil, wishing again that Thomas hadn't left him alone. If Campbell was about to give a confession, it would be beneficial to have it recorded by two police witnesses.

"Other than his murderer, of course," Campbell continued, puffing steadily at his cigar with a furrowed brow.

Bernard's eyebrows rose.

"His murderer?" he repeated. "I don't believe I told Mrs. Campbell he was murdered, merely dead." Though she, too, had jumped to that conclusion, what with his connection to the President.

Campbell shook his head and took another pull on his cigar. "No one told me he was. But I know." He sighed.

"May I ask how you know?"

Campbell rotated in his chair to study Bernard fully. "Certainly you may ask. It's your job, isn't it?" Campbell shook his head, but then apologized. "I'm sorry. That was rude of me. But, tell me," he opened his hands expansively, "why else would a man to whom I'd just offered a full-time job be dead?"

Bernard grunted.

"See." Campbell pointed at Bernard with his cigar. "That's my point. You thought it might be suicide, didn't you? I take it he wasn't shot then?"

Bernard just shook his head. He wanted to see if the man would get there himself.

"Must've been strangled or fell someplace, I suppose."

That hadn't taken him long. Bernard scribbled on his notepad, but watched Campbell's face.

"Terrible news," the older man repeated for a fourth time, his brow furrowed, his whole demeanor downcast.

"I hadn't realized you knew Mr. London so well," Bernard said, switching tacks. "I was given the impression he only started work for you a month ago."

Campbell nodded. "Yes, but when you've been in business as long as I have, you're able to get a notion for a man from that first handshake. And the notion I had from the beginning was that London was a brick. He may have come across as...nervous or incompetent to some—I know Mrs. Campbell never took to him—but then, she's not a man. Women notice different things in people. Men may not have 'womanly intuition' but we still have the better ability to sniff out a good'un when we see one."

Bernard supposed they'd see if that was true or not. "I take it he came with impeccable references then?"

"The very best," said Campbell, turning toward his desk. He placed his cigar on an ash tray before pulling open a drawer and then swinging back around with a piece of paper in his hand. "I suppose you can keep this. Won't be needing it anymore, then, will I?"

Bernard took the paper and glanced at it. The name across the top and bottom of the page was a recognizable one: Mr. Antonio Pavoni.

"Tony Pavoni recommended Mr. London?" Bernard asked, surprised.

The man was well-known in town. He'd come all the way from Tacoma, even while in the midst of his first year as the State Labor Commissioner, to assist in making McKinley's entire trip across Washington seamless, from Tacoma to Spokane.

Bernard had happened upon him on the streetcar once, and Pavoni had been kind enough to give him a firm handshake and a "Thank you for your service, Detective," after Bernard introduced himself. And wasn't their new boarder from Tacoma? Perhaps their exchange of information could be a two-way street.

Campbell nodded. "You see what I mean? If Tony approved of him, I knew he'd be better than some random chap I picked out to assist me. London got right down to business. It was clear he'd come from a service background and took to it with a fire at his heels. There was nothing I couldn't ask him to do."

"What sort of things might that entail?"

"Oh, everything from delivering a message to the cook about dinner to taking down a dictation of a letter to typing up a list of figures for Finch to look over. I've never had a butler or a valet in the house. Never needed one."

"How many staff do live in?"

"Two maids, they live upstairs; one cook, one gardener, and one coachman," Mr. Campbell listed on his thick fingers, "but those men all live above the carriage house." He waved a hand toward the mullioned window out of which the roof of the carriage house could just be seen. "Don't care for men living in the house, no matter how young my daughter is. London boarded elsewhere, and yet he was still here at six a.m. on the dot every morning, straight as a pin and ready to work. Hell, sometimes he'd finished work I'd meant for him to do the next day, but he always said he liked to keep busy." Campbell shook his head and laughed. "My kind of man, I tell you. He could've gone places with me. He really could've." The smile fell from his face. "It's a real shame."

Again, Bernard was surprised to see the sadness on the older man's face. He supposed it might be real, no matter how odd it seemed to him for such a bond to have been created in such a short matter of time.

"So you said you were the last to see him? Was that when you offered him the job?"

Campbell returned to his cigar before answering. "Yes, just after dinner last night I asked him to meet me in here."

"Did he take the offer?"

Campbell shook his head. "No, which surprised me. He said he had to think about it. He seemed pleased, however. What man wouldn't be?" Campbell smiled expansively like an offer from him was better than finding gold. "I was hoping the news would cheer him, as he'd seemed a bit down in the mouth since I'd told him about the telegram from Secretary Cortelyou expressing the regrets of the President. We were very much disappointed that the President would not be visiting us after all. It is a great disappointment to the entire northwest country."

"So you knew McKinley was no longer coming before Chairman Black?"

Campbell nodded. "I understood. When the wife is ill there's not much can be done, even when you're the President of the United States."

Bernard nodded. He would never forget what it had been like when Roslyn had gotten ill—and she hadn't even been his wife yet.

"So Mr. London seemed down before you told him of the offer. I suppose he thought he was done working for you after you received the telegram?"

"Yes, he'd only been offered a temporary position originally, until after the McKinleys left."

"So what was the new position?"

"Oh, just more of the same," Campbell said, waving a heavy hand. "I could tell after just one month that he was the kind of man I wanted working for me permanently. He was ambitious, hard-working, neat...and he didn't back down from Mrs. Campbell." Campbell laughed heartily.

Bernard wrote it all down. When he looked up, he realized Campbell was now studying him with a serious eye.

"London didn't kill himself," he said, his voice low and firm. "I know he didn't." He pointed his diminishing cigar at Bernard once more. "You find his killer, Detective. The man deserves justice."

* * *

Thomas could still feel the warmth of Marian clutching him at the police station.

It had been a long time since he'd had a woman hug him so firmly, so closely. And that hadn't ended well.

He glanced over at Roslyn in her chair. Well, maybe it had ended well enough. Roslyn was better as a sister-in-law than a wife, anyway. And when she and Bernard looked at each other—well, no one could stand between that.

He sighed and stretched his long legs over the end of the Chesterfield, his head resting on a pillow, his hands across his middle.

"There's an awful lot of sighing coming from that couch," Roslyn said quietly.

Thomas lifted his head slightly so he could see her face. Her thin mouth was twitched to the side as she studied the *Scientific American* before her, a cross-section detailing of some sort of boat across the cover.

He let his head fall again. "It's been a long day." He could feel his cheeks warming as auburn curls molded into his shoulder in his memory. It had been quite nice to suggest Prescot order his own carriage home so he could escort Marian back to the Carews' alone. Falling for the girl currently boarding under his own roof had its merits, he supposed.

"This wouldn't have anything to do with the young woman I had to send to bed so suddenly? Leaving me without a companion yet again for the rest of the evening?"

Thomas scoffed softly. "Don't tell me you're put out, Roz. I know that smile." He didn't need to look at her to know he was right. "Besides, she was quite shaken."

Roslyn gave up all pretense and set down her magazine, leaning forward but still keeping her voice low. "She went out for baskets of food and came back with a patrolman—and then left again to see her friend who just happens to be in jail. For murder. Would you care to tell me how that transpired?"

Thomas pressed his elbows on the couch to lift himself up again. "We ran into each other on the porch as she was leaving and I offered to escort her out to the House." He fell back on the pillows. "You know I can't resist Mrs. Curry's muffins."

"Nor a redhead in distress, I take it."

Thomas's cheeks warmed again. "A gentleman would never ignore a lady in distress. No matter her hair color."

"Indeed," said a deep voice from the doorway.

Thomas bolted upright on the couch, scattering pillows, his booted feet landing back on the Swiss rug. "Good grief, Bernard!" He picked up a pillow and threw it back in the corner of the Chesterfield.

"Did I interrupt something?" his brother asked, looking at Roslyn, not at Thomas, who kept himself busy returning the pillows to the couch.

Thomas didn't have to send any sort of signal to Roslyn, as he'd always known her to be the best secret-keeper.

"Oh, nothing much. Just hearing the latest update on Eleanor," she said. Thomas breathed out gratefully. "Thomas took Marian and Mr. Prescot to visit her today."

"You did WHAT?!" Bernard bellowed, turning on Thomas, who suddenly wished he had more pillows to hide behind. But then he remembered he was not a child any more and didn't have to cower before Bernard, who was not their father.

He stood and straightened his officer's uniform, which he hadn't had a chance to change out of. "I took Miss Kenyon and Mr. Prescot to visit Eleanor today." He matched Bernard's glare —from a couple inches farther down than he would have liked, but he made up for it with the firmness of his jaw which he could jut out without the hindrance of extra chins.

Bernard seemed surprised by his straightforwardness and dimmed his glare from a new lightbulb back down to an oil lamp. "I see," he muttered.

Bernard leaned down and kissed his wife softly. "Good evening, my rose."

It was nice to see his anger at Thomas didn't diminish his instinct to show affection to his wife, but then he followed it up with, "You and I are going to have a talk later." He practically growled it out between his teeth as Thomas made his way to the large armchair by the fireplace.

Thomas had to force his hand down from a salute.

* * *

After dinner, Bernard stomped to his bedroom, knowing full well that Roslyn was at his heels. He started a fire in the fireplace once he arrived, busying his hands while he tried to calm down.

It had not been a good evening. First learning what Thomas had done, and then being forced to sit at the dinner table with a reporter who managed to twist every word he said back to the Baker. It hadn't helped that somehow Bach had known Thomas had visited her this afternoon, while Bernard had needed to be told by his wife.

What had Thomas been thinking? How daft could he be? He knew better than to take civilians down to meet the Baker.

Bernard took a deep breath and let out his frustration into the fire, which only crackled more angrily in response.

How could he ask Thomas to help him on this case when he insisted on being an idiot around a pretty woman? For he knew without a doubt that he'd walked in on a very different conversation between Thomas and Roslyn earlier. He was a detective, for heaven's sake.

"You really mustn't grind your teeth so," Roslyn said, rolling up beside him. "You'll never know when I finally do find the perfect cook, as you won't be able to eat anything she prepares."

Bernard smiled and turned to her, taking her small, beautiful hand in his.

"It was a lovely meal tonight, my rose. Whoever you've found cooks by far the best cherry pie I've ever tasted."

Roslyn's mouth twitched at the corner. "It was cooked by Mrs. Curry. As you would well know if you'd heard any of our dinner conversation this evening."

Bernard's smile fell. "I'm so sorry, my dear. I—"

"You have a new case." She waved her free hand and smiled encouragingly. "Naturally you're distracted. Let me tell you what you missed: Marian and I made a stew this morning with vegetables and rolls, thankfully, as she returned too upset to do more than finish the meal we'd started. Then we enjoyed one of the pies Mrs. Curry had been kind enough to send over by way of Marian and Thomas this afternoon."

Wait. "Miss Kenyon and Thomas went to see Mrs. Curry today? Alone?"

"Of course. Someone had to collect the enormous baskets of pies and fruit and vegetables."

Bernard let go of her hand. "Is that where Thomas disappeared to? When he should have been working?"

Roslyn's brow furrowed. "He was supposed to be working? Doesn't his shift end at noon on Fridays?"

"Not when we have a case!" Bernard yelled.

Roslyn put her finger to her lips and glanced at the closed door. "Hush, my dear. He'll hear you."

"He damn well better hear me," Bernard cursed.

"Then for the sake of the reporter now boarding with us, perhaps you'd better speak more clearly so he can write it all down for the morning paper," Roslyn said through gritted teeth.

Bernard threw up his hands and went into their private adjoining bathroom, narrowly avoiding slamming the door in his frustration. He turned on the sink and threw cold water on his face until it dripped from the tips of his mustache.

Did no one in this house think he knew what he was doing? He clenched the edges of the new porcelain sink, thankful for the cold running water he took for granted already. He grabbed a towel and rubbed his face till it stared back at him redly between the thick black hair that outlined his forehead, above his eyes, and under his nose.

Roslyn was right. He shouldn't have shouted. And he shouldn't have cursed in front of her. That was very disrespectful. He owed her an apology. He took a deep breath and had just put his hand to the door when he heard a soft knock on the door to their bedroom.

"Who is it?" Roslyn called out softly in response.

"It's Thomas," he said, clearing his throat. "Is Bernard still decent?"

Bernard swung open the bathroom door and Roslyn looked at him with raised eyebrows. "I don't know. Is he?" she asked him so quietly Thomas couldn't hear.

Bernard leaned down and kissed her hand. "I'm sorry, my rose."

"You are forgiven. Now go make amends with your brother so you'll get some sleep tonight."

Bernard kissed her hand again. She knew him too well.

He pulled the door open and found Thomas wearing only his banded collared shirt, navy pants, and stockinged feet without boots. Clearly he'd been in the process of getting ready for bed when he'd heard Bernard's outrage from the floor above them. Bernard rubbed a hand down his face. He worried who else had heard.

He closed the bedroom door behind him and motioned toward the kitchen—the one room in the house from which sound didn't carry.

The warm oven lit the room enough that Bernard was able to find a match to light a lamp for the table.

Thomas took a seat across from him but waited for him to speak first.

Bernard sighed. "I suppose you heard something of what I said just now?"

Thomas shrugged. "I heard you yelling and figured it was

probably on my account, seeing as how I kind of abandoned you this morning."

Bernard didn't point out that he didn't "kind of" abandon him, but had indeed left him alone with a dead body. "I was upset," was all he said.

Thomas nodded. "And you have every right to be. That wasn't very professional of me to leave you there. I'm afraid I got a little...sidetracked." He rubbed his neck and avoided Bernard's eyes.

"By a pretty redhead, I take it?" Bernard asked with a smile.

Thomas grinned foolishly. "And a basket of Mrs. Curry's lemon muffins."

Bernard shook his head. "That still doesn't account for why you felt the need to take Miss Kenyon and Mr. Prescot down to see the Baker."

Thomas's grin slid to the side. "I know I shouldn't have. But...she asked nicely?"

Bernard almost laughed. "At least tell me what happened, would you?"

"That's the thing: I don't know exactly what happened." Thomas scratched his head and then his chin. "One minute Marian—"

"Oh, it's 'Marian' now is it?" Bernard shoved Thomas's shoulder lightly and Thomas grinned in response with a shrug.

"One minute she's asking to be alone with Eleanor, and everything seemed fine, so Prescot and I stepped out—but I kept the door held open so I could hear if anything went awry. And then suddenly there was this nun and—"

"Wait, a nun?"

"Yeah, give me a minute. This nun comes in and says she's here to see Eleanor, been sent over from that Catholic hospital—"

"Sacred Heart?"

"Yeah, that one. And I'm still questioning the nun when suddenly I hear running echoing off the walls of the cells, but before I could get through the door to Marian the nun goes bolting through and Marian comes rushing out and...well..." Thomas opened his arms and smiled, leaving Bernard to guess to where—or to whom—Miss Kenyon had run.

"Where was Smith? Wasn't he supposed to be guarding the cells?"

"Exactly," Thomas said, as though it was Smith's fault for letting him in with two visitors in the first place. "I left him to handle the nun, told Prescot to call a cab for himself, and took Marian home."

Bernard nodded. "So you don't know what the Baker said to Miss Kenyon?"

Thomas shook his head.

"Then I think your duty tomorrow is to find out what was said."

Thomas nodded and smiled. "Gladly."

"And then," Bernard continued, "I'd appreciate your help on this new case."

Thomas nodded again. "Fine." Then he grinned. "But only if I get to eat all the lemon muffins."

* * *

Roslyn sat before the fire in her bedroom and read more of her magazine, waiting for Bernard to reappear and help her undress for the night. She wasn't sure what it was like for other couples, where both individuals could dress and undress at will, but for her and Bernard it had become an intimate ritual of affection. She was so dependent on him, it felt almost wrong, in this era of women's suffrage movements.

But what else could she do, stuck as she was? She thought of her companion, whom she'd had to comfort and send to bed, rather than the other way around.

Marian had been quite disturbed upon her return from City Hall. Roslyn hadn't thought it was a good idea, but also felt it wasn't her place to question Thomas's plan when Marian had informed her of it this afternoon.

She'd been unable to discover exactly what had been said, but she had gathered that Eleanor had turned into the Baker at some point, and this had seemed like the end of everything to Marian. Because Roslyn had never heard of this sort of thing before and couldn't be sure if Eleanor had changed in countenance, manner, speech, or all three, she wasn't certain how to comfort Marian.

The door opened behind her and Bernard came in, closing the door again as he entered.

"I'm sorry I had to leave you like that, my dear."

"I understand. Did you and your brother find a common ground?"

"Yes," he leaned over and kissed her on her forehead, "for now. I still don't understand what's bothering him, though. He's so distracted lately. It's not just Miss Kenyon. I've never seen him like this."

Roslyn stopped herself from hitting Bernard over the head

with *Scientific American.* "Bernard...dear...you've never seen him like this before?"

"Well, not since childhood at least. It's like he's jealous of me."

Roslyn almost raised her hands in praise. "That's exactly what he is," she said softly, grasping Bernard's hand where it hung by her shoulder. "He's always lived in your shadow, Bernard. You may have been born at the same time, but you have advanced further than he in the same amount of life."

Bernard stared at the fire.

"You are a detective, he is a patrolman. You are married, he is not. You are getting all the fame and glory from this Baker case, and he is getting none of it."

Bernard cocked his head toward her. "That can't be it. He's never been so prideful as all that."

"Perhaps. But didn't you say you would never have solved the case without his help?"

"Yes."

"And have you said such a thing in front of reporters? Or Captain Coverly? Or Chief Witherspoon?"

Bernard grunted. "You sound just like Thomas." He pulled his hand away. "Yes, I have, and the chief made it quite clear that we need all the good publicity we can get with the mayor and city council threatening cutbacks."

Roslyn nodded. "Then you've done all you can do, my dear." She reached out and grabbed his hand again, giving it a comforting squeeze.

He turned back to her. "I wish I could do more. You know that."

Roslyn smiled and squeezed again. "I do. Now," she set down

her magazine, "perhaps you could help me out of this corset, my love?"

And finally, Bernard smiled.

* * *

Archie lay in bed tossing and turning. He half-dozed into a sort of crazed hallucination where the Baker's face turned into Marian's and then into the nun's.

The nun. He sat up and rubbed his eyes. He knew he'd seen her face somewhere before. But where?

He started thinking through all the ladies he'd met since coming to Spokane. It had only been a little over a month so it didn't take him long. But none of the women he could think of had that long, beak-like nose. Aquiline or Roman he'd heard it called before. He could almost place the face just on the nose alone...

Marian had a nice nose. It was small and lightly freckled, and she wrinkled it when she laughed or was trying to make a face.

Thomas had a nice nose, too. Unfortunately. They'd probably get married and make very handsome babies with adorable little noses.

He couldn't very well blame Thomas for his interest, but part of him had hoped... What? Marian had been nice to him. That was all. A woman had to be allowed to be friendly without worrying about a fat frog falling in love with her.

Archie sighed. If he kept along that line of thought he'd never get to sleep.

He lay back and tried counting sheep, but they all had cute little button noses. And that got him back on the aquiline nose.

And suddenly all the sheep were looking down at him with a frown, peering pretentiously over their prodigious noses like—

Wait.

Archie's heart stopped. He knew where he'd seen the nun's face before.

Jennings the butler.

Two

Saturday, May 18, 1901

Spokane, Washington

It was Saturday, so technically Thomas could do what he liked, but he had agreed to help Bernard with his case, so instead he sat up in bed and tousled his hair, stretched, scratched, and prepared himself for the day. A vision of green eyes above a speckled nose floated before him and he recalled the rather delicious dream he'd been having. Marian had been in the kitchen baking up a batch of Mrs. Curry's blueberry scones...

Even now he could practically smell them as he shaved in the bowl and pitcher he'd filled with hot water from the bathroom down the hall. He tried to shave everyday to avoid any growth that might enhance his similarity with his twin brother, but this was more difficult than one would think as they both suffered from facial hair that didn't give up easily. Having done all he could on that front, he dressed in trousers, shirt, vest, jacket, and tie, opting for casual rather than his officer's uniform on his day off. Someday, perhaps, he'd make detective and then he could discard the uniform forever.

As he walked down the stairs, the smell of blueberry scones became more pronounced, and he almost gasped with delight when he entered the dining room and discovered his dream had become a reality.

Marian smiled at him shyly as she placed a steaming basket of scones in the center of the table. A few curls hung loose, framing her heart-shaped face. Her cheeks were pink, either from cooking or seeing him, he couldn't tell, but he hoped it was the latter. He smiled at her and then at the scones.

"Good morning!" he said heartily. "Don't tell me Mrs. Curry's scones were hidden among those baskets?"

Marian nodded. "It's a good thing they were hidden, too, it seems." She placed her delicate hands on her hips, the apron tied over her black dress emphasizing her waist. "You wouldn't happen to know where all the lemon muffins have gone, would you?"

Thomas grinned sheepishly. "Guilty." He waved to the table laden with eggs, bacon, toast, jam, pears, potato cakes, and hominy with sugar and cream, not to mention the blueberry scones. "Will you join me for this most welcome feast?"

Marian lowered her hands and looked along the table. "Yes, I think that's everything." She pulled the string at the back of her apron and lifted it over her head before carrying it to the kitchen. When she returned, Thomas made sure he was standing behind her chair.

He pulled it out for her and she took a seat, thanking him as she sat.

"You're welcome," he whispered, surprised by her thanks; most women just sat without a sign of gratitude.

He admired the way her curls rested on her slender neck before finding his own seat across from her.

She served him a full plate and then helped herself. "It was so wonderful of Mrs. Curry to bless us with so much in our time of need," she said, taking a bite of toast.

"I somehow doubt Mrs. Curry had much to do with cooking half of this," Thomas said, looking at his plate of cooked food and taking a large bite of egg, bacon, and potato cake all together. He swallowed and let his pleasure show on his face. "I think we should alert Roslyn that her search for a cook is over. You'll do just fine."

Marian blushed happily.

"She'll do just fine for what?" came Roslyn's voice as Bernard pushed her chair into place at the table.

Marian's face turned a shade brighter as she stood to make a plate for her employers.

"Try a bite of those perfectly cooked eggs and you'll see what I mean," said Thomas, waving a piece of bacon in his brother's direction.

They both did and joined in the smiles around the table. "Indeed, Marian, my dear, these are better than those watery eggs of Mrs. Hill's any day," said Roslyn kindly.

The conversation continued congenially, with even a few laughs thrown in, until the sound of footsteps in the hall warned them they were about to be joined by Bach.

Bernard stood quickly and excused himself, and Thomas followed his lead, much as it pained him to leave the ladies to the mercy of the reporter. But their worry was misplaced, for Bach stopped them in the hall.

"Good morning, Mr. Carew, Mr. Carew," he said, nodding to each of them. "Off on the hunt already?"

Bernard nodded and grabbed his derby and overcoat from the stand. "Yes, sorry we missed you at breakfast."

"Not at all." He ran a hand over his beard. "I've never been one to eat first thing in the morning. I'll just tag along with you now, then, shall I?"

Thomas glanced at Bernard and read clearly on his face that this was the last thing he wanted. Even though he was still a bit miffed with Bernard, he knew what he had to do.

"You run along, Bernard, and I'll catch up," he said, waving his brother out the door.

Bernard left with a look of astonished gratefulness peeking from behind his mustache.

* * *

"Aren't you going with him to the station?" Peter asked, grabbing his hat and coat along with Thomas as Bernard shut the door in his hurry.

"Yes, but since he's the detective on the case, best to let him get in and organize his thoughts before bringing me in."

"That's not how I heard the last case worked out. You were both there soon after the body of Miss Mitchell was found, and inseparable ever after."

Thomas nodded and opened the door for him. "Yes, but this is a new case. I can't expect it to go like the last one."

"Perhaps that's better, anyway," Peter said, taking the steps slowly down to the front walk.

"What do you mean?" Thomas came up alongside him.

Peter shrugged. "Maybe this time you can get the glory and Detective Carew can remain in the shadows."

Thomas's brow furrowed. "That's not how it works. There's no 'one for you, one for me' system when it comes to police work. There's just the detective and the—"

"Sidekick?" Peter supplied.

Thomas snorted. "Yeah, something like that."

"Looks to me like your brother is already ahead of you on this one once again."

Thomas shrugged. "Like I said: he'll bring me in when he's ready." He started walking, trying to show he didn't care, but it was clear he did.

"What if I helped you?"

Thomas stopped and turned. "What?"

"Well, I just happened to come across some information about the dead man, information I understand Detective Carew has yet to share with you."

Thomas rubbed his brow. "I feel like you're not hearing me. Bernard is about to fill me in as soon as I catch up to him at the station and lose you."

Ouch. But Peter could appreciate blunt honesty. "Perhaps. Or you could solve the whole thing without him and the next time you see him could be with the murderer in handcuffs before you."

He could see Thomas imagining it now, the image before him probably as tangible as the beard on Peter's face. But then the patrolman's face cleared and he asked, "What's in it for you?"

Peter ran a hand over his beard nonchalantly. "A story. I am a reporter. It is what I live for."

Thomas narrowed his eyes. "That's not it. What are you after?"

He was too perceptive. Peter came closer and lowered his voice. "I want to meet the Baker."

Thomas immediately started shaking his head. "Nope. Nuh-uh. My ears are still ringing from the last time I made that mistake. I'm lucky Bernard isn't taking it to the captain. I could lose my job."

Peter smiled. "There are ways around that, you know. I could dress as a nun, for example? I understand they are being allowed in to see her for medical purposes."

Thomas's eyes narrowed again. "How did you know that?"

Peter shrugged. "I'm a reporter. My cousin is a reporter. Spokane's a small town." And an insomniac with good hearing could hear quite well through heavy kitchen doors when given the opportunity.

Thomas shifted his feet. "It doesn't matter. I'm not doing it. The answer is no."

Peter nodded. "That is fine. I will still help. For the story." He extended his hand.

Thomas studied it. Then clasped it and they shook.

* * *

Bernard had only just reached his desk when he found a note from Hollway telling him Coroner Baker wanted to speak with him as soon as possible.

Without even removing his hat or his coat, he turned on his heel and headed back out to the coroner's office in the Hyde Block.

As he entered the office, he heard Baker call out from the back room, "I'll be with you in a moment!"

It was certainly much longer than that before the man himself appeared, rubbing his clean hands on a white towel and removing his pince-nez.

"Ah, Detective Carew. I'm glad you came so quickly."

"Has my seemingly simple murder gotten complicated already? Don't tell me the man was strangled before he fell," Bernard said with a twitch of his mustache, referring to the last time he'd met with the coroner in this office.

Baker shook his bald head, the electric lights reflecting off it and giving him a slight halo above his tiny ears.

"Poisoned?" Bernard pursued. "Knifed? Perhaps signs of a mugging gone wrong?"

Again Baker shook his head, rubbing his thick mustache beneath his pointed nose. "If you're quite finished, Detective, I'll tell you what I found."

Bernard stood silently, crossing and uncrossing his arms impatiently.

Baker made his way to his desk, where he sat down and pulled open a drawer, slowly removing a small collection of items. "I found these in London's pockets: a cigarette holder, a pocket watch, a handkerchief, and some loose coins."

"No matchbook? Then perhaps this was his." Bernard pulled out the one he'd found in his search amongst the rocks the day before, along with his collection of coins, key, pencil, and smashed spectacles. "I've never known a man who carried cigarettes to be without a matchbook."

Baker nodded. "These interest me, as well," he said, pointing to the spectacles.

"Yes, they seem to have been London's defining feature," said Bernard, recalling the maid and Mrs. Campbell's immediate reaction to them.

"I see," sniffed Baker, "but, the man on my table did not wear spectacles."

Bernard studied the coroner, who was tapping his pince-nez on the desk. "What do you mean?"

"Do you see these?" Baker pointed to the almost imperceptible divots on either side of his nose where his pince-nez had left their mark. "The dead man did not have these."

"How could you tell? I thought his face was—"

"Yes," Baker interrupted with a wave of his hand, "but once the blood was washed away, and his face was cleaned as well as I could manage, I could see things much more clearly. Although his nose was, of course, broken, the bridge of his nose was intact." The coroner straightened his small shoulders. "It was just your luck that your coroner is so minute in his notations, Detective. I take great pride in my observation skills, and I always notice when a body has the markings of spectacles because I wear them myself."

"But you don't wear spectacles. Don't those, I don't know, pinch less?" Bernard asked, never having worn glasses himself.

Baker shook his head. "They may hook to the ears, but they rest on the nose often enough they should have left marks or bruising of some kind. A slight indentation, at least."

"Perhaps he only wore them for work?"

"It is possible, I suppose." Baker shrugged. He returned his pince-nez to his nose. "But I also wanted to bring your attention to the handkerchief." He picked up the white bit of cloth and turned out the corner with embroidered initials toward Bernard. The letters were quite clearly "A.P." not "J.L." for James London.

Bernard frowned. "Perhaps that handkerchief belongs to a lady friend?" he suggested.

Again, Baker merely shrugged.

Then Bernard picked up the pocket watch. There were no engravings, but he knew someone who could tell him all he'd need and more besides.

* * *

Archie felt like he'd spent the night slogging through water in search of a golden ball that had sunk to the bottom of a well.

He certainly hadn't slept, and he knew he'd feel it the rest of the day. But for now, it was time for breakfast, and ever since moving into the House where Mrs. Curry was cook, he'd begun looking forward to meals again.

He slid into his seat with a grateful sigh as he eyed the collection of buckwheat cakes with pure maple syrup, cheesy eggs, sausage and bacon, three kinds of jam and toast, steaming oatmeal with cream and sugar, and a bowl of fruit beautiful enough to tempt even him, who generally didn't care for berries that had arrived on the back of a truck rather than straight off the farm.

Matsumoto was already seated at the broad oak kitchen table, which was built to seat many more than simply the three of them. Matsumoto and Archie had insisted they'd much rather join Mrs. Curry downstairs for meals than stand on ceremony and eat in the large, intimidating dining room upstairs. It was quickly becoming a house that broke all the rules, from allowing a Japanese man to work his craft in peace to letting Mrs. Curry continue living in a house with two single men.

The cook bustled about the kitchen, grabbing a pot of green tea for Matsumoto and coffee for Archie. Her mix of brown and gray curls bobbed as she walked, and her hazel eyes twinkled merrily as she sat across from the two men.

Archie took his time eating, allowing his tired mind to wake up with a cup of coffee and enjoying a little of everything Mrs. Curry had prepared for them.

"You sure do know the way to a man's heart," he finally said, patting his belly appreciatively, and knowing Thomas and Bernard would give their left feet to be here in his place.

Mrs. Curry smiled and offered him more, but he declined.

"If I eat anymore, my fingers will swell up and I won't be worth a thing!"

His work as a clockmaker required meticulous planning and placement, when he wasn't out at the blacksmith forge with Matsumoto creating prototypes, or down at Havermale Island sketching his plans for the depot clock tower.

The Japanese sword-maker was the slow and steady sort of eater, so when the blind man asked Archie how he'd slept, Archie took the opportunity to ask his opinion.

"I had a terrible night," Archie answered honestly. "I was overcome by a realization from my visit to the Baker yesterday."

Matsumoto nodded. "Yes, I could tell you were quite agitated at dinner last night. Did the Baker say something to you?"

"It wasn't the Baker that bothered me—though for all intensive purposes, yes, that was rather...unpleasant," Archie said with a gulp. "It was the nun that came in just before we left."

"The nun?" Matsumoto asked, his dim eyes focused on the cup in his hand, which Archie knew he couldn't see and could only feel, though Archie could have sworn he was studying the steam rising from his tea.

"Yes. She was tall, taller than Thomas, with broad shoulders, and her voice was deep. But it was her face that distracted me. She had heavy-lidded eyes and an aquiline nose." Archie set down his fork and turned to Matsumoto, clearing his throat. "Now, don't laugh, but I think it was Jennings dressed up."

Matsumoto didn't laugh. This was why Archie had trusted him with his concerns.

Mrs. Curry, however, did. "I'd have paid good money to see that!" she said, wiping where her laughter had caused her to spill her cream-colored coffee. "Jennings as a nun—ha!" She shook her graying brown head at the pleasant thought.

"I know it sounds augmented, but I swear it was," Archie insisted. "I think he was trying to get in to see Eleanor. They're not letting anyone in but police so far—and nuns from Sacred Heart."

Matsumoto nodded and set down his cup. "Did you smell anything?"

Archie considered and almost immediately he recalled the

smell of smoke that had followed the nun into the cells. He'd noticed the smell of pipe smoke on Thomas often enough, but the nun had smelled different, like cheap cigarettes. His subconscious at the time had figured it was due to her work with the poor, or that perhaps even nuns had vices that were difficult to break.

"She smelled of cigarette smoke," Archie said aloud. "Didn't Jennings smoke?"

Matsumoto nodded again and asked, "Did the nun breathe in just before speaking?"

Archie searched back to that brief moment in the jail. "Yes, I think she did. Just a soft breath in. Hardly noticeable."

Matsumoto nodded again. "Jennings had a habit of doing that as well, most likely caused by his smoking."

"I never noticed him doing that."

"You noticed his mannerisms, though, did you not? The way he lifted his nose or narrowed his eyes when he spoke. You have eyes that can see such things. I have ears and a nose." He picked up his tea and took another sip.

"Then you think I'm right?" Archie asked, his heart thumping. "That it was Jennings who snuck in to visit Eleanor?"

"He did always seem ready to defend her," said Mrs. Curry. "I think he would have killed Mr. Sigmund himself if she hadn't beaten him to it." She sighed heavily and shook her head. "That poor woman."

"He had feelings for her?"

"Certainly," said the cook. "He may have even loved her. Or thought he did."

Archie shook his head. "I can't imagine loving someone and then finding out she was crazy—beyond crazy. Insane."

"You've never fallen in love with someone before getting to know them? All their secrets? All their faults?" Mrs. Curry asked. She shook her head and stood to begin clearing the dishes. "You're younger than I thought."

Archie blushed as his thoughts turned to Marian. It was true he knew *one* of her secrets. Did she have others? Would she tell Thomas about her past life as a thief? Archie would never tell him, of course, for it was her secret to tell.

Unless he had to protect her.

Archie sighed. He needed to tell Thomas about Jennings and the nun. It was the right thing to do, no matter how aggravated he was with the man at the moment.

* * *

Roslyn was pleased to see she and Marian hadn't been abandoned to play hostess to the bearded reporter after all, feeling unsure as to whether she could fend off the young man's impertinent questions much longer. She hoped Marian felt the same and hadn't been drawn in by his charming manners and chiseled good looks. Especially when it was clear Thomas had indeed begun forming an attachment to her new companion. The quickest way to Thomas's heart, Roslyn knew, was through his stomach, and so she thought she may have found a way to kill two birds with one stone.

She decided the time had come to pose the question in the front parlor after breakfast as they sat together reading quietly, she with the latest edition of *Century Magazine* and Marian with another of Bernard's recommended Sherlock mysteries, *The Sign of the Four*.

"Marian, I've been thinking. Mrs. Hill acted as both cook and housemaid, and as we have Mary to do the housework now, I was wondering, might you consider taking on the cooking duties as well as acting as my companion? I assure you, it wouldn't put me out should you desire to stretch your talents in other areas."

Marian closed her book over her finger, marking her stopping place, and gazed inwardly. Roslyn could tell Marian was considering the idea most deliberately. She thought she'd decided to say yes, so she was very surprised when Marian declined.

"I'm afraid I'd disappoint everyone in the end," she said. "I am very grateful to Mrs. Curry, and for the new ice box in your pantry, as it made it possible for her to bless us with so many prepared meals. I have never had a talent for creating new foods without following a recipe book to the letter—much to Nain's dismay. I seem to always be distracted and to end up with an overly boiled egg or burned bread, which makes me no better than Mrs. Hill."

"This morning's breakfast was superb, though, my dear. And the stew and rolls we had last night—though you may have been unable to appreciate them at the time—were quite excellent. And, really, the person you have to impress most is Thomas, and you've already done that."

Marian blushed a crimson that almost matched the curls framing her forehead. Roslyn was quite pleased to see just his name induced such a physiological response.

But before Roslyn could question the young lady further, the doorbell rang. Marian answered it and shortly returned to say, "There's a woman here to see you. She says she's a friend of Mary's?"

"Mary, the maid?" Roslyn asked, setting her magazine to the side. "Please, show her in."

Marian nodded and returned to usher in a very slight, very timid middle-aged woman. Her straight, black hair was pulled back in a tight bun beneath a simple, crumpled hat. She wore an old calico dress in a fashion from at least the previous decade, with just a thin crocheted shawl wrapped about her shoulders. Her small, pointed nose and thin face claimed Italian through and through, reminding Roslyn of Bernard and Thomas's mother, who'd blessed them with their olive-tanned skin and dark hair. When the woman spoke, Roslyn was not surprised to note a strong accent still clinging to her vowels and shaping her sentences.

"Mrs. Carew," she said with a deferential bob. "I come from Mary, who is great friend, who say you need cook. I good cook. *Sono una cuoca meravigliosa...* I need work." The small woman kept her eyes lowered and her voice was so soft, Roslyn found herself leaning forward in an attempt to hear her better.

"*Benvenuta,*" Roslyn replied, pleased to see her Italian might finally come in handy. The woman's head tilted up just a little more, her shoulders relaxing just a tad at the greeting. "*Il tuo nome,* Miss..."

"*Signora* Magro. Teresa Magro, Mrs. Carew." She bobbed again.

"*Signora,* I am pleased Mary sent you to me—*sono contento.* I am indeed looking for *la cuoca.*" She glanced at Marian. Perhaps her companion wouldn't have to cook after all. "May I see your references?"

Signora Magro glanced up and then down again. "No references," she said so softly Roslyn had to guess at her words based on the sad shake of her head.

"*Nessun riferimento?*" Roslyn waved her hand. "Mary's reference is good enough for me, for you see I am in desperate need of someone who can prepare a decent cornbread, of all things. You wouldn't happen to know how to make such a thing would you?"

The sad-looking woman brightened, though she did not smile as she turned back to Roslyn. She nodded and said, "*Pane di granturco? Sì, certo!* I cook many things. I very good cook. I only need *cucina.*"

Roslyn nodded. "*Molto bene.* That's good enough for me. Marian, please take Signora Magro to the kitchen and show her where she can find what she needs." Then she turned to the signora and asked her if she might prepare luncheon for them at one. "*Proverò la tua cucina a pranzo e vedremo se puoi restare. Mangiamo all'una, se ti va.*"

Signora Magro bobbed and nodded, this time with something that wanted to be a smile but wasn't quite sure of itself yet.

Roslyn smiled to herself as the door closed behind the two women, eager to see what the woman would cook up, and wondering what Italian cornbread would taste like.

Perhaps this was better in the long run. Now she could contemplate Marian as companion and possible future sister-in-law, rather than resigning her to kitchen duties.

* * *

Marian showed the signora where everything was located in the small kitchen, grateful it was already stocked to bursting with whatever the silent woman might need, and then left her to her duties. Signora Magro had not spoken since leaving Roslyn in the parlor, and had merely nodded when Marian asked if that was all she needed. But it didn't matter if the woman didn't care to speak, all that mattered was if she could cook well enough to please the Carew brothers, and Roslyn, of course.

Marian had been tempted by Roslyn's offer, greatly tempted, since as a young girl she'd spent hours with Nain in the kitchen, but she'd known she'd never be able to hold a candle to Mrs. Curry, especially with recipe books that started with "kill the chicken and prepare in the usual way."

She was much better suited to being a companion. Someone to help around the house with things one took for granted when not confined to a wheelchair. Someone to read to you, embroider with you, and simply talk with you when you're forced to remain in the house all day waiting for company to come to you. Marian sadly realized that in the month since she'd begun working for Mrs. Carew, no one had stopped by for tea with her employer. She wondered if Roslyn had any friends to speak of. Not that Marian could help her much there. She'd never been much of a socialite herself, and since she'd left Spokane five years ago and only recently returned, she hadn't yet connected with old friends.

Other than Eleanor, of course.

Marian stopped by the indoor bathroom for a brief respite before joining Mrs. Carew again. It was still such a modern marvel to have running water and plumbing inside the house. Nain had only just added a bathroom off the back of the house before Marian left for Seattle. She hoped she'd never take it for granted, but knew deep down she probably would some day. She hadn't yet enjoyed the luxury of a bath in the claw-footed tub, instead restricting herself to the everyday use of the bowl and pitcher in her room, as she'd always done. But she had assisted Mrs. Carew in a bath, which was one more thing to get used to as a companion.

At least as a companion she'd never be in want of time to read, and the Carews were a wonderfully literary family. She smiled, recalling her conversation with Thomas the day before. She wondered when he found time to read with his work as a policeman. She'd seen the hours he was forced to work, and couldn't imagine him, or Bernard, sitting down to read, in fact had yet to see them do so. Yet, both of them were fully capable of holding the most intellectual discussions, and not just about the latest news in *The Spokesman*. And Mrs. Carew insisted on reading the most scientific books and articles of any woman Marian had ever met. Nain hadn't enjoyed reading, often saying she couldn't seem to make the letters line up properly for her, but she'd loved listening to Marian read to her while she embroidered.

Marian returned to the front parlor and picked up her embroidery from her work basket in the corner. She'd always enjoyed the rather womanly task, taking pleasure in the way the thread moved across the fabric. Marian sighed, moving the needle in and out with a strand of vibrant yellow. Nain had called it "painting with thread"...

Even though she hadn't seen Nain for five years before her death, the loss was still poignant. Perhaps more so, even. She'd missed out on five whole wonderful years with her dear grandmother because of her own stubbornness and pride. She'd run away to Seattle to "discover herself," only to discover that what she missed most was her home. And Nain.

Why did it always seem to take the largest mistakes to realize what one had at the start?

"Marian, what's wrong?" Roslyn's voice was tender and soft.

Marian wiped the tears from her eyes that had been welling gently, blurring the daisies she was stitching into something reminiscent of an impressionist painting by Van Gogh.

"Nain," she murmured softly.

Roslyn folded her magazine. "I'm so sorry."

Marian reached for a handkerchief from her chatelaine purse. "There are so many people in this world, and chances are there's someone out there very similar to Nain...but not *my* Nain."

Roslyn nodded sadly. "In this great, big world it feels like the loss of one person shouldn't affect us as much as it does. But that doesn't change how much it hurts when they leave us."

Marian wondered how she had missed the Nain-shaped hole in her heart when it was filled, and only now noticed it when it was empty?

"Be thankful for the time you knew her," Roslyn said quietly. "For all the times you had the chance to speak with her, to tell her you love her."

Marian bit her lip. "I just wish I had come home sooner." She might have been able to nurse her back to health, or at least hold her hand at the end.

Roslyn was quiet a moment before saying something Marian was certain she'd once heard Nain say. "God uses all obstacles to His glory. When bad things happen, and it's difficult to see how Someone so loving and powerful could let such things happen, remember: He's not finished yet. He can still use us. In the end, there's nothing and nobody He can't use."

Marian bit back a scoff. God. But before she could stop herself, the thought escaped her lips. "If God was loving, he wouldn't have taken my grandmother before her time. She was perfectly healthy when I left her five years ago. She was only sixty-five when she died. I should have had another lifetime with her."

She looked at the woman in the wheelchair across from her. How could someone destined to live the rest of her life with no legs believe in a loving God? Surely she felt the same way.

But Roslyn rolled closer and reached out, taking Marian's hand lightly in hers, her penetrating blue eyes locking with Marian's. "Marian, God's plan outweighs our obstacles. Think of Zechariah and Elizabeth, too old to have children, yet when they obeyed amidst their pain, God made it happen. Or Jonah—he tries to run from God, and God uses his disobedience to speak to the city of Nineveh, leading to the largest revival ever recorded in history! Or Joseph, disowned and sold by his brothers, and yet God takes his pain and uses it not only to drive him out of jail and into the highest position in Egypt, but it eventually saves the lives of those same brothers who once betrayed him. God doesn't make the pain go away, he just gives the pain a purpose."

"But death?" *Or my past as a thief?* Marian thought to herself. "How can He use Nain's death?"

"I don't know." Roslyn squeezed her hand. "But I believe He does."

* * *

Thomas walked into the first floor of City Hall with Bach still in tow, having been unable to find a way to shake him. Thankfully, the man had wanted to grab a smoke outside before entering so Thomas figured he could forewarn Bernard he'd been unable to lose the reporter.

But it turned out not to matter anyway, as Bernard had already left again on a lead.

Perhaps Thomas was the sidekick after all. The nameless narrator to Bernard's masterful mind as the detective. There was no way he was going to allow that. It was time he took this mystery into his own two hands and became the detective himself. And perhaps win the heart of the fair maiden, as well.

Thomas tried to hide his extreme annoyance as he asked Hollway, "Do you know where he went?"

The thickly mustached man scratched his chin as though pondering but then shook his head. "Afraid I don't."

Thomas clenched his jaw. "Did he leave anything for me?"

Hollway leafed through some notes to the right of the registration book. "Afraid not," he said.

"Of course not." Thomas thanked him curtly and joined Bach out on the sidewalk, a cigarette between his lips.

"Those things will kill you, you know," said Thomas, who'd always preferred pipe smoking over cigarettes, especially after Roslyn told him about an article she'd read revealing that some cigarettes mixed opium with their tobacco, or soaked their wrappers in arsenic. He figured it was much safer to stick with a decent pouch of tobacco that he knew to be only that—tobacco.

The reporter scratched his thick sideburns nonchalantly. "We've all got to die someday," he said, pulling on the cigarette before removing it to speak. "Did Detective Carew decide he didn't need your help after all?"

It seemed to Thomas the reporter kept emphasizing the "detective" part of his brother's name in his presence to get a rise out of him.

"No, as a matter of fact he's taken off on a lead without me."

"Ah, that is a shame." Bach shook his blonde head. "Do you think, in that case, now would be an opportune time to follow your own lead?"

Thomas knew what he was trying to do. If he wasn't going to let Bach meet the Baker, the man was going to try his best to get a worthy story out of this new murder.

Then again, it sounded like a good idea to Thomas.

"Fine. Tell me what you know."

Bach practically jumped in glee as he dropped his cigarette butt and pulled out his notepad, his breath catching in his excitement. "London worked as personal secretary to a Mr. Campbell here in Spokane."

Thomas squashed the cigarette end that Bach had simply left to roll across the sidewalk, shaking his head. The last thing they needed was *another* Great Fire.

He nodded at Bach's statement and looked west, toward where he knew the Campbells resided in Browne's Addition. "Campbell, eh?"

Bach scratched his mustache. "Do you know him?"

"Not personally." Thomas started making his way toward the nearest streetcar that would take them that direction. "But everyone knows who the Campbells are. They just built a new home a few years ago, relocating from Wallace."

"Wallace?"

"Idaho. But I believe they're originally from the midwest—Ohio."

Bach kept up with Thomas's long strides after they disembarked from the streetcar, once again finding themselves in Browne's Addition just a few blocks from the bluff that dropped into Hangman Creek. Thomas was thankful for the walk from the stop, for his frustration had only grown during the ride on the streetcar.

Didn't Bernard remember what happened last time? How many times had Thomas helped him solve the case? Bernard had thrown out ideas of Thomas's that he'd said were inane, only to have them proved right. Thomas had discovered the blackmailer, and had even known who the murderer was, or at least one of them.

The problem was all that fame. It had gone straight to Bernard's head. Now he thought he was as great as Sherlock and didn't need Thomas. Well, Thomas didn't mind playing Watson since, to him, Watson was the smarter of the two anyway. Watson was the one who always offered the ideas that brought Sherlock back to the real world, where understanding real people was often necessary, sometimes even in spite of what the facts seemed to suggest.

Real people had real feelings, real passions, real frustrations. Like him.

Thomas had gone out of his way to help Bernard by trying to lose the reporter for him, and instead he'd taken off without him again. And yet Bernard had offered to include him last night. Had he just been trying to assuage his guilt?

Fine. Thomas didn't need Bernard. He would solve this case on his own, and *before* Bernard.

They reached the steps of the Campbells' front door quicker than Thomas had anticipated, and he took a moment to look around for Bach, who was panting a few yards behind him.

"Perhaps you should give up smoking after all. Don't you Tacomans exercise?" Thomas asked, shaking his head.

Bach pulled a handkerchief from his coat pocket and wiped his brow. "Do Spokanites all walk with such purpose?"

Thomas grinned. "Yes. Now, let me do the talking."

Bach shrugged and pulled out his notepad and pencil. "Then I will do the noting."

Thomas turned and rang the front bell.

* * *

It wasn't long before a blonde housemaid answered. She wasn't German, though her blue eyes and nose were almost right for it. Peter guessed she was Swedish, that little bit of Norwegian spiking her chin and cheekbones.

"May I help you?"

Thomas tipped his derby. "Good morning, I'm Officer Carew with the Spokane Police Department, and this is my assistant, Mr. Bach. We were wondering if we might speak with Mr. Campbell about Mr. London."

The housemaid shook her head, lifting a rather pert little nose as she took in Thomas's plainclothes. "You're no police officer. I know a reporter when I see one." She glared toward the notepad in Peter's hand. "Besides, Mr. Campbell has already spoken with a *Detective* Carew." And then she slammed the oak door in his face.

Peter let loose a burst of laughter.

Thomas glowered, his cheeks red with embarrassment. Peter kept laughing as Thomas turned and walked toward the carriage house to the east, heading up the drive with purposeful strides, ignoring Peter's mirth at his expense.

A couple yards outside the carriage house, Peter began to smell the horrid scent of horse manure and hay. Horses would always be a sore spot for him. He was quite happy automobiles were becoming more plentiful in Washington, but chagrined to find they hadn't yet made their presence known on the eastern side of the state.

Could it really be that the Campbells hadn't bought an automobile yet? Given the size of their house, he would've thought them one of the few families in Spokane who'd have one.

Clearly, this was not the case, as they opened the door to the stable and the smell only strengthened.

He pulled out his handkerchief and held it to his nose.

"Hello?" Thomas called out.

A whinny answered and they followed it back into the bowels of the stables, past a beautiful carriage, the top down thanks to the warming spring weather, with gleaming rims and seats pin-tucked and fit for a king. This seemed to confirm Peter's theory of a lack of automobile.

"Grrrrr, roaf, rufff!" The bull terrier surprised him, growling fiercely enough to intimidate most men, including himself. But Thomas just put out the back of his hand for the dog to sniff.

"Excuse me?" he called out over the dog's continuing barks

of alarm. "We're looking for the coachman of Mr. Campbell? I assume this fella isn't him?"

A rather square head poked out from inside one of the back stalls before stepping out, revealing a clean-shaven young man, a curry comb in one hand.

"Bobby, heel," he said firmly, and immediately the dog came to him and sat at his feet obediently, though he continued to study Thomas and Peter warily.

"Good guard dog," Thomas said pleasantly, offering his hand to the coachman. "Officer Carew, at your service."

The man scratched his high forehead. The sleeves of his white shirt were rolled up to reveal massive forearms. Suspenders held up his black trousers, criss-crossing his broad back and wide shoulders. His eyes focused on the two of them with all the intensity of a horse, revealing the man was in the right trade.

"Gladding," he finally said, moving the brush to his left hand before shaking Thomas's hand firmly. "Joseph Gladding."

Thomas apparently didn't mind that his hand now smelled of horse.

"This is my associate, Mr. Bach," Thomas said, nodding over his shoulder at where Peter stood with the handkerchief over his nose. "I see you have a way with animals." Thomas pointed toward the stall with the horse in it, and then the dog at Gladding's heel.

Gladding nodded. "Been a horse-trainer from a young age, grew up around 'em back home."

"Where are you from?"

"Youngstown," he said, "Ohio."

"Ah, is that where you met the Campbells? I believe they come from Ohio stock, as well."

"Yup. Met Mr. Campbell while he was in town to buy some horses and a pony. We hit it off, so he offered me a job as coachman out here."

"How long ago was that?"

"Ninety-eight, back when the house was first built."

"And you've been here ever since?" Peter asked from behind the handkerchief.

"Ever since," Gladding said, giving Peter a wary look before returning his focus to Thomas. "Carew, eh? You related to the detective in the paper?"

Peter smiled at Thomas's discomfort. The man just couldn't get a break.

"Why, yes, I am," Thomas replied. "I'm his brother."

Gladding crossed to some hooks where he hung the brush and wiped his hands on a towel. "Well, how can I help you?"

"I'm looking for anyone who can tell me more about Mr. London."

"Yes, sir, he was found at the bottom of Hangman Creek. It's not too far from here." He pointed in the general direction over his shoulder.

"I heard he worked for Mr. Campbell."

Gladding nodded. "Yes, sir, he did. But you'd best talk with Mr. Campbell about that."

"My brother already has. I'd like to hear what you knew about him."

Gladding shrugged. "Didn't speak much with him. Just gave

him a ride when Mr. Campbell traveled with him on business. He was always with Mr. Campbell."

"Did you ever give him a ride home?" Peter asked through his handkerchief, thinking maybe they could get a leg up on Bernard by beating him to the dead man's house.

"No, sorry. He always walked home, though that doesn't mean much these days since the streetcar can take you most places just as quickly as a coach."

Peter couldn't tell if the man was trying to be helpful or purposely unhelpful. "Is there anyone else who might know more about him?"

Gladding scratched his forehead again. "You might speak with Chung Lee, I suppose."

"Chung Lee?" Peter repeated.

"He's the cook."

Thomas gave Peter a smile. "Perfect."

* * *

Bernard was beginning to realize he sort of missed the slower pace and lesser paperwork of thefts, hold-ups, break-ins, and the like. With a murder, there was so much more to consider.

Like what to do with the murderer after he, or she, had been caught.

The Baker was an exception in that no one in Spokane quite knew how to handle her rather unique case. Chief Witherspoon had told Bernard and Thomas to keep an eye on her, and speak to her at least once a day, to see if they couldn't get a better handle on the situation, and how it would be best to move forward with prosecuting her case.

As he rode the streetcar up to the House, the watch the coroner had given him rested in his palm with a weight of indecision, and he found his mind turning not to his current case, but to the middle-aged woman already locked in a cell.

One of the first times they'd talked with her in jail she had shared something from her past that had stuck with him. He was pretty sure it was Eleanor speaking at the time, since she'd seemed lucid and had told a story from before the Baker's first appearance in 1889.

She'd started by saying she'd grown up on a farm. "My father had a small one-man forge for fixing horseshoes and tools and such on his own. One day I saw him leave the forge to go attend to some emergency. The fire called to me. I snuck inside and studied the apparatus. I'd seen my father working it before, but knew better than to touch anything. And yet... The fire called to me again. So I reached out to touch the tongs, which were stuck in the sand beside the glowing pit. It *burned*. I plunged my hand into the slack tub, but it wasn't enough. Just a brief touch of the still-hot metal had left a line of irritated, melted skin across my hand, a clear sign of my disobedience."

She'd held her palm up then for him to see. She'd hidden the hand from her parents, she'd said, afraid what her father would do to her if he found out. And so she still had the scar. A constant reminder of why fire was no laughing matter.

She'd traced her fingers over the red line. Tenderly. "So many scars...," she'd murmured. "Mr. Sigmund, my first husband...Fire." She'd seemed to forget then that he was still standing out there, memorandum book in hand, writing down every word she said. "Sometimes I wonder how God, if he exists, can allow so much pain to happen to just one woman. Why not spread it out amongst the populace? Surely there are enough people in the world. But no, I seem to gather them all on my own. Like some terrible lodestone, magnetically drawing all the pain to myself."

She'd turned away from him then, folding in on herself as she sat back down on the cot. "Perhaps someday the stone will become heavy enough to drag me under, and I can escape, finally, for good."

Bernard had made doubly sure afterward that she didn't have access to any shoelaces or small knives or even a hatpin with which to finish the job on her own, though something told him the Baker would never allow Eleanor to kill herself. The Baker side of her—if that was how one thought of it—had gone to too much trouble to allow her to take her own life.

But then, Thomas had taken Miss Kenyon down... Bernard suddenly realized he hadn't checked on the Baker yet this morning, and he'd meant to. As much as he hated to think it, he needed to be certain Miss Kenyon hadn't accidentally—or purposely—handed the Baker something through the metal bars.

Escape from this new prison would be much more difficult, of course, in comparison to the old jail, which the *Review* had once described as looking "like a poor man's overalls. It is patched in 100 places." The new, thicker brick walls enclosed separate steel tanks for males and females, though they still didn't have matrons, something they were unlikely to get anytime soon with cutbacks on the horizon.

Bernard sighed. He was too far up the hill to go back now. He'd have to stop by on his way back in. Just one more thing for him to handle on his own.

On his own. The first time, Thomas had helped him. And he most certainly *had* helped, no matter what the papers said, or how overlooked Thomas felt. Bernard wondered, not for the first time, if he'd be able to figure out this newest one without Thomas's assistance.

Part of him wanted to. The part of him that had jumped on the streetcar without waiting for Thomas to arrive after being so gracious as to try to shake the reporter for him.

But the other part of him really missed his brother. They were twins, after all, so he couldn't imagine a world without him.

That part of him kept asking if he might have ever solved the Baker murder without him, without Eleanor explaining it all and the Baker revealing herself in a moment of truth. He'd had all the clues, but would he have eventually gotten there himself? To the complete truth?

Would Thomas?

* * *

Thomas thought things were finally looking up as he followed the coachman into the main house. He held cooks in a special place in his heart, and just knew this Chung Lee would have the answers he needed to beat Bernard to the punch this time.

It was a short walk out of the carriage house and up the back steps to the door of an enclosed porch. Inside stood a large ice box along the back wall, an appliance that seemed common enough in America these days. Here they were asked to wipe their boots thoroughly on the outdoor rug before entering the kitchen.

"Chung Lee does not take kindly to those who come tromping in with mud on their heels," explained Gladding.

After checking to be sure they'd followed his instructions—it was clear the man feared he'd be blamed should they not comply—he opened the door and let them into the kitchen.

White-and-red-patterned wallpaper covered the upper half and ceiling of the room, with white tile and moulding covering the bottom half of the walls and floor. Everything sparkled as though it had been whitewashed with paint, rather than scrubbed with vinegar and borax. A white marble sink stood in the corner, though clearly no dirty dishes dared to remain there long. The only black item was the massive wood and gas range along the wall to their left, its size declaring it to be the master of its domain.

Standing at it was an Asian man dressed all in white, who whirled around as they entered.

"Can I help you?" the cook asked sternly, the spoon in his hand held at the ready like an executioner's axe.

Gladding introduced them and left quickly, muttering something about getting back to the horses.

"May I say: it smells quite delectable in here." Thomas looked pointedly toward the enormous pot on the stove.

"You may." Chung Lee did not smile or elaborate, or offer a taste, much to Thomas's chagrin. But they were only getting started.

"We're here about Mr. London."

"Yes, I hear he is dead," Chung Lee said.

Thomas nodded. "Yes, I'm afraid he is. Anything you can share with me about him would be most helpful."

Chung Lee turned and stirred the delicious-smelling something in the pot, replacing the lid before turning back to Thomas to reply.

"Mr. London was not to be trusted. Everyone but Mr. Campbell knew that."

Thomas's eyebrows rose in surprise. "May I ask what made you believe he was untrustworthy?"

"Mr. London took smoke breaks practically every hour, and he always did it out back, behind the carriage house, where Mr. Campbell could not see him from his study windows upstairs. But I could see him."

"You don't trust a smoker?" Bach asked, no doubt concerned his own yellowing teeth might give him away.

"Not when he continually does so in order to meet with certain persons without Mr. Campbell's knowledge."

"Like who?" asked Thomas.

Chung Lee returned to his pot on the stove for a minute, and then turned back to face him, as though giving himself a chance to decide whether to answer the question. "People like Mr. Pavoni."

"Pavoni?" Thomas repeated. "I know that name. He's on the McKinley Reception Committee. He's from Olympia or Seattle or somewhere out west."

"Tacoma."

Thomas turned to Bach. "Tacoma?"

The reporter nodded. "He's from my neck of the woods."

"Do you know him personally?" Thomas asked, for once interested in what the bearded man had to say.

"As much as any reporter might do. I had the pleasure

of making his acquaintance at a Fourth of July parade, and I attended one or two of his speeches. He's a great orator. Very persuasive."

"I see," murmured Thomas.

Bach pulled out his handkerchief and blew his nose loudly. Chung Lee glared at him and pointed toward a door with a little round window in it for peeking out, or in, as the case may be, but said no more.

Bach nodded—clearly *no one* blew their nose around Chung Lee's food—and made his escape while Thomas shook his head after him.

"I apologize for him. He's getting over a cold," he lied. Why was he bothering covering for a man who irritated him so much? Thomas cleared his throat. "I guess I don't understand the dilemma," he said, turning back to the cook. "If Mr. London was Mr. Campbell's secretary, then wouldn't it make sense for them to meet?"

Chung Lee sniffed. "Yes, it would not be odd for them to discuss things in Mr. Campbell's presence. Indeed, Mr. Pavoni has often been a dinner guest of this house in the past month."

Chung Lee set down his spoon and opened the top of the range to stoke the fire. "What *is* odd is for Mr. Pavoni to say good evening to Mr. Campbell and exit by way of the front door, only to return to have a private smoke with his personal secretary behind the carriage house."

Thomas agreed. That was certainly odd. "I take it you enjoy working for the Campbells?"

"The Campbells are ever so kind. Mrs. Campbell, in particular, is very considerate, especially with the menu. She is willing to try new suggestions, and always lets me know well in advance when plans have changed."

"Like when McKinley's visit was canceled?"

Chung Lee nodded, though Thomas noticed his shoulders slumped a little.

"That must have been a great blow to you. I'm sure you had many wonderful meals planned for him."

Chung Lee returned to his pot for one more stir before setting down the spoon and crossing to a small white table that sat along one wall of the kitchen, which hid a few small drawers just under the lip. Opening one, he removed a piece of paper covered in scrawling handwriting and handed it to Thomas.

"This was what was planned," was all the cook said.

Although both breakfasts were pretty standard with eggs, toast, potatoes, steak, fruit, and coffee, the lunch and dinner menus were extravagant, including things like boiled fish, red flannel hash, and hot lobster salad.

"Food fit for a king, or a President, as it seems," Thomas said encouragingly.

"Indeed." Chung Lee returned the list to the drawer and then crossed back to the range. "And now, if you would please take your investigation elsewhere, I am in the midst of luncheon preparations and cannot be disturbed further."

Thomas's face surely revealed his feeling of utter sadness as he thanked the cook and exited through the swinging door.

As the door swung to, he found himself in the servants' entryway. Bach was ascending the stairs that led down into the basement, where he must have found a bathroom.

"Shall we?" Thomas said with a wave toward the back door, leading the way out into the yard.

"What rotten luck," said Thomas as he walked away from the house.

"I'm certain you'll find a lead elsewhere," Bach said helpfully.

Thomas stopped and shook his head. "Not that. He didn't even invite us to stay for lunch!"

* * *

Roslyn shuffled the articles before her. She'd taken it upon herself to learn more about the psychology behind the Eleanor/Baker dilemma. It was clear neither Marian, Bernard, nor Thomas knew what to make of the whole thing, and so for the past month she'd been combing through every old and new edition of her favorite magazines searching for something helpful.

She may be confined to a chair, but that didn't mean she couldn't help in that one particular gift of hers: researching.

Her fascination with all things medical and scientific was finally going to pay off and prove that she had a lot to offer in assisting her detective husband.

What she'd learned was far more enlightening than she'd imagined, however. She'd finally found what she wanted in an older edition of *The Journal of Nervous and Mental Disease*, a collection of them having been donated to her by someone in the church who'd thought she might find them interesting.

The article was about a young French woman named Felida, entitled "*Amnesic periodique ou de dedoublement de la vie.*" It had been translated into English from the *Revue Scientifique*, and published back in 1876 by a Dr. Azam.

Felida was described as an intelligent, ordinary young lady, who occasionally suffered from intense headaches and a form of hysteria. Then in 1858, she began showing far more worrying symptoms, including falling into a sleep state from which she'd awake with a personality very different from her normal one.

"Her character is completely changed; formerly melancholy, she has become cheerful; even gay, her vivacity something even bordering on wildness. Her imagination is very vivid. From the slightest cause, she is overcome with emotions of sadness or joy. Instead of being indifferent to everything, as she was, she has become sensitive in the extreme.

"In this condition, she remembers perfectly all that has passed during similar preceding states, and also during her normal life.... Felida remembers not only that which has taken place during previous attacks, but also during her entire normal life, whereas...during her normal life she has no recollection of that which took place during the attacks....

"Some minutes before, she sings a romantic song, and if we ask her to repeat it, she does not know what we are talking about. They speak to her about a visitor whom she has just received, but she has seen no one.... The forgetfulness relates only to those things which transpired during the second condition. Every general idea acquired prior to this, is unaffected. She knows perfectly well how to read, write, and keep accounts, cut out work, sew, and a thousand other things..."

Once Roslyn realized she might need to be looking in the French magazines, rather than the English, she was pleased to find a second article, "*Un cas de dedoublement de la personnalité; piriode amnesique d'une annie chez unjeune homme,*" in the *Annales*

Médico-Psychologiques and authored by Dr. Camuset. It took a little more time, as it required she translate the French to English on her own.

According to Camuset's article, his patient, Vivet, also existed in a primary and secondary state. Strangely enough, Vivet was even paralyzed in one state, and fully capable of walking in the other. Also, like Felida, Vivet was able to recall everything when in one state, but suffered from amnesia when in the other.

Roslyn finally set down the articles, tapping her fingers upon them as she gazed at nothing, thinking about what she'd just read.

From what Bernard and Marian had told her, it seemed to Roslyn that it was very likely there were certain similarities between Eleanor's case and those of poor Felida and Vivet.

If the Baker only appeared to defend Eleanor, to help her do "what was necessary" to remove the terrible husbands in her life, then it made much more sense for the Baker to be secondary and Eleanor to be primary. But if Eleanor could not remember becoming the Baker, then that meant that her Baker side most likely *could* remember everything. Which made Eleanor a secondary state, and the Baker her primary state—something too horrifying to maintain.

Roslyn bit at her lip, avoiding looking at Marian, who was reading beside her, as she wasn't ready yet to present these new ideas to her companion. She'd need to make a list of questions for Bernard to ask Eleanor the next time he interviewed her. It was possible that he might be able to teach the attending physicians a thing or two when it came down to it, as the likelihood of local psychologists being familiar with anything remotely similar to this was highly doubtful.

At least she was finally getting somewhere with her research. If Eleanor really did suffer from this "double consciousness," she stood a very good chance of ending up in Medical Lake asylum, which, although not good, was far better than ending up at the end of a hangman's noose.

* * *

Peter looked down the bluff into Hangman Creek and the world swirled before his eyes.

It was all too similar. Too familiar.

Suddenly he could hear it again: a screech, a pop, screaming, a crash. Many had thought it fireworks, it being the Fourth of July and all. But no, it had been the screech of trolley car brakes trying to slow the wheels that were picking up too much speed coming down Tacoma's Delin Street, the popping of the electrical line disconnecting from above the track, and then the desperate screams of people.

He'd heard the crash from two blocks away. He and his cousin Daniel had been interrupted in their conversation with a very important man—Tony Pavoni. The same man Campbell's cook had just mentioned.

How ironic that it had been the three of them who'd run to the edge of the ravine, just like this one, and peered down a hundred feet onto wreckage too difficult to access in order to assist in any rescue attempts.

They'd stood there, looking back and forth between the upside-down car at the bottom of the ravine and the dozens of injured passengers who'd had the gumption to leap from the runaway car on its way down the hill. Later, they'd learned the car had reached almost thirty miles an hour by the time it hit the sharp curve at the bottom, allowing it plenty of speed to jump the track, clearing the guard rail, and plunging, down, down, down—

Peter's stomach plummeted along with the memory.

Over one hundred passengers on their way to the parade: forty-three dead, the remaining sixty-five injured.

It had almost been a year since the accident, almost a year since Peter had decided he was going to change his life because of what he'd witnessed. He'd decided to try his hand at a variety of different jobs, finally landing on reporter and getting shipped out here, so determined was he not to waste his life or die meaninglessly in a runaway trolley accident.

And now he was here, in Spokane, looking down into another ravine, and all he could think was: had he really managed to move on from the past? His cousin would say that he needed to get out there and get himself a story no one else had. And he had done exactly that, only to find himself confronting his darkest memory anyway.

He knew he should tell Thomas what he'd found in the den of the Campbells' house, but a part of him—the reporter part—wanted to keep it to himself. After all, it might just be the advantage he was looking for. He'd only get one chance at a first article for *The Spokesman-Review*, and he intended to start off with a bang.

From the moment he'd entered the basement den—after he'd so cunningly found an excuse to take a look around without

Thomas—he'd known he was on to something. The walls were papered in a dark maroon shade, but not so dark that the Japanesque pattern in the wallpaper couldn't be noticed. A large brick fireplace filled one corner, and a low-hanging lamp in an Arabic style hung over a large table in the center of the room. The windows were made of bottle glass—privacy glass—which meant whatever happened in this room, Mr. Campbell didn't want others to find out about.

Then, his luck still holding, inside a closet door he'd found a fireproof National Safe from Cleveland, Ohio, which he'd just happened to have been able to unlock with a few deft movements—a worthy skill he'd picked up in one of his last jobs. Inside the safe he'd found some rather intriguing papers.

Anarchist papers. Flyers calling for the downfall of the moneyed elite. A folded newspaper with articles circled in bold pen outlining how to build bombs. A crumpled letter that had been smoothed and folded that was addressed to Mr. Campbell and signed by "A.C.M.—A Common Man" that called for better pay and protection for the miners. Another letter from a Levi Hutton, dated 1899, who claimed he'd been held at gunpoint and forced to drive his train hauling dynamite into the concentrator at Wardner. Letters from a Pinkerton detective reporting notes from a private union meeting. Letters between Mr. Campbell and someone named Finch, as well as letters with Pavoni, whom he now knew was also somehow linked with the dead man, London. Peter hadn't had time to read, though his quick eyes had caught on words like "the President" and "McKinley."

There was money and jewelry in the safe, too, but those didn't interest Peter.

The papers were quite enough for him.

Like Daniel once said, "You don't need the whole truth and nothing but the truth. You're a reporter, not a judge. It's up to the people to decide. Not you. Report what you know, report what you don't know, then let the people make the final decision."

Suddenly, Thomas came up behind Peter where he stood on the ledge, interrupting his thoughts and scaring the wits out of him. He cursed and then grimaced, running a hand nervously over his beard as Thomas continued to lean out, taking in the view down the bluff to the river.

"Such a long, rocky way down."

Peter nodded and crossed his arms. "How easy would it be? It wouldn't even have to be on purpose. Just a trip, a stumble, and down you go."

Thomas scratched his chin. "You know, we might not be looking at a case of suicide, but just an accident. Perhaps London was out here smoking, looking at the stars," he looked up himself, removing his derby, "and then *oops!*" He looked out and down.

It made Peter's knees tremble just to consider.

He needed a cigarette.

Thomas made a face. "Another one?"

Peter looked up at him as he dropped his match. "All that walking," he said around the cigarette, waving his hand behind him, "and this." He waved toward the bluff's edge.

Thomas studied him a moment, replaced his derby, and then gave in, pulling out his own pipe and tobacco pouch.

Peter gave him a look.

"You've got a point. I need to think," Thomas admitted, lighting his pipe, which took considerably longer and made Peter wonder why the man wouldn't just go for the simplicity of a cigarette.

"So tell me more about Pavoni," Thomas said after they stood together puffing a short while in companionable silence.

Peter considered. "Well, for one thing, he doesn't like McKinley."

"What makes you say that?"

"Pavoni's the State Labor Commissioner, whereas McKinley's a friend to the elite, the business owners who make their money off the sweat of the laborers beneath them."

"Didn't McKinley say, 'I am for America because America is for the common people'?" Thomas asked.

"You shouldn't believe everything you read in the paper."

"I take it you see the irony in that statement coming from a reporter's mouth?"

Peter took a long draw. "Pavoni isn't afraid to say what he thinks. In fact, I think he delights in getting a rise out of people. Like most politicians, what he says and what he means are often at odds with one another."

"But he's a good orator, you said—persuasive."

Peter nodded and scratched at a sideburn. "Yeah. He's definitely that. If you ever get the chance to hear him speak, I recommend it. But be ready to hear some things that may be difficult to swallow...until you've had time to really consider them."

"I take it you've had this experience?"

Peter shrugged. "I don't pay much attention to politics, myself. Other than to write about it. It's best not to get so involved you get an opinion as a reporter. Makes it harder to be unbiased in your writing."

Thomas scoffed. "An unbiased reporter, now that's something that's difficult to swallow."

Peter smiled. He sort of liked Thomas.

* * *

Thomas couldn't believe it, but part of him was starting to like Bach. He'd never been big on reporters, had always thought of them as an acknowledged evil. His father had encouraged this dislike from a young age, filling their heads with how reporters were only out for a story, nothing more, nothing less, and at whatever cost.

"Just the other day," he'd say, "I was at the deathbed of a friend, when this reporter fellow comes in, all solicitude and sadness, only to lean over the dying man and ask, 'Have you anything to say about this disgraceful report concerning your son?'" His father had simply shaken his head in a manner that said, "What more can you expect from a reporter?"

The term had been a curse, a derogatory, vulgar name for someone worth less than the scum beneath your boot.

But maybe, just maybe, his father had been wrong. After all, his mother had said, "It pays to be polite to all." And if he was honest, Thomas had met his fair share of decent reporters in his time. Perhaps some of them were just trying to earn an honest living...in a disagreeable way.

"So, what do you think?" Thomas waved his pipe toward the incline before them. "An accident?"

Bach threw the butt of his cigarette onto the ground. "Like you said, it would be easy." His eyes focused on the creek beneath them, then he took a step back and looked at Thomas. "Perhaps the hobo did it?"

Thomas scratched his chin and began to tamp out his pipe onto the ground. "Perhaps. You're thinking he accidentally tripped London, he fell to his death, and then the hobo felt so guilty about it he came in to ensure we found the body?"

Bach shrugged. "I know it's not likely, but maybe we should speak with him again?"

Thomas shook his head and replaced his pipe into his coat pocket. "That hobo's long gone, probably snuck onto the first train out of town. Especially if he just accidentally killed a man."

"You're right," Bach said.

"However, if it was an accident, it's also possible London had enemies that might turn an 'accident' to their advantage."

"Like Mr. Campbell?" Bach suggested.

"Hm," Thomas said.

Bernard had a tendency to get impressed by the big wigs, by the upper crust, but to Thomas's mind they were no different from middle-class like himself, or even the hobo. They were still people. And people had motives.

He had no problem suspecting Mr. Campbell, especially as it was possible he'd found out about whatever Pavoni and London were discussing behind the house at odd hours. But to go so far as killing?

It would only take a simple accidental shove. It wouldn't even dirty his fancy evening dress shoes...

It was a possibility, though he was hesitant to mention it to Bach. The reporter may be growing on him, but that didn't mean he intended to give him a story like that to run in the paper. The last thing he needed was the Campbells calling for his head.

Thomas scratched his ear. "I'll have to ask Bernard what he learned when he interviewed him."

"That would require getting him to share the investigation with you," Bach pointed out.

Thomas growled, but then he realized the sound hadn't come from his throat, but from his stomach. "We'd better head home. At least Mrs. Curry would never leave us to fend for ourselves."

* * *

Archie watched out the streetcar window as it sailed down Howard Street—a route he was becoming increasingly familiar with, as his new lodgings were quite a commute from where his work on the clock tower was located downtown.

Just yesterday, he'd spent several hours studying plans for the depot with the architects, remarking on the idealistic...that wasn't the word...idol...*idyllic* nature of the design. Unlike the other railroads that criss-crossed through downtown, the Great Northern wanted their depot to stand out from the rest. With their rail yards already situated on Havermale Island, slightly removed from downtown with the Spokane River on either side, it would make for a magnificent placement. The depot would hug the edge of the island along the river, so that a reflecting pool would stand before it. It meant passengers would disembark to be met not by the clanging dirtiness of other railroads but by the reflection of the sandstone depot and clock tower in the water. The station's grandeur would give a worthy first impression of Spokane, Washington.

And then, as his clock chimed the hour, they would follow the roadway from the depot across the bridge, passing over the roaring, rushing, wonderful Spokane Falls, and into the beautiful brick buildings that made up downtown Spokane.

He'd come to love the falls. The way they drowned out the busyness of the world around him with the simplicity of nature.

Yeesh. He was starting to sound like Matsumoto.

He grinned to himself and glanced about the car to see if anyone else had seen his foolishness. Nope. Everyone was too busy with their own thoughts. It was Saturday, so the streetcar was slowly filling up as it made its way down the hill. Families and couples and singles all headed to Natatorium Park for an enjoyable afternoon visit, no doubt. He had yet to make it out that way himself, but he'd had hopes of taking Marian...before Thomas moved into play.

There was no way he could compete with such a guy: smart, handsome, witty, and he had to admit, he was kind. It wasn't like he'd *had* to bring Archie along on the visit to the Baker, even if Marian had asked for him. But still, he had brought Archie. Because he was a gentleman.

Archie sighed. And Marian deserved a gentleman.

He shook his head slightly and tried to switch thoughts but he just landed back on the nun. He kept replaying her—or his— entrance into the jail, trying to recall every detail.

He really, really, *really* hoped Thomas didn't laugh at him. He wasn't sure how he'd handle that. Especially if it was in front of Marian...

With that terrible image in his head, he finally dismounted from the streetcar at the stop nearest his old lodgings and walked down to the green house with the red shutters at 1423 W Mallon Ave. He took a deep breath and straightened his tie and waistcoat under his jacket—it was warm enough he hadn't bothered with an overcoat, thinking he looked rather dashing in a simple suit, with his pocket watch hanging on an elegant chain, even if the buttons did strain a bit across his middle. He cleared his throat and strode up the walkway. He almost walked straight in, like he was still lodging there, but remembered himself in time to knock on the front door.

A smile framed by freckles and red curls answered the door.

"Archie!" she exclaimed happily.

He removed his hat as she waved him into the foyer. "Good day, Marian. I actually came by to speak with Thomas. Is he in? Or is he at the station?"

"He left this morning with Mr. Bach, the new boarder." Marian leaned in just slightly. "He's not nearly as wonderful as the old boarder, in my opinion."

Archie felt his mouth turn up in a stupid grin. But then he straightened and put his homburg back on in preparation to leave. Before he could make his excuses, however, Marian stopped him with a hand on his arm.

"Please, stay. We're about to test our new cook's luncheon menu. You know Thomas won't be gone for long with food on the table." She laughed, but this time Archie had to force the grin. "Please, come in. Mrs. Carew will want to see you."

Archie wasn't so certain about that. Not that they hadn't gotten on well, but he barely knew the woman. When he'd lodged here she'd mostly kept company with her companion, and he'd been rather distracted by a murder investigation.

"I suppose I could stay for a short time. Until Thomas returns. I just had a small question for him."

Marian was discreet enough not to ask him what his question was, for which he was grateful, since he wasn't certain what he'd say. She hung up his hat and then led them into the front parlor, where Mrs. Carew was seated in her wheelchair before the fireplace, a stack of papers in her hands.

"Mr. Prescot," she said kindly, placing her reading material onto a side table and offering her hand to him. "What a pleasure to see you again."

"The pleasure's all mine," he said, taking her hand before seating himself on the Chesterfield.

"Shall I call for some tea?" Mrs. Carew asked.

"Thank you, but I heard your new cook is working on luncheon, so I'd hate to disturb her."

"Nonsense," said Mrs. Carew with a smile, and Marian nodded in agreement before leaving to see if tea were possible.

The room seemed to shrink in size as Archie and Mrs. Carew were left alone.

Mrs. Carew turned her attention to Archie and studied him. "You look well, Mr. Prescot. I see Mrs. Curry is taking good care of her household."

Archie smiled. "Indeed. As well as this one, I know, for I assisted in the delivery of the baskets yesterday. I hope you found her profferings to your liking."

Mrs. Carew waved a hand. "Naturally. No one can compare to Mrs. Curry," she said with a sigh and in such a way as to intimate she'd heard this said far too often in the month since her husband and brother-in-law had met the cook and sampled her wares. "I do wish she would do us all a favor and come to work for us here, rather than hiding her talents up in that mansion."

Marian returned with a tray laden with tea things, her eyes wide as she addressed her mistress. "Roslyn, I think you will be most pleasantly surprised by the coming meal, if the smells emanating from that kitchen are anything to go by. Not to mention, Signora Magro said she always keeps a kettle boiling on the stovetop so it was no trouble at all to prepare tea while she worked."

Mrs. Carew breathed out a sigh of relief, her hand to her chest. "How thoughtful of her." She smiled happily at Marian as she poured a cup for each of them, handing the first to Mrs. Carew, then Archie, then taking a seat with her own in hand.

"Magro?" Archie repeated. "Italian, I take it?"

"Yes, indeed." Mrs. Carew nodded. "My maid sent her to me after I asked her if she knew anyone she'd recommend as a cook. We have been in desperate need, as you well know." She tipped her head to him.

"I feel like I've heard the name before," said Archie. "I don't know why. I wish I had a photogenic memory. I seem to be having a lot of these moments lately."

"Moments of forgetfulness?" Marian asked with a laughing smile.

"No, of feeling like I've seen someone or heard something before."

"'There is nothing new under the sun,'" quoted Mrs. Carew.

Marian's face lit up and Archie expected her to say that was something her Nain used to say. But she didn't, surprisingly.

"What do you call that again? When you feel like you're experiencing something you've experienced before?"

"Promnesia, though I believe the French call it, '*déjà vu*,'" said Mrs. Carew, handing her finished cup and saucer to Marian.

"I feel like I just saw you," said Thomas from the doorway.

Marian's face lit up again, but this time Archie knew for certain the cause.

"Humorous, dear brother-in-law," said Mrs. Carew.

"Uh-oh. She only ever calls me that when I've stepped over the line." He chuckled. "Prescot, good to see you again, even if it's only been a matter of hours. There can only be one reason why you felt the need to stop by again so soon."

Archie's eyebrows rose, his cheeks flushed, and his eyes shot to Marian and back to Thomas as his heart tried to make a break for the door.

Thomas rose only one eyebrow in response, but it was clear he'd seen Archie's reaction. "Mrs. Curry must have accidentally sent the last of her blueberry scones to us, and you've come in search of them." He smiled and rubbed his stomach. "I'm afraid you've just missed them."

Archie blew out and pretended he was taking a sip of tea instead. What a gentleman.

"You'll either be pleased or put out to hear we'll be sampling a new cook's menu for luncheon this afternoon," Mrs. Carew cut in.

Thomas's forehead furrowed for a moment, but then brightened. "Perhaps you wouldn't mind inviting us up to the House again then?" he said to Archie.

It was clear he was joking, but it had been rather rude to ask such a thing before Mrs. Carew.

"Nonsense. He'll be joining us here," said Mrs. Carew. "Won't you?"

There was no polite way to decline an invitation from the mistress of the household, so Archie agreed, covering his discomfort with another sip of practically nonexistent tea. He decided he'd keep the last swallow until luncheon was served so he could continue to have something to do with his hands.

"You can count me in," said another voice from the hall.

Into the doorway stepped a tall man with blonde hair, blue eyes, and one of the most magnificent beards Archie had seen in a long time. But it was the smell of cigarette smoke that made Archie thankful he hadn't taken a large sip of tea.

And the man's nose: it was aquiline.

* * *

The fat man on the couch was staring at Peter, and he wasn't sure why. They'd never met before, had they? Though the man did look vaguely familiar...

He nodded his head to him and put out his hand. "Peter Bach."

"This is Mr. Prescot, our previous boarder," said Mrs. Carew by way of introduction.

"And now a good friend," said Thomas, taking a seat beside the larger man on the Chesterfield.

"Ah, yes, the clockmaker?" Peter asked, his breath catching slightly. He really did need to cut back on those cigarettes. Not that it helped that Thomas insisted on walking at a stride that kept pace with the carriage horses on the street. "Detective Carew told me about your involvement in his last case."

He took a seat in a small armless chair a little outside the circle of friends and family. Peter's fingers itched to pull out his notepad and pencil, but he knew it would be frowned upon by the lady of the house.

"Yes, but he came to Spokane to build the new clock for the Great Northern depot," Miss Kenyon put in.

"Seth Thomas sent him all the way from Connecticut to do the work in person, isn't that right, Prescot?" Thomas added, giving Mr. Prescot's shoulder a friendly nudge.

Peter glanced about the room and then back to the clockmaker. Clearly they didn't want him delving into a certain topic of conversation.

"I see," he said politely. "It seems a bit odd for a company to send a clockmaker across this expansive country to build a clock. Is it not usual these days to simply send the clock by train to have it installed in the finished clock tower?"

Mr. Prescot lowered his teacup, which he'd been clasping firmly since Peter's entrance into the room even though it was visibly empty.

"Yes," he said softly, still staring at Peter like he'd seen a ghost.

Peter took a quick breath before returning to the more interesting subject at hand: "Detective Carew told me you had only just received patronage from the late Miss Mitchell when she was murdered. Tell me: What work of a clockmaker is worthy of such notice?" Peter asked with a smile.

"Now, now, Mr. Bach," said Mrs. Carew. "I will have to ask that you refrain from interviewing my guests."

Peter tipped his head to her respectfully. "Naturally, Mrs. Carew. I only wondered."

"I'm afraid Mr. Bach works for *The Spokesman-Review*," Thomas explained to Mr. Prescot. "It's like trying to break a bulldog of tugging on a bone."

The clockmaker still stared. His eyes must be getting tired.

"I'm sorry I took your rooms here," Peter said politely, trying to engage the man behind the thick glasses.

"Prescot has moved on to better things, haven't you?" Thomas said. "He's living the high life now up at the House—" He stopped and glanced at Mrs. Carew, as if realizing his mistake.

Too late.

Peter leapt at the bone. "Ah, so now you live in the former Mitchell mansion? However do you do it?"

Mr. Prescot's eyes narrowed.

Had he said too much? "I merely wondered how you could live and work in such a place after all that excitement. I would love to see where it all happened."

The clockmaker's mouth turned up into a smile. Almost unnerving in its way, to see his face finally transform from a silent, staring monument to a theater mask fit for a *commedia dell'arte*.

"Surly...um, surely you've been there yourself," Mr. Prescot said.

Peter shook his head.

"Then, perhaps, you would care to join me after lunch?" the clockmaker asked with an almost sadistic grin.

The invite sounded more like an invitation to be baked in the forge alongside Mr. Sigmund than to visit the house where two people had been murdered—neither of which was very enticing.

But he was a reporter now. A reporter who always got his story.

He'd do whatever it took to get the answers he was looking for.

* * *

Bernard knocked at the front door of the house that had changed his life, recalling his first introduction. The butler, Jennings, had opened the door and immediately led him and his brother to the workshop where the dead woman lay. Everything had changed in that instant.

One thing had led to another, discoveries had been made, and the murderer had been caught. It had been a successful case, in some respects. But in other respects there were still loose ends... Like the fact that the butler had faked his references and then disappeared into the night—he was still wanted by the police for falsely representing himself. And the whole reason they'd knocked on the door in the first place—in response to the report of a burglary—had never been solved, in fact had only grown as Bernard had begun to make a connection between that burglary and others reported in the area that same week.

He had a lot on his plate, to say the least. Yet here he was again, back at the walnut front door that would lead to a foyer and then a front parlor overwhelmingly stuffed with Japanese memorabilia and ephemera.

While he considered all this, it was certainly taking a long time for someone to come to the door.

Then it finally occurred to him: there wasn't a butler anymore. Mrs. Curry wouldn't hear the knock from downstairs in the kitchen and the inventors would be where they were always found: in the workshop.

At least he knew the way.

He lengthened his strides, hoping to make the long walk to the little stone building on the edge of the property as quick as possible, and praying Prescot would be there.

But all he found was Matsumoto, his white shirt sleeves rolled above his elbows revealing his scarred forearms. He stood outside the workshop before a table covered in drinking glasses of all shapes and sizes: wine glasses, flutes, ice tea glasses, beer mugs, brandy snifters, shot glasses, goblets, water glasses, and more. With a steady hand, the blind man finished pouring water from a large carafe into the final glass.

As Bernard came over the hill, he could hear the inventor rubbing his finger along the rims of the glasses, each one emitting a slightly different tone.

He turned to Bernard as he neared and bowed his head slightly in greeting. Bernard was not surprised when the blind man spoke before he came close enough to hail him.

"Good afternoon, Detective Carew."

"Good afternoon, Mr. Matsumoto," Bernard said, stopping beside him and bowing his head respectfully. "I am pleased we meet again, though I must ask how you knew it was me? It might have been anyone coming over that hill."

Matsumoto shook his head and smiled, continuing to wipe a glass as he spoke, causing it to hum. "Only you walk so heavily with the impatience of a horse awaiting its feed."

Bernard grunted at the comparison. "I *am* in a hurry, as usual. I am looking for Mr. Prescot. But I don't see him here with you, and I know he'd prefer never to set foot in that workshop again if he can help it." He smiled as he recalled the man's faint at the sight of the dead woman's leftover blood.

"I believe he went into town to find you, Detective." Matsumoto straightened, the soft hum stopping as soon as his finger left the rim of the glass.

Bernard's eyes were drawn to a sword sheathed in its scabbard hanging from Matsumoto's belt. On the opposite side of his belt was a gun that was, according to Prescot, a prototype of what the two of them hoped to accomplish: a way to shoot sound.

It was just his luck to have crossed paths with Prescot. Their streetcars had most likely passed each other on Howard.

Matsumoto seemed to sense his frustration. "Perhaps I might be of assistance?" he asked, pulling a handkerchief from his pants pocket and drying his hands on it.

Bernard shook his head. "I'm afraid it's in reference to something which I cannot discuss at present."

"It would not have to do with a nun who visited the Baker, would it?" Matsumoto asked.

Bernard blinked. The nun? "I'm afraid not."

His hand hovered over the pocket watch in his coat, but he didn't pull it out. Instead he tipped his derby and excused himself, figuring if he went directly home he'd most likely catch Prescot there.

"Detective, I believe it is almost time for lunch," Matsumoto said, beginning to roll down the sleeves of his white collared shirt from above his elbows, where he no doubt preferred to keep them while working. "I am certain Mrs. Curry would be greatly saddened if you did not stop by on your way out."

Bernard smiled. Yes, indeed. It was his duty to join the inventor at Mrs. Curry's table. He might just as easily meet up with Prescot here rather than back down the hill. He thanked the blacksmith for the suggestion and joined him as he made his way to the kitchen.

As he walked, he told himself his eagerness had *almost* nothing to do with catching up with Thomas on the number of delicious meals he'd obtained.

* * *

Archie would not be surprised to learn the new Italian cook would be staying on at the Carews. One bite into the fluffy, buttery cornbread—who knew Italians could make such good cornbread?—and no one would question Mrs. Carew's decision. Unfortunately, he'd embarrassed himself by mistakenly remarking that it seemed Signora Magro was getting along "like a horse on fire." Just another fabulous blunder for Mr. Prescot in front of the marvelous Maid Marian.

After thanking Signora Magro for the delicious lunch, Archie led Mr. Bach to the streetcar to head back up the hill to the House. He was irritated—but not surprised given the "reporter" was clearly Jennings in disguise—to find the man wanted to light up before they boarded. Archie didn't care for smoke: gave him a headache. He realized suddenly that in Washington he hadn't observed quite so many smokers as in Connecticut, and wondered if it was one of the states fighting to put a ban on tobacco.

While he smoked, Bach didn't say much except to comment on the fact that, like in his beloved Tacoma, the upper-class had literally built their homes above the lower-class working stiffs. "Though here, the hill is to the south, and in Tacoma it's to the north."

Archie wasn't certain what to say to this, since he'd never been to Tacoma, but he felt it notable that Bach, or Jennings, seemed eager to drop references to his past at every opportunity, for he'd done so not once but *four* times at lunch. He knew, because his stomach had leapt each time, wondering if the man was about to say something that would indicate he was a liar and a conman.

When the streetcar finally made its clanging approach, Bach took a last long draw before flicking the butt into the street and pulling himself aboard behind Archie. Luckily, there were not so many people heading up the hill as there'd been in the morning heading down, and they were able to find seats.

It didn't take long for the reporter to whip out his pad and start peppering Archie with questions.

"So, tell me," he said, and again Archie thought he noted that slight intake of breath before he began, "how did you feel when you learned your patroness had been butchered by a madwoman?"

Archie felt the blood drain from his cheeks and get lodged somewhere in the region of his tie. He could still see that terrible red stain...

He shook his head and realized the reporter was writing something down even though Archie hadn't said anything in response.

"May I ask what you're writing?"

The man looked up quickly and smiled beneath his Roman

nose. "You may, but it is a reporter's duty to keep his notes to himself until the article is published. I am sure you understand. You are a clockmaker, yes?"

Archie nodded slowly.

"You would not want someone to see the insides of your pocket watch before it was complete—they might not understand the chaos required for creation."

Archie pushed his glasses up his nose. "Actually, the design of a clock relies rather more on order than chaos—"

"Of course, of course," Bach said, waving the hand that held the pencil. "As I was saying, I imagine you were quite distressed, so I find it quite interesting that you have since taken up residence in your late patroness's home."

Archie shrugged. "I have to stay in Spokane a couple more months to complete my plans for the Great Northern depot clock. It made the most sense to stay with Mr. Matsumoto, since he was lucky enough to inherit the mansion. In some ways, Miss Mitchell is still our patroness even in death, as she's enabled us to continue our work."

"Ah, yes, I find that most curious." He tapped the end of his pencil against his luxuriant, most-likely-fake beard. "Why him? No other family, or perhaps dutiful servants, she might have left it to?"

Archie's eyes widened and he had to push his glasses back up his nose again before they slid down. Was that why Jennings was playing a reporter? Was he hoping to dislodge Matsumoto from his inheritance? Did he plan to fight Mr. Westfall's attempts to uphold Miss Mitchell's dying wish? Perhaps he'd suggest she made the new will under duress since she'd been blackmailed at the time, even though it wasn't by the Japanese inventor?

Archie felt his stomach clench. He dearly hoped this wasn't the case, but what other reason would Jennings have for dressing up as a reporter with a fake beard and following Archie up to the House?

In fact, it might not even be for himself that he was fighting the will. The most "dutiful servants" to Miss Mitchell had been Mr. and Mrs. Sigmund—Eleanor Sigmund, whom he was certain Jennings had also visited as a nun. Had he snuck in to tell her he wouldn't let this rest? That he would somehow give her the inheritance she deserved and spring her out of jail at the same time?

The reporter's hand was flying across his pad as he watched Archie's face. Meanwhile, Archie tried to decide on his next move.

He should've told the Carews what he suspected back at their house, not allowed himself to be cornered by the masquerading Jennings. Alone. What was he supposed to do?

"Why are you so interested in the Baker?" The question popped out without his meaning to, but once it was out, there was no reeling it back in. "Eleanor Sigmund, I mean?"

"Who is *not* interested in the Baker?" the reporter countered with a shrug, his pencil pausing once again. "It is the most interesting story to come out of Spokane since—"

"It's pronounced 'spo-CAN,'" Archie corrected. He may be the one to often trip over the wrong word, but he knew from experience that "spo-CANE" would get you nothing but dirty looks around town. "How long have you been in town?"

"A couple weeks, I guess," the reporter shrugged again.

Archie nodded. It had been a month since the closing of the Baker case, so it was conceivable that Jennings had simply come up with a backstory to support his sudden "appearance," which neatly coincided with the butler's disappearance. He'd even mentioned at lunch a cousin who'd gotten him the job at *The Spokesman*—most likely a partner in crime, if the man even existed in the first place. He'd heard before how conmen would often create elaborate backstories and live them so completely it was difficult to tell where their reality ended and their lies began.

He really had to give it to him. When Jennings inhabited a role, he went all for it, even down to buying a massive beard to cover his face—a face that must be kept clean-shaven in order for him to also play his role as a nun.

It occurred to Archie that if Jennings ever decided to become a spy rather than a conman, he would make quite an admirable one. Archie shivered to himself at the thought. If Jennings became a spy, he hoped it was for their side—whatever side that was.

Jennings had given every indication of being a butler, too. He'd boasted of his past to Bernard and convinced the entire household he was who he said he was. So why not a bearded reporter? Why not make the next identity so completely the opposite of the first as to throw off the people around him? After all, he'd have to get very cozy with the same people, and yet they couldn't think they'd met him before.

And there was the breathing thing. He definitely took a small breath sometimes before he spoke. And he smoked like a chimney.

Archie distinctly recalled Jennings leaning against the wall outside the kitchen as he and Thomas approached from the workshop a month ago. The way he'd tilted his head back and looked down over that aquiline nose of his and sneered. Just like Bach had done before they'd boarded the streetcar.

But perhaps what Archie saw as a marvelous performance was not good enough to fool those he knew well. Archie, Bernard, and Thomas were less familiar with the butler, whom they'd only met a few times, and then under strained circumstances. Whereas Matsumoto and Mrs. Curry had known him for six months. He looked forward to hearing their opinion when they met up at the House.

"You came to Spokane to write about the Baker?" Archie asked.

"Yes. And then there's this new murder."

"Another murder?"

"Yes, the body at the bottom of Hangman Creek."

Archie wondered why *this* hadn't come up at lunch.

"Did you not see it in the paper? There was a most excellent article on the front page, right beneath the announcement that Mrs. McKinley took a bad turn overnight."

"I'm afraid I didn't have the pleasure this morning. I was distressed...*distracted* by other thoughts." About a nun with an aquiline nose, quite similar to the overly bearded reporter who now strutted his supposed writing capabilities. But as the articles in *The Spokesman* did not include its writers' names, anyone could claim to have written the words—even Jennings.

"Here. I have a copy on me." And the man pulled out a typewritten sheet headlined "Hangman Creek Claims Another."

Archie had to admit this made it a little more difficult to suggest the man hadn't written the article himself.

* * *

Peter watched as the clockmaker read his thrilling version of events. This Mr. Prescot was a marvelously easy person to read, now he'd gotten him alone. He still couldn't be certain why the man had been staring at him so confoundedly in the Carews' parlor, but perhaps he'd just never seen such a perfect beard before. It was clear *he* couldn't even grow the simplest mustache.

Peter wondered if Prescot could tell he was new at being a reporter, even though he thought the role fit him like a glove. He expected the clockmaker to ask him something when he finished with his read, but the first question was not what he'd anticipated.

"What did the hobo look like?"

Peter took back the proffered piece of paper and shrugged. "I don't know, I didn't see him."

"Of course you didn't."

"What do you mean?"

"Nothing. Just...a feeling."

"You are thinking the hobo killed London accidentally, reported the murder, and then left town? We already thought of that."

Prescot's eyebrows furrowed irritably at this statement.

Ah, how Peter loved figuring out what triggered people. Each person was so unique. It was like a game, finding the one thing they didn't like pushed in their face, and then pushing it right in.

Peter flipped open his pocket watch to check the time, being sure to let Archie see it clearly. He had a feeling one glimpse of his Martens 18K gold watch, engraved by Jess Hans Martens for his successor Georg Wessel, would be the push Prescot needed—

The clockmaker's eyes lit up at the sight and he leaned forward slightly, his mouth open. But just as quickly he sank back into his seat, his shoulders sagging and his entire body deflating as he turned to look out the streetcar window.

"We're almost there," he said sulkily.

Peter shook his head again and placed the watch back in his pocket. He'd find the thing that pushed Mr. Prescot into action, or he was done as a reporter.

Peter replaced his notepad and pencil and reached for his cigarette box, but then Prescot announced they'd arrived at the end of the line and Miss Mitchell's house. They disembarked and Peter started to ask if they might begin where the murder took place—in the workshop.

The clockmaker beat him to it. "I thought we'd start at the house," he said, leading the way up the long drive to the impressive front door.

The house reminded Peter of the Campbells', and he wouldn't have been surprised if they were designed by the same architect: Kirtland Cutter, whose homes he'd often admired in the Tacoma area, as well. The Tudor style was offset by a white-columned front porch, similar in look to the house a couple doors down from the Campbells'. The stained glass windows were completely unique, however, complete with cherry blossoms adorning the windows beside the front door.

They entered the front hall, but before Peter could take in his surroundings properly, the broad form of Bernard Carew came stomping up to them, his thick eyebrows raised at the sight of Peter.

"Detective Carew, I'm glad to see I've found you," Prescot said, shaking the policeman's hand.

"Me, too," Bernard said, then flicked his eyes toward Peter. "May I ask why you brought Mr. Bach with you?"

Peter smiled congenially, enjoying the obvious struggle Bernard had gone through to phrase his question as politely as possible.

"Mr. Prescot kindly offered to give me a tour of the place where the Baker's story began," he offered.

Bernard looked to Prescot, who nodded, but then seemed to be rethinking his decision as he shrank, nervously pushing his glasses up his nose over and over again and shifting his feet.

"I mean, only if you...that is if you...I mean..."

"No," Bernard said firmly, and motioned toward the front door.

"Excuse me?" Peter asked in mock surprise. "This isn't a crime scene anymore, Detective Carew. You have no right to bar my entry."

"You're absolutely right," Bernard said, turning to the clockmaker. "Mr. Prescot, I have been waiting all morning for you to return to your home so I could speak with you about a rather important matter. I would find it very considerate of you and be most appreciative if you would do me the honor of taking the time to speak with me before entertaining."

Prescot pushed his glasses up his nose yet again. "Of course, Detective Carew. I'd love to be of assessment...assemblance...*assistance*," he finally choked out.

For a man of supposed intelligence, he certainly had a difficult time with finding the right word sometimes.

"I understand," Peter said, with a tip of his hat. "Thank you for your time, Mr. Prescot. I will return another day. I enjoyed our conversation on the streetcar, if nothing else."

There was no way Peter was going all the way back down the hill without a fair bit of snooping, but when he glanced over his shoulder he could see Bernard watching him from the front porch, his arms crossed.

Perhaps, now that he knew how to get here, he could return at a later time to make his own unimpeded investigation. With a jaunty wave at the detective, he turned and made his way toward the streetcar stop.

* * *

After ensuring the reporter really had left the House grounds, Bernard finally rejoined Prescot in the Japanesque parlor, pulling out the pocket watch for the clockmaker's perusal.

"Thank you, Mr. Prescot. Now, what can you tell me about this?"

Prescot took it gently into his hands, his large fingers at once becoming nimble and delicate. "14K gold, 48 mm case, enamel dial, Patek Philippe, Swiss, 1880 I'd guess..."

Bernard wrote down each word Prescot said, though he couldn't be certain of their importance just yet. Something told him it was a rather nice watch for London, though.

"Would you say this is the usual watch one might find on a personal assistant?"

Prescot continued to turn the watch over in his hands.

"Perhaps. It might have been gifted to him by a family member, I suppose, but it seems to be in too fine a condition to be something carried about and used on an everyday basis by someone of the working class."

Bernard nodded. He needed to do some digging into London's past, and for that he could sure use Thomas's help. With a stab of guilt he thought again of asking for Thomas's help last night only to abandon him this morning. And still the reporter had managed to contrive a way up to the Baker's territory. At least Thomas hadn't let him see her in the jail... Right?

Prescot had popped open the back where one could access the inner workings of gears and whatever else it was that made clocks tick.

"There's an engraving here."

Bernard perked up and leaned over as Prescot held it out for him to view.

He grunted. "I missed that before."

"Watch repairmen usually leave their mark here on the inside to note their work. Looks like it was fixed by someone on 5-3-1901. So, earlier this month."

Bernard nodded. "That might be helpful if it was done locally and I could track down the watchmaker. Maybe they could tell me something about London."

"London? Is that the man they found at Hangman Creek?"

"Yes. Be glad you weren't there for this one. Even I had difficulty stomaching it." His mouth twitched beneath his mustache.

Prescot's cheeks reddened. "Is Thomas assisting you again?"

Bernard's almost-smile disappeared completely. "In a way. When he's not distracted by...other things."

Prescot's redness spread to his forehead and his throat, which he cleared nervously before closing the watch with a forceful *snap*. "I think that's about all I can tell you on my own. Sorry I couldn't be more help."

"That's all right. You helped plenty. Too bad you're not more familiar with the watchmakers of Spokane."

"You know, I might be able to assist you with that. I don't know them personally, but they're more likely to spill to a fellow tradesman. I could ask around if you like."

Bernard's eyebrows rose. "Thanks, Prescot. That'd be incredibly helpful."

Prescot placed the pocket watch in his jacket pocket.

"Did you have anything you wanted to ask me?" Bernard asked.

"What?" Prescot furrowed his brow.

"You went down to my house to ask me a question while I came here to ask you a question."

"Ah." Prescot blushed again. He opened his mouth and then closed it again.

Bernard shook his head and patted the large man on the shoulder.

"It's all right, Prescot. You're not the only one who's noticed my wife's new companion."

Prescot's face grew even redder.

Bernard shook his head again. He was glad he was no longer on the hunt for a wife. He didn't miss the days of fighting his brother for a woman, though he was still eternally grateful he'd won Roslyn's heart in the end.

* * *

Thomas sank onto the Chesterfield patting his belly, as contented and satisfied as Bagheera after an entire wild boar.

He had never eaten such incredible Italian food, which, if this meal was anything to go by, was going to be his meal of choice in future. No more meat and potatoes for this guy. Fresh, homemade noodles with tomatoes, olives, and mushrooms, bread that was crispy on the outside but chewy on the inside and slathered in garlic butter, garlicky green beans that still had some snap to them, and cornbread—because Roslyn was crazy sometimes. All of it finished off with a cake that had been soaked in coffee with this delicate caramel on top... And this had just been lunch!

He wondered if it was dinner time yet...

He closed his eyes and drifted off into a happy daydream where he imagined eating such a meal every day...

Roslyn wheeled into the front parlor, pushed by Marian, who placed her next to the fireplace. This was her customary spot, where she could be warm and command the attention of anywhere in the room.

"Well, I vote she stays." Thomas was attempting to sit up a bit more properly, even though his belly really didn't care to be in an upright position at the moment.

"I second that," said Roslyn.

"I agree," said Marian. "I'm so glad we didn't settle for my sad attempts when there were miraculous fingers just waiting around the corner."

"Amen," said Thomas. Then he realized the comment might

be misunderstood and apologized. "Not that your attempts were sad by any means—I mean, wasn't the bread yours?"

"I suppose it must have been, though I can hardly believe it! My bread never turns out so perfect! I'll have to ask her what she did to it... Though it's probably all down to the baking. I have a tendency to forget bread in the oven, so I end up with a loaf better suited to holding doors open."

Thomas laughed at the image.

"Well, I think I'll turn in for a short nap," said Roslyn with an obviously faked yawn, and Marian immediately stood to take her to her room. "Oh no, no, you two stay out here and don't mind me. After such a wonderfully delicious meal I feel the need to rest for a little while."

Thomas quirked a brow at his sister-in-law. She'd never been one for napping after a meal before. If he didn't know better, he'd guess she was attempting to allow him and Marian some time alone.

Roslyn turned to Marian. "When Signora Magro is finished cleaning the kitchen I asked her to come to the parlor to discuss her future. Please inform her we'd love for her to remain as a part of the household, and she and I can discuss the details after I wake."

"Rest well, Roz," Thomas called out as she wheeled herself to her bedroom.

Marian sighed as she seated herself across from him on the edge of the large armchair with wooden bears climbing up the legs. "She really is quite marvelous."

"Who? Roz?" Thomas followed her gaze where she'd been watching her employer maneuver herself without assistance.

"I'm sure you take it for granted by now, but it really is wonderful how she's able to do most things herself with that chair of hers."

"It hasn't been that long since she's had the wheelchair, really. It was a donation from the church. Before that she was simply carried by Bernard in the mornings and evenings out to this parlor, and then she spent her days in this room with her companion doing all the fetching she required."

"How long has she been..." Marian left the delicate question hanging.

Thomas looked up as he calculated. "It's been about eight years, I think." Eight years. Had it really been that long? Thirty-two only ever felt old when he looked back. They were so young then.

Marian's eyes widened. "Eight years in a chair?"

Thomas nodded. "The doctors still aren't quite sure what it is. Some form of muscle paralysis. She and Bernard were married a year after she became permanently wheelchair-bound."

Even then, Bernard had had to propose six or seven times before she'd finally accepted him. Roslyn had been quite a stubborn young woman. When she'd found out she'd probably never be able to walk, much less bear children... She hadn't wanted to take that away from him. From either of them, since Thomas himself had also pursued her. The discovery had been enough for him to look elsewhere, since one of the things he still yearned for was children of his own. He hoped he wasn't getting too old for such things. Of course, if he found a young wife—he glanced at Marian across from him—then there was a much higher chance of his dreams coming to fruition.

"It hasn't taken the edge off her intelligence, though." He whistled. "That woman is a voracious reader. Sometimes I envy the time she has to read. Makes me wish *I* could be her companion."

Marian laughed. "I certainly have had more time to read in the past month than I've had since I was a child. It's been wonderful, I admit!" She smiled and her eyes twinkled at the thought. "'I like good strong words that mean something.'"

"Nain?" Thomas asked.

Marian laughed again. "No, Louisa May Alcott. In *Little Women*."

Although he desperately wanted to take the bait and dive into a discussion of books again with her, the thought of Bernard's request was weighing on Thomas's mind. He needed to turn the conversation to the Baker, and somehow get Marian to confide to him what had been said between them at the jail.

"So how's the new case going?" Marian asked.

Thomas looked up in surprise. Perhaps it would be simpler to broach the topic than he'd thought. "I honestly don't know. Bernard wasn't too pleased about our little excursion yesterday and so we haven't really had a chance to discuss the new case or compare notes, that sort of thing."

"I'm sorry if I caused a rift between you and your brother." Marian's brow furrowed in distress.

Thomas waved it away. "The tension between us right now is not your doing. It was there already for other reasons."

"From what Mr. Prescot told me, it was thanks to the two of you working together that the last case was solved, no matter what the papers say."

Thomas glanced at the fireplace. This conversation was not going the route he'd intended. "It was our first murder case together. I think it's natural for there to be kinks still to work out. It's difficult to remember exactly how it happened." He smiled at Marian. "And really it was you who brought us the murderer."

A look of sadness crossed her face for a moment before she straightened and responded, "I never would have realized the importance of the ash bucket, nor made the final connection, if I hadn't heard that you were currently sifting through the ashes looking for bones as proof of a second body."

Thomas nodded. "I figured that one out." He tried not to say it too arrogantly, but it was difficult not to be proud of that deduction. "The body in the forge was a pretty amazing leap, to be honest. I'm not really sure what got me there." He struggled for a moment to think of the exact order of events, but he couldn't. He only recalled when all the pieces fell into place.

"I suppose that's what makes real life different from detective novels," Marian said. "Sherlock is always able to go back and explain the exact chain of clues that led him to his final deduction."

"Precisely!" Thomas laughed at her ability to read his thoughts. "At least with that case Bernard and I were always on the same page. We both had all the clues to work from." His gaze fell on the fireplace again. "This time I feel like I've only got half the notes. I haven't heard what the coroner found and I left too soon to search around the body. The only people I've interviewed are the staff at the Campbell House, and that was thanks to a lead from Mr. Bach, not Bernard."

He shook his head. "Mr. Bach says I should try to solve the

case before Bernard, but I haven't got a thing to go on. Besides, I'd never do that to my brother." Even as he said it, he knew it was true. It didn't matter if Bernard had followed a lead without him. What else did he expect him to do? Thomas would have done the same in his place. This was about solving a murder, not about their petty rivalry.

"I admire my brother. He's got a good head on his shoulders. There's a reason he's made detective and I haven't. If he wanted to, I'm certain he could solve this case without me."

"That doesn't mean you can't help him." Marian leaned forward as though she was going to take his hand comfortingly, but then thought better of it, and instead merely straightened her skirt where it fell over her knees. "Is there something you learned at the Campbells' you could follow?"

Thomas thought through his notes, landing on the man who'd been meeting London secretly behind the carriage house. "I suppose there's one name I could look into: Tony Pavoni."

* * *

"I recognize the name, but I can't think why," Marian admitted.

"Pavoni's on the McKinley Reception Committee," said Thomas, which explained it, "but that's really all I know about him."

"Oh, yes, Pavoni. Roslyn and I were just discussing an article about a speech he made in Tacoma. I believe he's a state representative or commissioner."

Thomas's face clearly showed he was impressed that she, a lady, would know about such things. He should have known better, given his sister-in-law was the one who'd led their conversation about the article in the first place.

"Tony Pavoni," Marian repeated. "You certainly wouldn't forget a name like that when it came time to vote. It rolls of the tongue rather well: Tony Pavoni."

"PAVONI?!" screeched a voice from the hall. Signora Magro rushed in, her face flushed with anger. "Pavoni you say?" Suddenly a torrent of Italian words came spilling out, her hands flying about her.

Marian looked at Thomas but it was clear he didn't understand what was happening either. The only thing for certain was their new Italian cook was furious, and it had something to do with Mr. Pavoni.

Thomas rose from the couch. "Signora Magro, please." He indicated she take his seat. She finally took a deep breath and did so. He sat across from her in the other armchair and looked at her steadily, leaning forward with his elbows on his knees. "Please, slowly: Do you know Mr. Pavoni?"

"*Signore* Pavoni is bad—*cattivo*. '*Pavone*' mean peacock, and he is this bird. He is proud—*molto orgoglioso*. He think he can do whatever he please. He not worry he hurt people."

"Signora Magro," Thomas said slowly. "Did he hurt you?"

"No, no," the Italian woman waved this idea away. "*Mio fratello*. My...brother."

"He hurt your brother?"

"*Sì, sì*." She nodded, her eyes never leaving Thomas's, as though hoping this would help him understand her. "My brother, he is in jail because of this peacock."

"Jail? Did Pavoni have him arrested? Did he steal from Pavoni?"

"No, no. He...he..." Suddenly she gave up trying and broke into fluid Italian again. "*Pavoni è un anarchico. Ha fatto mio fratello lavorare per lui, e quando il complotto non ha avuto successo, ha incolpato mio fratello. Mio fratello è in prigione mentre Pavoni è libero.*"

Marian didn't understand her words, but she understood her actions. She admired Thomas's patient manner with the woman. She could tell he was quite interested in what Signora Magro was saying, and wished desperately to understand.

"She says that Pavoni is an anarchist," came Roslyn's clear voice as she wheeled herself back into the front parlor. "She says he made her brother work for him and when the plot was not successful, he blamed her brother. Her brother is in jail while Pavoni is free."

Signora Magro turned to Roslyn like she'd found her long-lost sister, her anguished face flashing to joy briefly at this interpretation. "*Sì, sì!*" She rippled off more, her hands emphatically waving this way and that. Marian was impressed she was capable of remaining seated while the entire upper portion of her body was so animated.

"She says Pavoni is trusted, that no one would say he is a crook when he is one," translated Roslyn slowly. Now she was the one whose eyes never left Signora Magro's. "She knows because of her brother. No one believes her brother but her. He would not lie to her. Pavoni is the anarchist. Not her brother."

"Does she have proof?" Thomas asked Roslyn, and then his gaze turned back to the woman who was really speaking. "Do you have proof?" he asked.

The Italian woman snorted and waved her hands about.

"Of course not," said Roslyn. "If there was proof, Pavoni would be in jail and not her brother."

Thomas nodded. "I had to ask," he said with a sigh. He ran his fingers through his dark hair. Marian hated seeing him so ruffled. "Well, I suppose that's no worse than I expected. What with his connection to the President." His cheeks puffed out as he leaned back in his chair. "What we have here are the makings of an anarchist plot, and from what I've heard of them, what they'd like more than anything is to do away with McKinley. McKinley's a Republican through and through, and in this day and age that means industrialism, commercialism, and capitalism."

"What do the anarchists hope to gain by assassinating McKinley?" Marian asked.

It was Roslyn who answered. "There is a great division between the ruling elite and the lower classes, and it is only growing bigger." Even Thomas turned to her with a look of surprise, though by this time Marian figured if the woman knew Italian, she shouldn't be surprised to learn she also knew what the anarchists believed. "They say the moneyed elite control the economy and are building on the backs of the little people. The anarchists feel the only way to correct the problem is through violence, by tearing the whole system down."

"And building it back up again?" Marian asked.

Thomas shrugged. "Given their name, I doubt that."

Roslyn shook her head. "They preach the downfall of the U.S. government. Their papers include instructions for how to build a bomb out of everyday supplies, and they've been successful in creating chaos across the nation."

"You've read these papers?" Thomas asked, a note of either shock or admiration in his voice.

Roslyn straightened herself in her chair, resting her elbows on the armrests. "I feel it is my duty to be informed concerning all sides of an issue, so that *when* women finally get the vote, we do not make fools of ourselves at the polls."

Marian's jaw dropped and she had to stop herself from standing and applauding. Roslyn Carew was her hero.

But in the meantime, they had a more urgent issue to solve.

"So what happens now?" she asked Thomas.

Thomas stood up. "Now Bernard and I compare notes. If Pavoni is an anarchist, and London was working with him, and they were both working for Campbell... This is definitely one of those moments where two heads are better than one."

* * *

Peter stood and quickly moved behind the door to the dining room. It swung open as Thomas marched past and out the front door. Peter mulled over what he'd heard as he waited for the door to stop swinging to and fro.

Perhaps his return to the Carews' house, rather than sticking around up on the South Hill, would pay off after all. Along with the information he'd uncovered at the Campbells', he'd heard enough to write an article. Whether that article would be full of conjectures rather than truth—well, as his cousin Daniel said, "The truth is what we print in the paper." Someone's truth, at least.

He shook his head and leaned back against the dining room wall.

"If Pavoni is an anarchist, and London was working with him, and they were both working for Campbell..." then the natural conclusion was that all three were anarchists, and Spokane should be eternally grateful Mrs. McKinley's health had kept the President from visiting their fair city. It was only right that the people of Spokane knew of this close shave.

He needed to get something written today. It wouldn't do for *The Spokesman*'s newest reporter to deliver nothing but an article reporting the same details already known about the Baker's case. He'd gathered less than nothing from his excursion up the hill, except that Mr. Prescot was keenly interested in him for some reason, and that Bernard Carew trusted him about as much as a stray cat who'd shown up on his doorstep looking for free milk.

He sniffed without thinking and then stood as still as could be, straining his ears to determine if someone might have heard it.

He'd better pack his things. If the Carews found out he was here and had overheard their little discovery, they wouldn't let him leave until they closed the case. He'd have to type up the article at the Review Building.

He pressed his ear to the door and then opened it a crack. Time to slip away from yet another housing situation for the good of the people. And the good of himself.

* * *

Bernard came back down the hill with Prescot, though they parted ways at City Hall: Prescot to uncover what he could about the pocket watch and Bernard to go by the jail to check on the Baker.

He walked into the bowels of the station trepidatiously, prepared to be told the Baker had slit her throat with a hatpin or hung herself by a shoelace. But Officer Smith merely stood as he entered and reported all was well, though there'd been a couple of drunk-and-disorderly types who'd spent the night in the cell next to hers.

"They smarted right up after whistlin' at her and gettin' the Baker in return!" he said with a barely visible grin from beneath his thick mustache. "Perhaps we should keep the lady around."

Bernard personally couldn't wait for her to move to the Medical Lake asylum where she could be properly cared for—and away from prying eyes.

"Has a reporter tried to nose his way in? Tall, blonde, heavily bearded, goes by the name of Bach?"

Smith shook his head. "Not as yet." He frowned. "You don't want me to let him in if he comes by, do you?"

"No," Bernard said, shaking his head forcefully. "He's been trying to get 'the scoop' as he calls it and I don't want him anywhere near. How about a nun?"

"Just the one yesterday." Smith leaned in conspiratorially. "One of them types as you can tell why she chose the order over marriage."

Bernard suddenly recalled Matsumoto had said something about the nun when he'd first gone up this morning. Made it sound like Prescot had wanted to ask him about her, but he hadn't, so it must not have been too important.

"How long was she here?"

Smith shrugged. "Not long. By the time I got back from usin' the W.C., your brother and his lady-friend and the big gentleman was leavin' and all's I heard was there was a nun speakin' with the Baker. Soon after they leave, the nun comes out, bobs a thank you kindly and leaves."

"How often does a nun from Sacred Heart visit?"

Smith bit his lower lip and shook his head. "None too often. Since the Baker's been with us, maybe twice, three times. I'd have to check the log book to be sure."

Bernard waved his hand. "That's not necessary. I only wondered. So you weren't here while my brother and his friends were here?"

"Nah, I stepped out, like I said. Figured if an officer was here it weren't no problem. Good thing, too, as I'd had a bit much over me lunch and—"

Before Smith could give him a full report on his eating habits and more, Bernard walked to the door of the cells and said, "I think I'll just go check on the Baker..."

He walked along the cold cells to the last one and peeked through the iron bars. The woman was curled into a ball, hugging her knees to her chest beneath a gray blanket, her face calm and placid as she breathed in and out slowly, evenly. Her brow was unlined and she looked at peace. Bernard prayed this meant Eleanor was getting some much-needed rest from the machinations of the Baker, and wondered how frequently she was able to overcome her other side.

Such a strange case. A convoluted mess of multiple victims and multiple murders and then multiple personalities within one person. And yet, somehow, he and Thomas had been able to untangle it all right up to the final knot.

He shook his head at himself and turned away. What did it

matter who solved what or what might have happened if? The case was over. It was time to turn his focus to the new one, and pray it wasn't a similar convoluted mess.

Bernard left the downstairs cells with a tip of his hat to Officer Smith and a reminder to let him know should anyone else wish to visit the Baker. Then he headed up to his desk to make telephone calls where he could and send telegrams where he couldn't in an attempt to find out more about Mr. James London.

It was a slow business, and Bernard considered returning home for tea in hopes of finding Thomas and making another plea for assistance. But he knew his brother was most likely miffed over his heading up the hill without him this morning. He should've left a note with Hollway telling Thomas to join him as soon as he'd shaken the reporter.

Bernard ran a finger over his mustache. He had to stop replaying the same lines over and over again in his head.

It was difficult not to let his mind wander when he kept hitting dead ends, however. No one seemed to know anything about Mr. London. He wasn't staying at any of the hotels in Spokane and it would be impossible to contact every boarding-house. He'd have to place an ad in the paper, he supposed.

He groaned at the idea of going to Bach in need of help.

He picked up the reference for Mr. London that Mr. Campbell had given him and read through it again, but there were no references to past work, other than for Mr. Pavoni himself, or anything that might assist him in his search. It was time to hunt down Mr. Pavoni and ask him what he knew about the dead man. Bernard had hoped it wouldn't come to this, as politicians were known for withholding information. Pavoni would never share something that might threaten his precious election somewhere down the road.

Bernard pulled out the long sheet of committee names they'd been given, which listed the contact information for each of the men. He ran his finger down the list to Pavoni and found he was staying at the Montvale when he was in town. The Montvale did not have a telephone, but no matter. After sending a telegram to the hotel requesting that Mr. Pavoni stop by the police station at his earliest convenience, Bernard went back to his notes on the case.

He was surprised when only half an hour later, Hollway approached his desk and introduced the short, stout, balding man behind him as the manager of the Montvale.

"Mr. Myers, pleased to meet you," Bernard said, waving for him to take a seat as Hollway returned to his post. "You didn't have to come all the way down here. I was hoping to speak with Mr. Pavoni, a guest at your hotel."

"Ye-es," Mr. Myers said nervously, holding his hat by the brim and shifting it around and around. "I'm afraid I'm here in regards to that. We received your telegram. We did not open it—naturally, we take our clientele's privacy very highly—but as it came from the police station I thought you should know that, well…"

Bernard waited patiently.

"Mr. Pavoni has not been seen since Thursday."

Bernard grunted. "Thursday? Did he leave town?"

"No, sir. At least, he has not checked out from our establishment."

"Why were we not informed?"

"Well, sir," the man paused uncomfortably, "as it has only been one full day I did not think it necessary to inform the police. I would have done so if he had not appeared by this evening. I informed the owner of the hotel, Mr. Binkley, and he agreed I should bring the matter to the police, given your interest."

Bernard rose and the manager followed him. "Thank you, Mr. Myers. Please let the station know immediately if and when Mr. Pavoni returns."

Bernard led the manager to the front and out the door before returning to Hollway's front desk and requesting the telephone. He pressed the receiver handle until he got the operator.

"Please connect me with Mr. Campbell."

* * *

Thomas barged past Hollway and into the conglomeration of desks, straight up to Bernard.

"We need to talk," he said, seating himself in the chair next to Bernard's desk. "I'm sorry I haven't been forthcoming, but we need to get on the same page about this London murder. I know he worked for Mr. Campbell—I went up and spoke to his coach-man and his cook this morning."

Bernard's thick eyebrows rose but he didn't interrupt.

"I learned that Mr. London would often meet with Tony Pavoni secretly after leaving Mr. Campbell. Pavoni is—"

"I know who he is," Bernard cut in, but waving Thomas onward. "Continue."

"Well, I just learned from our new cook," here Thomas couldn't help but rub his belly in appreciation, "that the man is an *anarchist*."

Bernard leaned forward. "Which man? Not Campbell."

"No, no, Pavoni."

Bernard sat back in his chair. "An anarchist. That's a pretty serious claim. Who told you this?"

"Our cook, like I said."

Bernard's mouth quirked beneath his mustache, which Thomas knew meant he didn't think much of such an informant.

"I believe her, Bernard. You had to be there. She got quite upset when she heard Marian and me talking about him in the front parlor."

Bernard's eyes narrowed. "Why were you two talking about Pavoni?"

Thomas waved it away. "He just came up. But then the cook, Signora Magro, came in and whirled into Italian and it took Roslyn translating to make it clear: Signora Magro's brother is in jail for anarchist activity, but he was put up to it by Mr. Pavoni."

Bernard blew out through his mouth. "That's pretty thin, Thomas. I know you know that. But I can see you really believe her. I'll speak with her myself this evening. In the meantime, I'd like to talk with Mr. Pavoni, but I can't seem to find him."

Thomas cocked his head. "What do you mean?"

"I mean nobody's seen Pavoni since Thursday. I just got off the telephone with Mr. Campbell who says Mr. Pavoni dined with him Thursday evening and left at ten o'clock. He hasn't heard from him since."

This time Thomas was the one to quirk his mouth. "Did you ask the coachman, Gladding?"

"Of course not. I was on the telephone. I couldn't very well ask Mr. Campbell if I might speak with his coachman to verify his story."

Thomas stood up. "I'll go ask him myself. He and I had a decent conversation this morning so he might be willing to tell me more."

"I'll speak with Chairman Black to ask if he's seen Pavoni, and telegraph to Tacoma in case he's simply left town and headed home without notice. Thomas," Bernard leaned across his desk, "it's good to have you back."

Thomas grinned. "I knew you'd never solve the case without me. Thanks for letting me help." He thrust his hat jauntily back onto his head. "I'll be back before you can say 'Mrs. Curry's muffins.'"

* * *

Archie looked in the display window at the fourth clock shop on the list. Before he and Bernard had headed back down the hill, he'd taken a look through Polk's City Directory for a list of all the local watchmakers. Under the heading "Watches, Clocks, and Jewelry" he had found ten listings, six of which were all to be found on Riverside, meaning he could walk down the sidewalk and simply turn in at each location. The first had been Elbertson at 326 Riverside, followed by Schacht and Riorden at 403, then Sobol at 507, and now he turned in to try Dodson's at 517 Riverside Ave. It was the Mohawk Building, one of a line of buildings filled with storefronts on street level, offices on the second, and apartments above.

None of the previous stores had recognized the maker's mark within the watch's casing, though they'd attempted with great skill and aptitude to sell Archie a new watch, even offering to buy the old one for twice its worth.

He pushed open the door to Dodson's, escaping the dusty street outside and wiping his boots on the mat inside the door. It was quiet within. Archie couldn't hear the hum of street noises—streetcars and carriages, horses and people, construction and trains—outside on busy Riverside.

He was greeted by a young man with brown hair parted in the usual style, down the middle, with round-rimmed spectacles that matched Archie's own. Archie self-consciously pushed his up his nose.

"How may I help you, sir?"

"I'm looking for the watchmaker," Archie said. "I have a question about a piece that recently came into my possession."

"I see," the young man said, giving Archie a once over with his eyes and glancing at the satchel slung over his shoulder. "One moment, please. Let me see if Mr. Kratzer is available."

Archie turned to admire a case of fine watches displayed, but he found himself instead looking at his own appearance in the reflection, wondering if he'd made the right decision on his mustache. Perhaps he shouldn't have given up so easily on the accoutrement.

He shook his head at his reflection. He needed to stop caring so much about what other people thought of him. It was probably Thomas's confidence that made him so appealing to Marian, after all.

Archie straightened his shoulders and turned to look through the stacks of books that bordered the opposite side of the store, which was apparently half jewelry store, half bookstore, with a sign on a bannister pointing downstairs for the toy department.

He'd just picked up a copy of Edgar Allan Poe's collected poems, smiling to himself as he recalled Marian's feelings about Poe's attempts at mysteries, when a man cleared his throat behind him and Archie turned around.

A shorter man with a large black mustache and piercing eyes held his hand out in greeting. "I am Otto Kratzer, the watchmaker at Dodson's. I hear you have something you'd like me to see?"

"Yes," Archie said, replacing the Poe collection. He pulled himself up and pointed his chin out with authority, confidently shaking the man's hand. "My name is Archie Prescot and I'm in town to design and install the clock for the new Great Northern depot under construction."

He handed over his calling card, which listed him as a watchmaker for the Seth Thomas company of Connecticut.

Kratzer's eyes widened just slightly and his entire demeanor changed toward Archie as he examined his card. "Welcome to Spokane," he said warmly. He held his hand toward the back of the store. "Please, let me take you back to my desk where we can speak more conveniently."

Archie removed his satchel and set it beside his chair as he took a seat across from Kratzer.

"So, what can I help you with today?" the man asked.

Archie realized there was a slight accent behind the words, but one which had been cultivated carefully into the background of speech.

"I came across this watch and would like to track down the

owner," said Archie, pulling out the pocket watch Bernard had given him, but choosing to avoid mention of the police, in the same manner as he'd done at the other three jewelry stores. "I found the maker's mark inside indicating it had been serviced earlier this month and have been in search of the watchmaker since. Do you recognize it?"

He held out the watch and Mr. Kratzer took it, putting on a pair of pince-nez across his nose as he did so. "Yes, in fact, I do. An 1880 Patek Philippe. I serviced this watch a couple weeks ago." He turned it over in his hands and opened the back casing. "Yes, that's my mark."

Archie exhaled in relief. Kratzer raised an eyebrow at him as he removed the pince-nez. "I'm afraid our customer records are private, however, so I cannot divulge the owner's name or address."

"Naturally," said Archie, holding his hand out for the pocket watch. "But perhaps you could describe him to me, or give me an idea of where I might find him in town?"

Kratzer held onto the watch. "I could return it for you, if you like. It belongs to a man of some status, and I am certain he would be pleased to have his watch returned to him."

Archie frowned. "I'm afraid I need to return the watch myself."

Kratzer quirked a brow at him. "And why would that be?"

"Because...," said Archie, searching for some reason other than the one he didn't want to give. But he didn't see he had much of a choice in the matter and knew he had to get the watch back to Bernard. "To be quite honest, I'm assisting the police in an investigation, and this watch is evidence."

Kratzer's eyes widened. "Really?"

"Yes," said Archie, as confidently as he could, holding Kratzer's eyes and willing him to see his truthfulness. "I'm working with Detective Bernard Carew."

Kratzer smiled. "Ah, yes, Detective Carew. And his brother?"

"Thomas, yes," said Archie.

He got the impression Kratzer was just checking his facts. Kratzer nodded and handed back the pocket watch, so Archie figured he must have passed the test.

"I most certainly will offer any assistance I can give the Carews."

Archie wondered how he knew them, but figured they were probably just steady customers, though the more sensationalist side of his brain wondered if maybe they'd helped the man out of a tight spot once before.

"I will tell you the man was most certainly Italian, olive-skinned like yourself, but tall and dark with a thin mustache," said Kratzer.

"A tall, dark Italian?" Archie repeated. "I'll pass it along. You can't give me his name? Perhaps a Mr. London?" he asked, re-calling the name Bernard had mentioned.

Kratzer's brow furrowed. "No, it was—" But he stopped himself and shook his head. "I really can't say. But it was definitely not a Mr. London. It was someone who is a person of some rank in the community and it wouldn't do for me to go spreading his name about, especially if this watch is associated with an investigation."

"Even a murder investigation?"

Again Kratzer's brow rose, but then fell again as he shook his head. "I'm afraid I can't." He stood behind his desk. "But be sure to tell Detective Carew that if he really does need that name, he's welcome to come ask me for it himself." He offered his hand.

Archie rose and shook the man's hand, replacing the mysterious pocket watch back in his pocket.

"Thank you for your assistance, Mr. Kratzer."

Archie swung his satchel back over his shoulder and made his way quickly to the first floor of City Hall, which was just a few blocks away. He was guided back to where Bernard sat at his desk, the end of his pen tapping methodically against a paper while he gazed into the middle distance.

He relayed the information to Bernard, who wrote notes as he spoke, but looked up when he described the man who'd dropped off the watch.

"Tall, dark Italian with a thin mustache?"

"Yes, sir," said Archie.

"Not a tall, nervous man with spectacles?"

"Um, no," said Archie. "Just what I told you. He said if you need the name, you're welcome to come speak to him yourself, as a police officer, but he didn't feel it right to share the customer's name with me."

Bernard stared at his notes, as if wishing they'd change. "I see." Then he nodded once and stood. "Thank you for your assistance, Prescot. You've been most helpful."

* * *

It was almost dinner time before Thomas got back to the station with what little news he'd been able to glean from Joseph Gladding. He knew because his stomach was rumbling again, reminding him he and Bernard should be returning home soon if they wanted to enjoy another round of Signora Magro's cooking.

"Gladding says Mr. Campbell called him to prepare the carriage for Mr. Pavoni to return to his hotel, but after saying goodnight to Mr. Campbell, Mr. Pavoni declared he'd rather stretch his legs for a bit and headed off for a walk."

"Which direction did he go?" Bernard asked, turning a pocket watch over in his hands.

"Toward the bluff. And if London's at the bottom of the bluff..." Thomas left the implication hanging.

"It only stands to reason it was Pavoni who helped him down, which explains why he's skipped town."

Thomas plopped back down into the chair beside Bernard's desk. "This is gonna be a tough one, Bernard. You don't just take down a man like Pavoni, even if he is an anarchist and a murder—"

Bernard pushed back his chair with a loud *screech* against the floor as he stood quickly, cutting off Thomas and tipping his head to someone approaching from behind him. When Thomas saw who it was, he also respectfully rose and stood at attention beside his chair.

"Mr. Black," Bernard said, extending his hand to the chairman of the McKinley Reception Committee.

George Black was the opposite of his name, with blonde hair, blonde eyebrows, and a blonde mustache that twisted up at the ends like a melodrama villain—only blonde.

"Detective Carew, how can I help you?" asked the chairman, taking Thomas's seat and not waiting for an introduction. "I'm in rather a rush but I'd take a cup of tea if you can manage it," he said offhandedly to Thomas.

Thomas clenched his jaw and stared at the man.

Bernard cleared his throat and sent Thomas a clear signal to get the man what he wanted, no matter his rudeness.

"Yes, sir," said Thomas, glad Mr. Black wasn't watching his face.

Bernard sat back down as Thomas went to get the man his tea.

Of all the— He steamed, realizing angrily that the kettle on the stove in the corner was cold. Luckily, the station was equipped with modern necessities like running water and indoor bathrooms, so he didn't have to pump the water as well as boil it for His Highness.

It was clear he'd missed quite a lot by the time he returned with the tea, however, as Chairman Black was standing, shouting at Bernard, who remained seated, his calculating dark eyes watching from above his dark mustache.

"You better find proof, Detective Carew, and fast," the chairman was saying. "I'll not let you slander that good man's name in this city without repercussions."

"Naturally, Mr. Black," said Bernard calmly. "I would not have mentioned it to you if I did not have good reason to do so."

"So do you have someone's word outside your...cook's?" He snarled the word.

"Signora Magro had no reason to lie, Mr. Black," said Thomas, and immediately regretted it when the chairman whirled on him, his eyes blazing.

"Who are you?" he yelled.

Bernard stood. "This is my brother, Officer Carew, who is

assisting me on this case. He was the one who took down the good lady's statement."

Thomas's stomach tightened as he realized he hadn't been taking notes during her spouting of information, but he wasn't about to admit that now.

"And what makes you think she's to be trusted against a man of Mr. Pavoni's standing?" Mr. Black asked, his eyes squintingly taking in Thomas from head to foot.

"Again, I do not see why she'd have reason to lie about such things," said Thomas. "She might just as easily have kept her mouth shut in order to keep her job. Instead, she took a chance and told us the truth."

Mr. Black whirled back to Bernard. "I don't want to hear anymore about this until you have absolute proof, Detective Carew. Hard evidence. I will not have the presidential reception committee dragged through the mud with implications that anarchists were involved. People are frightened enough of them without worrying that President McKinley might have been assassinated on our watch."

"You won't hear a thing until we've got this nailed down, Mr. Black," Bernard said firmly.

"Good, because if I do, I'll be speaking to Chief Witherspoon about ending your time on this police force."

* * *

Bernard sank back into his desk chair slowly. He closed his eyes and took a deep, steadying breath before opening them again.

"So, what'd I miss?" Thomas asked jovially, taking a seat and sipping the tea he'd made for the chairman.

Bernard massaged his temples. He was getting a headache. "Not much. The chairman didn't know where Pavoni had gone and was obviously quite threatened by the thought that the man might be an anarchist."

"I don't blame him, though he might have been more polite about it."

Bernard stared at the papers before him, picking up the pocket watch he'd been holding earlier.

"I've been thinking," he started. "There's a couple things that don't add up for me."

"Only a couple?" Thomas asked.

Bernard looked up at him. "This is no time for joking, Thomas. Our jobs are at stake."

"Aren't they always?"

Bernard grimaced. "Perhaps. But accusations like this one need careful thought and attention to detail."

"I was wondering when he would come along."

Bernard raised an eyebrow in question.

"Sherlock. He's always hiding just behind your next line." Thomas waved the teacup toward him as he spoke. "And as you've got your Watson back, it was only a matter of time before he'd reappear."

Bernard grunted. "Well, what's Watson without Sherlock?"

"I think you mean what's Sherlock without Watson, but let's not digress. This is a bigger issue than us."

Boy, did he have that right.

"Now, what were you saying about thinking?"

Bernard collected his thoughts, still turning the pocket watch over in his hand. "If the worst is true, and Pavoni is an anarchist and he and London were in cahoots together, why would Pavoni kill London?"

"It is possible Pavoni didn't kill London and has simply skipped town for other reasons," pointed out Thomas.

"I suppose that's valid, but it seems too coincidental to have a dead man and a missing man and not require some link between the two."

"You forget, Jennings the butler went missing for reasons other than his being a murderer."

Bernard nodded. "Again, true. And another missing man ended up being a murder victim himself. So does missing equal murdered in Pavoni's case?"

"Then the question becomes two-fold: Why kill Pavoni? And where is his body?"

Bernard nodded again and scratched his mustache. "We should check out Pavoni's hotel room. There may be something there for us."

"Where you go I will follow," said Thomas, standing and placing his empty cup and saucer on the table.

Bernard placed the pocket watch in his jacket pocket alongside the other things he and the coroner had collected from around the body.

As the brothers made their way toward the Montvale Block, they swapped further details from each of their investigations. By the time the building was in their sights down Monroe, Bernard heaved a sigh, relieved that he and Thomas knew the same things at last, from pocket watches to cigarette stubs.

"Interesting that Mr. Pavoni was staying here," Thomas said before they crossed First Avenue.

"What makes you say that?"

"I'm wondering why he didn't stay with someone like the Campbells or Chairman Black while he was in town. Why pay for a hotel room?"

Bernard shrugged. "Maybe he didn't know anyone well enough to be invited?"

"Perhaps, though I personally think it's more likely Pavoni stayed here from a political mindset of wanting to appear in step with the 'common working man.'"

Bernard shook his head. "He is the State Labor Commissioner, after all."

It wasn't like the Montvale was a bad place to stay in town. It was a newer endeavor on the part of Probate Judge John Binkley, built two years ago. He'd had an idea of helping the traveling working-class men and women who came to Spokane by providing a Single Room Occupancy hotel, with rent as low as a dollar a week.

Bernard and Roslyn asked more for staying at their house, but then, they provided both room *and* board, not to mention the friendly, homely atmosphere.

Bernard took a step back to get a view of the building, noting the sign that read "MONTVALE HOTEL-APTS" and another that read "HOUSEKEEPING" in big, bold print. The Montvale Block was a beautiful three-story building of red brick on the corner of First and Monroe, the hotel apartments being on the second and third floors, while the first floor boasted five commercial spaces.

The brothers entered via the impressive brick archway off Monroe Street, with "Montvale" lettered above the double doors. They entered the building from this east side and went up a flight of grand stairs to the main lobby. Bright, natural light spilled upon them from a magnificent skylight above.

At the front desk, the manager who'd spoken to Bernard was retrieved. Mr. Myers agreed to allow them into Mr. Pavoni's room, grabbing a room key from under the counter before leading them across the atrium lobby toward a second-floor corner room. Doors to rooms circled the central area. The staircase in the corner led up to a third floor with an overlook balcony so they could see the door of every room in the place by simply standing in the middle of the high-roofed atrium.

"The only way to access the residential second and third floors is the way you came in. It would be difficult for someone to enter the hotel without the front desk's notice," Mr. Myers pointed out as they walked.

"Or vice versa, I would assume?" Bernard said.

Mr. Myers nodded. "That's why I'm certain no one at the Montvale has seen Mr. Pavoni since Thursday. I asked the entire staff, just to be sure, after meeting with you."

"Is there a doorman?" Bernard asked.

The manager shook his head. "No, but the front desk is always manned."

"What if the clerk is called out on important business? Like a bathroom break?" Thomas asked, ever the realist.

Mr. Myers grimaced, either at the improper question or the suggestion that there was indeed a time someone could go in or out without notice, Bernard couldn't tell.

"No," Mr. Myers said adamantly. "If the desk is ever left unattended, the front door is locked from the inside. Only the staff have a key to that entrance." He shook his own collection of keys to illustrate his point.

A thief might still get in that way, thought Bernard. But they weren't looking for a thief this time. They were looking for a missing political figure.

"Could a guest with a secret visitor simply open the door and allow them in?" Thomas asked.

Mr. Myers grimaced again. "Yes, I suppose so, but I cannot be held responsible for the actions of all our guests."

So really, anyone could get in or out of this place quite easily, Bernard thought. But then, what did he expect? It was just a hotel.

"Downstairs is commercial only?" Bernard asked.

"Yes," Mr. Myers answered easily, obviously eager to move off the lack of security in his hotel.

"And there's two floors of rooms?"

"Yes. Sixty total, with thirty on this floor and thirty on the third floor."

The manager knocked before unlocking number 206 and opening the door onto a small, simply furnished corner room. There was a bed and not much else, unless one counted the dresser with a mirror next to one of the windows, and an armless chair with a suitcase set atop the seat. The two windows looked out across First and Monroe, the Review Building just visible a couple blocks north.

"Shared washrooms?" Thomas asked.

"Common ones, yes, one for women and one for men on each

floor. Each has two toilets and one bathtub, with hot and cold water provided at all times." Mr. Myers seemed proud of this, and rightly so.

"Thank you," said Bernard, leading the way in. "We won't be but a moment."

The manager took his cue, asked that they'd let him know should they find anything, and closed the door as he left.

Thomas went straight for the bed while Bernard searched the dresser.

On top lay the normal accoutrements of the traveling man: collar stays, a comb, a couple handkerchiefs. In the drawers were plenty of choices of shirt fronts, pants, socks, suspenders, and underthings.

"Nothing here," said Thomas from the bed after a few minutes, then went to check the suitcase. "Empty," he called out.

"Well, he hasn't left town," Bernard said, lifting one of the handkerchiefs off the top of the dresser to show Thomas.

"Ew, I wouldn't touch that if I were you," said Thomas. He wrinkled his nose and came to join him at the dresser.

Bernard ignored him, examining the starched, clean handkerchief closely. In the corner were embroidered two entwined letters.

"A.P.," Bernard read aloud.

"Yeah: Antonio Pavoni," said Thomas.

Bernard reached into his jacket pocket and pulled out the pocket watch, cigarette holder, matchbook, key, spectacles, and handkerchief, spreading them out beneath the mirror so Thomas could see them clearly.

Thomas pointed to the corner of the handkerchief Bernard

had just pulled out. "Same initials. Where did you find that again?"

"I didn't. The coroner found it in London's pockets."

"Why would London have Pavoni's handkerchief in his pocket?"

"As well as a watch serviced to a 'tall, dark Italian,'" murmured Bernard, recalling Prescot's odd report. "The body was wearing Italian clothes, too, and didn't have spectacle marks around the nose, even though I found those smashed spectacles beneath the body." He pointed at the ones that now lay atop the dresser.

"How did you identify the body as London's?" Thomas asked.

"His calling cards," said Bernard slowly, following the same line of thought as Thomas.

"I wonder if this key..." Thomas picked it up and walked to the door of the hotel room.

The key slipped in with a click.

Thomas whistled. "There's only one way this all makes sense."

"I agree," said Bernard. "We're not looking for the murderer of James London. We're looking for the murderer of Tony Pavoni."

Three

Sunday, May 19, 1901

Spokane, Washington

Sunday was the Lord's day as far as Roslyn was concerned, and to profane it with things like work before church was not to be borne. She realized they were in the middle of a case and Bernard had told her of their revelation concerning the body after their late return the night before. Still, she insisted they at least not read the newspaper until after attending Sunday school at ten and the service at eleven at the First Swedish Baptist Church.

However, that didn't stop them from discussing the case during the several-block walk to and from church. Although Roslyn did not take part, she listened with eager attention as Thomas told Marian what they'd uncovered, their voices carrying past Bernard as he pushed her in her wheelchair down the sidewalk back toward home.

"So the body *isn't* London?" Marian repeated.

Roslyn could hear the awe in her voice.

"It must not be," said Thomas, obviously enjoying her interest. "There are too many indications that it's not."

"I suppose Nain was right and you should 'believe nothing of what you hear, and only half of what you see.'"

A good motto for a detective, Roslyn thought.

"But what about the spectacles?" Marian asked. "Why were they under the body?"

"London must have placed them there, to mislead us, just as he must have replaced Pavoni's calling cards with his own in the jacket pocket. Other than those two items, everything else seems to be Pavoni's."

"But then why bother?" Marian asked, Roslyn wondering the same thing. "Surely he knew you'd figure it out eventually."

"Must've wanted enough time to skip town."

Roslyn glanced back at the pair of them, walking arm-in-arm comfortably, their heads tilted close to each other in an attempt to speak quietly, as though afraid she would condemn them for breaking her rule. She didn't tell them not to—the sharing of secrets in such an intimate manner could only encourage her notion that Marian would be a wonderful addition to the family.

She returned her gaze to the sidewalk in front of her.

"I am sorry our new boarder could not join us this morning," said Roslyn, speaking to Bernard in an attempt to give Thomas and Marian the idea that their conversation was not being overheard.

"It's my opinion Mr. Bach's left for good," Bernard rumbled behind her. "His room was empty of all his belongings."

"Did you argue yesterday?"

"Not that I'm aware of. He somehow managed to weasel an invite up to Miss Mitchell's house, but he didn't stay long. I made sure of that."

"Oh? I hope you weren't too rude."

"I was firm, was all. But it may be he realized he'd overstayed his welcome."

Roslyn could well imagine Bernard's response when the reporter turned up at the House. "I did wonder at Mr. Prescot's inviting him."

"I still wonder. What's with everyone inviting outsiders into our investigations?"

"Well..."

Bernard waited for her to continue.

"I mean," she hesitated, "you're the one who invited Mr. Bach to stay with us in the first place."

Bernard grunted, then sighed. "I admit, I don't know what I was thinking with that."

"You're a good man, Bernard. That's all. You trust people. Even reporters."

"Thank you, my rose," he said, giving her a kiss on the top of her head.

Roslyn had to admit, she was glad to be rid of the reporter. It had made her distinctly uncomfortable knowing he was staying under her roof. She'd be more particular when choosing their next boarder. She was starting to realize just how lucky they'd been with Mr. Prescot.

As they neared the house, Bernard began to slow. "I think I'll run and catch the next streetcar down to City Hall. Get right to work."

"Don't you want to stay for lunch? I gave Signora Magro the day off, but she said she left us a meat pie for luncheon, in addition to the delicacies we haven't yet finished from Mrs. Curry."

"Did I hear you say you're skipping lunch, Bernard?" Thomas asked, leading Marian up to them.

Bernard pulled to a stop at the bottom of the ramp that led up to their front door and came around so he could see Roslyn's face. "I'd rather get back to work so I can catch people while they're home this afternoon."

"It's Sunday, Bernard," she reminded him with a small frown. "Surely you don't intend to bother people with a murder on a Sunday."

"Crime doesn't close on Sundays, Roslyn," he said. "I've got to close this case as quickly as possible, before someone picks up one of the loose ends and draws the wrong conclusions—ones that lead to Thomas and me both being out of a job."

Roslyn nodded. She understood, even if she didn't like it.

"I'll catch up with you later," said Thomas. "I work better on a full stomach." He grinned that boyish grin that was sure to melt Marian's heart, and led the young lady up the front steps and inside.

Bernard leaned in to give Roslyn a quick kiss farewell. "I'm sorry, my rose," he said, close to her face, not caring that they were still outside for all to see. "I'll be home as soon as I'm able."

"You'll be home for dinner?"

"I'm sure Thomas will make certain we are." He grinned from

beneath his mustache in that way that told her he loved her. Then he leaned in and gave her a full, purposeful kiss.

She knew he'd be home every moment of the day with her if he could. But there was work to be done. Murders to solve and cases to close.

She sighed as he left with a wave. Thomas returned to push her up the ramp and inside; she was grateful he'd allowed them that moment alone. Perhaps next Sunday they'd be able to enjoy the entire day together without interruption.

After a delectable lunch, which only reaffirmed Roslyn's decision to hire Signora Magro, Marian offered to take some of the extra food from Mrs. Curry to the shelter around the corner. Thomas offered to join her, but she insisted she'd like to make this delivery herself.

Roslyn and Thomas adjourned to the front parlor. Thomas picked up *The Spokesman-Review*, no doubt glad Roslyn's mandate of "church first" had been fulfilled, but after all, it was Sun—

"'Assassination Plot Against President Foiled'?!" Thomas read the front-page headline aloud. "'While on the case regarding the body found in Hangman Creek Friday morning, new information has arisen to indicate that one or more of the suspected persons involved may have been connected with the McKinley Reception Committee while harboring anarchist tendencies...'" Thomas trailed off, his face draining of color. "Bernard is going to be *furious*."

* * *

Bernard was *furious*.

He had promised Chairman Black himself that nothing would

come out until they had definite facts confirming Pavoni's anarchist leanings. And yet someone—and he knew exactly which miscreant it was—had taken it into his blonde head that Pavoni wasn't the only anarchist.

Bernard flattened the paper he'd crumpled in his fists and read through it again.

"'Evidence suggests the involvement of two substantial community figures who were heading the plans for the President's visit to our fair city: Mr. Amasa B. Campbell and Mr. Antonio Pavoni of Tacoma. After discovering the anarchist beliefs of Mr. Pavoni, it has become quickly apparent that his cohorts, Mr. Campbell and the late Mr. London, were also working with him to plan a visit for the President that would never be forgotten. Chairman Black, head of the committee, was unavailable for comment...'"

There was no way *The Spokesman* would print such lies without confirming their reports...right? Thomas must have told Bach about the anarchist tilt and the reporter naturally went running to the paper with the story of his life.

He'd still said the body in Hangman Creek belonged to London, though, so they must have talked before Bernard and Thomas made their discoveries last night. Which was before he and his twin had finally compared notes and started working together again.

Bernard had thought last night was proof that they'd pushed past whatever petty jealousy was coming between them.

Apparently he'd been wrong. Thomas had already sided with Bach. Was he hoping to bring Bernard down with this and take his place in the spotlight by reporting the "truth?"

But why implicate Campbell? Bernard tried to slow his rampaging thoughts. He supposed it was possible Campbell, who openly admitted to working with Pavoni, was also an anarchist, but, as with Pavoni, they had no solid evidence this was true. To say such things in the paper was slander—or was it libel? No matter what it was, it was bad. Bad form and bad character to say such things without proof.

And stupid. His job was on the line for this. It wasn't worth the risk.

Damn it. Damn it to hell.

It didn't matter if it was Sunday, he had to vent his frustration at least in his own thoughts.

Bernard had taken that slimy good-for-nothing toad of a reporter and welcomed him into his home, shared his meals and his house with him. And for what? So he could write a misinformed article that would cost him his job?

ARGH!!

In the end, it was Thomas's fault. They'd finally been working together again. The fact that Tony Pavoni was dead should have been front-page news rather than this drivel.

This...this...

And the whole time, Thomas must have known, must have been thinking about how Bach already knew about Pavoni being an anarchist. Even as Bernard stood there defending him to Chairman Black, declaring no one would hear about their theory until they had proof, it was already too late. Thomas had already blabbed to his new buddy.

A reporter. A *reporter*!

"Detective Carew?"

He looked up to find Miss Kenyon.

"I hope I haven't caught you at a bad time?" She was looking at him like she was waiting for the Baker to leap out of his mouth.

He cleared his throat and took a deep, slow breath. "How can I help you, Miss Kenyon?"

She took a deep breath herself and settled on the edge of the chair beside his desk. "I know you're in the middle of this new case, but...it's about Eleanor."

Of course it was. "Eleanor, yes." He took a moment to rearrange his thoughts from focusing on the new murder and that...*blasted* article. There it was again. Yet another time Thomas had made a decision without thinking. "Has my brother found a chance to speak with you about whatever happened at the jail during your visit?"

"No." A look of surprise crossed her eyes, like she hadn't expected Thomas to speak with her about it in the first place. Perhaps they weren't as close as Roslyn had intimated?

"Oh." Bernard cleared his throat. "All right. Well, if you'd like to talk about it, we don't have to do it here. We could find somewhere more comfortable. Like the front parlor back at the house."

Miss Kenyon shook her head. "No, thank you, I'd hoped to catch you somewhere alone. I thought I'd just run out on an errand and then stop in at the station..." She studied her hands, twisting the ring on her pinky finger around and around. "I wanted to ask you a question."

Bernard nodded. "Go ahead."

Miss Kenyon took another deep breath. "I was wondering...about the inquest...for Eleanor. Shouldn't they have done that by now?"

Bernard rubbed his mustache. "Coroner Baker has said he doesn't need an inquest as Eleanor has pled guilty and explained —some might say a bit too thoroughly—the details of...what she did."

Miss Kenyon nodded. "But even if she's pled guilty...at her trial...how...will someone be defending Eleanor's...special case?"

Bernard shook his head. "I'm afraid I don't know the answer to that."

Her eyes met his. "But surely you have a theory?"

Bernard rubbed his mustache. Of course he had a theory. He also had an opinion. It was his opinion the woman was as mad as Professor Moriarty, and the world would be a better place if she came to the same end. But Moriarty had gone down with Sherlock. If the Baker hung for her crimes, Eleanor would take the fall with her.

"I get the impression Chief Witherspoon is hoping to send Eleanor to the Medical Lake asylum to seek medical treatment, rather than hang her for murders she didn't understand she was committing."

Miss Kenyon's face brightened.

"But," Bernard continued quickly, not wanting to get her hopes up, "as you say, hers is a very special case. I've never heard of someone with her...problems."

Miss Kenyon shook her head. "Neither had Roslyn, and she reads more psychoanalysis articles than any man I've ever met."

Bernard grinned beneath his mustache. "Yes, that's my wife for you. She tells me you are getting along fine?"

Miss Kenyon nodded. "Yes, most certainly. Thank you for letting me into your home and in…" She paused, but then stopped her next word. "…to see Eleanor," she finally said instead.

Had she been about to say "your family"? What would have been so bad about that? Too intimate? He thought again about what Roslyn had said about her and Thomas, and about Thomas's infatuated puppy dog look at the kitchen table the other night.

Hang Thomas. If he wanted to pursue his wife's companion, Bernard would rather he do that than continue to blab to reporters.

Miss Kenyon's cheeks reddened. "Thank you, Detective Carew," she said again.

"Call me Bernard," he said. "You're practically family now."

Her cheeks achieved an even redder glow that stretched to her forehead.

"Marian," she said, tipping her head to him as she stood. She turned and started to make her way toward the exit, tugging on her gloves as she went. Then she stopped and returned to him quickly.

"I think you should know that Thomas greatly admires you, and he appreciates when you allow him to help. It's that reporter who's the problem—he's trying to pit Thomas against you, but Thomas said he'd never do that to you. We were both very pleased to hear Mr. Bach has left. Thomas was so happy you two were able to work together again last night. He said you were most successful."

Bernard furrowed his brow.

"I just thought you should know." Then she turned and escaped before he could say anything in reply.

* * *

Thomas had practically flown out the door for the station, knowing immediately how Bernard was going to take this news.

And the answer was not well. Not well at all.

He'd probably be convinced it was Thomas's fault somehow. After all, he'd gone off with Bach yesterday morning and then returned full of information Bernard hadn't uncovered himself.

He felt guilty even though he knew it wasn't his fault Bach had written that article. He'd just started liking the man. Had just started to forgive him for choosing the life of a reporter. What Bach had printed was no less than his own musings on the bluff...

Maybe the man was psychic? More likely, he had been listening at the door and overheard Signora Magro's speech. But then he'd twisted it, deformed it, and mangled it along with what he'd learned while on the beat with Thomas that morning.

Why hadn't he just told the little creep to fend for himself? He should have shaken him loose and told him to go find his own story. He was going to strangle that reporter if he ever dared cross their threshold after pulling a stunt like this.

He was imagining throttling him until his high cheekbones turned blue when an evergreen coat came into view and he momentarily missed a step. But he made up his mind then and there he wouldn't be distracted. He had to speak to his brother first.

"I'm sorry, Marian," he began, "I—"

"You—," she began.

"—have to speak to Bernard," they both finished together. Then they laughed.

He could have kissed her for how wonderful she was just then, making him laugh, relieving the tension a bit before the difficult scene he knew was coming.

"I'm sorry," he said again.

"I understand," she said.

And they moved on from one another reluctantly, after exchanging one last smile.

Once Marian was behind him, however, Thomas felt the urgency of his situation again, and barreled into the station. He ran past the empty front desk that reminded him it was the Lord's Day, and up to Bernard's desk.

Bernard stood quickly as he approached, *The Spokesman-Review* lying crumpled before him. Thomas looked at the crushed paper and felt his regret deepen.

He slowed down and reached for the right words before saying simply, "I'm sorry, Bernard. I *swear* I didn't tell him anything. That mess of mistaken conjectures was all his. I—"

"I'm sorry, too," said Bernard. "I immediately assumed that you must have told him about Pavoni being an anarchist but he could just as easily have overheard half of a conversation and jumped to his own conclusions. But now both of our jobs are definitely at stake. We've got to solve this mystery quickly so we can present it in a neat package to the chief, or we're done for good."

Thomas breathed a sigh of relief. He agreed whole-heartedly. "Where do we start?"

Bernard's mouth twitched into a smile. "Let's go find us a reporter."

* * *

Peter called for another pint of beer for his cousin Daniel and himself. Daniel was three sheets to the wind already, and it wasn't even three in the afternoon.

He'd decided to celebrate his mayhem-inducing article by hiding out with a little bit of comfort between his hands, and between his legs if he could find it. Here at the Coeur d'Alene Hotel there seemed to be sins aplenty to choose from, and somehow it being Sunday made it all the more enjoyable.

"Fancy seeing you here," came a deep voice from behind him as a large hand slapped his right shoulder and squeezed.

Another hand settled onto his left shoulder with a firm grasp. "Mind if we join you?"

Peter gripped his mug of beer harder as the Carew brothers settled on either side of him like a couple of Mafia assassins.

"Hello there, twins! Please, do join me!" he said, forcing a smile onto his face and into his voice. "A round of drinks for my friends!" he called to the bartender. "I'm sorry I didn't get a chance to say farewell, but my cousin Daniel offered a bed in his home and I could not say no."

Peter looked about for said cousin, who he could've sworn was sitting next to him not two seconds ago.

"Naturally, naturally," said Bernard, keeping his hand on Peter's shoulder. He squeezed it slowly. "You left before we had a chance to update you on our investigation. I wish you'd waited."

"We have discovered something quite interesting you may want to share with the public." Thomas's hand was also slowly squeezing Peter's shoulder harder and harder.

Peter couldn't help the interest that shone on his face, though he had the impression the brothers were playing with him.

"Yes," said Bernard, "it's *real* information. You know, not the type you read in the papers these days."

"No," said Thomas, shaking his head, "*this* information is backed up by facts, but perhaps you're unfamiliar with that sort."

Peter gulped. "Carews, if you are in any way insinuating that what *The Spokesman* printed about your investigation this morning was *not* true, I must ask that you speak with the owner of the paper, Mr. Cowles. I do not know who wrote the article, but I am certain Mr. Cowles would be willing to speak with him should you have any concerns."

Their grips on his shoulders tightened again.

Peter tried not to squirm. "I wish I could help you more."

"I wish you would," said Bernard.

"I don't," said Thomas, and he leaned in close to Peter's ear. "We know you wrote that article, because no one else would be slimy enough to listen to a private conversation and then defame some of the biggest names in this city without proof."

Bernard leaned closer on the other side. "It's too bad you chose to print such lies just before we uncovered some rather remarkable facts. You might have raised yourself in the esteem of the paper, but instead, when they learn what you've done..."

"And they will because we'll have proof to back up our claims, unlike you..."

"Mr. Cowles will fire you like that." Bernard snapped his fingers. "And no one will hire you in this town to scrape mud from their boots."

Both hands squeezed so tightly Peter bit back a yelp, and then let go.

And they were gone.

Leaving Peter to his lonely thoughts, and two bruised shoulders.

* * *

"So, what did you think?"

Archie had been grateful to Mrs. Curry for inviting him to join her at her little church on the South Hill, but he felt ashamed that he didn't have an honest answer to her question. He could barely recall what the sermon had been about, let alone the name of the church.

He'd spent most of the sermon with his thoughts bouncing between trying to recall exactly what Jennings had looked like, and torturous imaginings of Thomas and Marian sitting closely together on the pew in front of him, their faces practically touching whenever they turned to whisper in the other's ear about something.

"No matter, I can see you're still pondering," said Mrs. Curry. "I'll ask you again after we've gotten some vittles in your belly."

She smiled, already removing her hatpin and untying her hat ribbon on the walk up the drive, so she was practically in her apron from the moment they stepped through the kitchen door.

After washing her hands and stoking the fire in the range, she removed the roast she'd put in that morning and murmured that it was "quite nice, quite nice indeed." She set it on the wooden countertop while she prepared the remainder of luncheon.

Archie took a seat at the table after his offer of assistance was turned down, and Matsumoto soon joined him.

"I have not yet had a chance to inquire," the inventor began as he took his seat. "Did Detective Carew agree with your theory regarding the similarities between Jennings and the nun?"

Archie shook his head glumly. "No, I haven't had a chance to speak with the Carew brothers. But I think I may have come across something else." He took a deep breath before continuing, but he had to tell *someone*. "I think Jennings is actually the Carews' new boarder, under the guide...*guise* of a reporter."

Matsumoto said nothing, simply stared at Archie's ear, so he continued. "I met 'Mr. Bach,' as he's calling himself, yesterday when I went down to the Carews. He's got a huge beard, claims to be a reporter from Tacoma, and even showed me an article he'd written as though that would prove he's who he says he is. But he's got an aquiline nose, he breathes in just before he speaks, and he smokes cigarettes," he counted on his fingers. "Plus he hot-footed it out of here when I brought him to the House yesterday."

"You brought him to the House?" Mrs. Curry asked, turning from her chopping block.

Archie nodded and pushed his glasses up his nose. "I thought if I brought him up here I'd find a way to make him spill the beans as to his true identity, and I could get your opinion on him. Detective Carew interrupted us, so I wasn't able to carry out my plans, but still—Bach skedaddled awfully quick for a reporter desperate for a story, as he claims to be."

"Perhaps he feared he'd be recognized," said Mrs. Curry.

Archie waved his hand. "That's what I was thinking."

"But," said Matsumoto, "why would he agree to come to the House in the first place, then?"

Archie was a bit stumped. "He may have had his reasons," he muttered, then brightened. "Perhaps he was so sure of his disguise he felt certain he *wouldn't* be recognized, but when Detective Carew asked him to leave, he began to doubt and thought it would be better not to risk it after all?"

Mrs. Curry furrowed her brow. "This reporter looks like Jennings?"

"If Jennings attached a massive fake beard to his face, yes...though I have to admit I only saw Jennings a couple of times. He disappeared pretty early on in the last case."

"Any other clues?" Matsumoto asked.

Archie considered. "He claims to have been in town for a couple weeks—which is within the length of time it's been since anyone's seen hide nor hair of Jennings."

"As they say, if it looks like a duck and quacks like a duck, it's probably a duck." The cook smiled at her witticism.

Archie laughed. That was one way of putting it. He was glad Mrs. Curry didn't seem to think the idea was too crazy, considering how she'd laughed at him the first time he'd suggested Jennings was the nun.

"What worries me is Bach is almost too reporter-y," continued Archie, musing aloud now. "A couple times yesterday I started to think maybe he wasn't Jennings playing a role after all. I wanted to ask you two if, over the six months he worked here as a butler, he ever gave any indication he might not be who he said he was. I know it's difficult to think about it that way now, when we know he's a conman. But did he give any false notes before we knew that for sure?"

Mrs. Curry shook her head. "Can't say that I took much notice, busy as I am with my own things. But then again, I never would have guessed at Eleanor's other side, either."

"No one could have guessed that," Archie murmured.

Matsumoto studied the table. "Mr. Jennings certainly played his part quite well."

As did Eleanor, Archie thought.

"I just don't want to make a fool of myself," admitted Archie. "I wish I could be sure before saying anything to anyone else. But short of asking him, 'Are you Jennings?' I'm not certain what my next step should be."

"I do not think you will know for certain until you speak with Detective Carew and Officer Carew," said Matsumoto slowly, his low, even voice making everything he said sound like motes of wisdom to be collected and cherished. "They are trained to notice such things and you may find they have had similar thoughts."

* * *

Marian prayed the entire walk back to the Carews' that Thomas and Bernard had been capable of reconciliation. She hated to see the tension between the two brothers. Although she wasn't certain it was her place, she felt the household would be better off if they could find a way to work together and solve this case like they had before.

Upon her return, she shared her thoughts with Roslyn as she

sank into her chair beside her employer, her eyes resting on the twin bear cubs decorating the sideboard.

"I do pray they paid attention to today's sermon," Roslyn replied with a nod. "Reverend Boberg's words on forgiveness are most applicable to their situation."

Marian smiled at this but did not say anything. She honestly couldn't be certain what the pastor had said, whether it had been about forgiveness or the church's need for a new organ, as she'd been quite distracted by the nearness of a certain young man seated beside her.

She'd clasped her gloved hands in her lap and focused her eyes on the pastor's as though soaking in his every word, but she'd been conscious of only the warmth of Thomas's right arm pressed against her left one. Her mind had been taken up with wondering if he'd offer his arm to her again for the return walk home, and he had done, much to her joy. He'd also insisted on whispering to her throughout the sermon, as well as on the journey home, his breath brushing against her ear and tickling her with the intimacy.

"...reminder that 'while we were yet sinners, Christ died for us,'" said Roslyn and Marian blushed at the realization that, once again, her thoughts had been far from the moment.

She nodded and hoped Roslyn had said something worth a nod in reply.

"I did wonder if you'd agree after your meeting the other day," said Roslyn.

Marian's breath caught. What had she just agreed with?

"I didn't want to pry, but I hope that you found some peace in seeing her again."

"Her?" Marian asked.

"Eleanor, dear. She is the one I pray for the most. I do so hope that somewhere in her broken state she is still capable of seeking and finding forgiveness."

Marian's face heated. "*She* forgave *me*," she murmured quietly.

"Forgave you? For what?"

"For..." Marian's throat was so dry. She looked about, her eyes landing on the glasses and pitcher of water on the cabinet by the door. "Would you like a drink?" she asked, standing to get herself one.

"Thank you, Marian, yes, please," said Roslyn.

Marian poured and then returned to her seat, handing Roslyn her glass while she focused on drinking her own. Roslyn did not speak and Marian knew she was waiting for an answer, and Marian owed her one.

"I wanted to see Eleanor to ask forgiveness for turning her in," she finally said. "If it hadn't been for me...I do not know for certain that she would be there now."

Roslyn brought her glass down after taking a sip of water. "I don't think that's true. I believe Bernard would have reached the truth eventually, especially if he'd found the ash bucket as you did. He's a very intelligent man, after all."

"Yes, but..." Marian paused to take another drink. "Eleanor didn't kill anyone. The Baker did. Why should Eleanor suffer for the actions of someone else?"

"Someone else?" Roslyn repeated. "The Baker *is* Eleanor."

"But when I visited her...I was speaking to Eleanor and then suddenly..." The flashing blue eyes haunted her. They had changed. They had changed in intensity of color and expression, proving once and for all that eyes were truly the windows to the soul. And in that instant the soul she'd been looking at had changed from Eleanor's to the Baker's. And if their souls were different, shouldn't they meet different fates?

Roslyn was nodding as Marian tried to describe what she had witnessed.

Then Roslyn asked, "Have you ever read *The Strange Case of Dr. Jekyll and Mr. Hyde* by Robert Louis Stevenson?"

Marian was a little surprised by the change in topic and shook her head. "No, I don't think I have. Isn't that a horror story?"

Roslyn smiled. "To some. To others, it's a mystery. Now, in order to share how this book reminds me of your friend's predicament I'm going to have to reveal the twist at the end—a twist that shocked me so much I couldn't get it out of my head for weeks. In fact, I had finally managed to forget it when this Baker business came about, and, at the time, I had nothing else with which to compare it."

Marian nodded numbly, uncertain what this book could have to do with Eleanor.

"It's about a man named Dr. Jekyll," Roslyn began, "who's gotten mixed up with a terrible beast of a man called Mr. Hyde. Hyde murders someone and then disappears, and yet Jekyll has rewritten his will to provide for him. His friend, a lawyer, is curious as to why this is and is determined to get to the bottom of the mystery. The truth that is finally discovered is this: Dr. Jekyll and Mr. Hyde are *the same person*."

Marian shivered involuntarily and looked away, staring out the front bay window.

It was just like her. She was Jekyll and the Red Rogue was Hyde.

Roslyn misunderstood the look on her face and continued. "Yes, I found it quite surprising, as well. And you can see why I immediately thought of it when I heard about Eleanor and the Baker. In the book, Dr. Jekyll has been attempting to separate what he believes to be his two souls: his Evil self and his Good self. When his Evil self murders someone and then tries to hide behind his Good self, it becomes tired of doing so and eventually tries to kill the Good self so that all that remains is Evil."

Marian's eyes widened. She tried to speak calmly but felt her voice struggle to find words that wouldn't reveal her actual fear: that if she continued to indulge in the Red Rogue side of her personality, she might end up as confused as Eleanor. "But...there's not really a way to separate our Good side from our Evil side... Right?"

Roslyn nodded. "Not in the way Stevenson describes. *Jekyll and Hyde* is more of a fictional study of humanity. It is about the struggle between Good and Evil internally, and less about double consciousness, the disease Eleanor suffers from, which does not divide by Good and Evil."

"She has a disease?"

"Yes, it's called 'double consciousness' or 'multiple personalities.'"

* * *

"'Multiple personalities?'"

Roslyn gathered her thoughts as she sipped her water. "Yes, that's the term I've been researching of late, in an effort to understand Eleanor's state of mind. It's something that's only recently come to light through the research of some very unique individuals: Felida and Vivet."

Roslyn was excited by Marian's undivided attention. There was nothing quite so exciting as revealing one's research to an interested individual.

"It's important to note that not all those who suffer from multiple personalities are dangerous in any way, but are in fact, people struggling to understand and come to terms with a rather unique and paralyzing illness of the mind.

"Multiple personalities usually manifests in a very slight difference between the personalities, though in the cases I've been studying there were some personalities that were quite distinct from one another: one a flamboyant, flirtatious, outgoing woman from the streets, complete with a different accent, while the other is a quiet, demure woman of high learning. Or in the case of Vivet: he was unable to walk in one state, and had quite a kind personality, but when awaking in his other state, he was able to move about on his own and had violent tendencies. Here, let me read you part of it."

Roslyn reached for the articles and searched for the one by Camuset, translating it into English for Marian's benefit. "'Noteworthy is also that the character of V...has changed completely. This is not the same subject. He has become quarrelsome and an epicure. He replies impolitely. Having never liked wine and giving his ration mostly to his comrades, now he steals theirs.'"

"That sounds like Eleanor." Marian nodded. "One the sweet, kind Eleanor I grew up with, and the other a threatened, malevolent butcher willing to do anything to protect herself."

Roslyn knew it was a lot to take in. She was still digesting the implications herself.

"But...I guess I still don't understand how this is any different from a conman," Marian finally said. "A man dressing up as one man and playing a part so he can go murder someone, then dressing up as another man with a different personality in order to hide in plain sight. For that matter, in the end, aren't we all like that? Wearing masks to hide our 'true' identities?"

"Ah, but the difference lies in the fact that Vivet and Felida and Eleanor have no control over their change." Roslyn leaned forward in earnest. "A conman can choose his next identity; someone with double consciousness cannot."

"What do you mean?"

"I mean, Eleanor cannot choose *not* to become the Baker. She can't wake up and decide, 'Today I will become an Italian cook' instead and then don the mask of one—only to take it off at night and go back to being Eleanor. When Eleanor wakes, she doesn't know if she's the Baker or Eleanor."

Of course, there was still the question regarding primary and secondary states, and if either state offered a complete awareness. But Roslyn hesitated from presenting this idea to Marian just yet.

Instead she said, "Eleanor may not even *know* when she's made the switch. Many double consciousness victims suffer from amnesia when they cross over."

Marian shook her head. "My poor Eleanor." She rubbed her hands together, worrying, fiddling with the ring on her pinky.

"The good news is, it gives me great hope that if the Baker side of Eleanor's personality finds it capable of forgiving you, perhaps, with a little help from doctors, there is the possibility of complete recovery."

"So Dr. Jekyll's good self," Marian asked, "is he saved in the end?"

Roslyn tightened her lips and glanced at the mantel clock. "I think it's time for tea."

* * *

Thomas followed Bernard back to the station, wondering if they'd accomplished anything by cornering Bach. Luckily they'd found him at the first watering hole they'd searched: Dutch Jake's Coeur d'Alene Hotel.

The audacity of the man to set up his gambling den, casino, bar, and Turkish bath directly across Front Street from City Hall just showed the kind of power he held. It never made Bernard happy when the place was mentioned, even though it was said everybody in Spokane went there eventually. Now, to have set foot in the establishment, and on a Sunday no less? He hoped Mr. Bach appreciated the lengths to which he'd forced them.

"Of course..."

"What?" Bernard asked, taking a seat once again before his desk.

"Well, I was just thinking..."

"Good to know you're practicing that more."

Thomas clenched his jaw. It was good to know Bernard couldn't just let a thing go. "I was just thinking that we don't know for sure that Campbell *isn't* an anarchist."

Silence.

"I mean, just because Bach missed out on the more important

fact that the dead body is Pavoni and not London still leaves us with a missing man—London—and the fact that an anarchist was working with Campbell and his assistant. Closely."

Grunt.

"London is still missing. Mightn't he have killed Pavoni on Campbell's orders and then skipped town?"

Bernard sat back and pulled at his mustache, which Thomas knew meant he was at least considering what he had said.

"Campbell certainly gave a convincing portrayal of surprise, anxiety, and sadness when I told him of London's death," Bernard finally said quietly.

"Well, sure," shrugged Thomas, taking a seat and removing his derby. "He's a businessman. That's like an actor who gets paid to act all the time."

Bernard grunted, but this time it was a grunt of appreciation at a good point. At least, it appeared so to Thomas. He was starting to doubt if he could read his twin brother as well as he'd always thought he could.

"Perhaps we should speak with Mr. Campbell," said Bernard. "He won't be pleased about this article, and he might take it into his head that it's my fault, since I spoke to him."

Thomas nodded in agreement. "Thankfully, it's Sunday, so we won't have Captain Coverly breathing down our necks, wanting to know what we think we're doing."

"What in the hell do you think you're doing?!"

At least it wasn't the captain; it was worse, it was the chief.

Both brothers stood at attention as Chief Witherspoon himself marched up to them, his face purple above his long, gray mustache and matching French fork beard.

"You better explain some things real fast or you're both outta here," he said, jabbing so forcefully with his forefinger that he threatened to punch holes in their chests.

"Sir—," began Bernard.

"Sir, it was my fault," said Thomas, literally feeling like he was jumping in front of a bullet for his brother. That finger was powerful.

The chief glared. "Explain."

"I'm afraid a reporter from *The Spokesman* overheard me questioning a witness and wrote an article misconstruing some of the facts of the case."

The chief nodded. "I see. You're suspended." He pushed past Thomas and up to Bernard. "Tell me about this case, Detective. Succinctly."

"Yes, sir." Bernard laid out all the facts as they had them, from the reporting of the body down to the matching handkerchiefs in Pavoni's hotel room.

"So Pavoni is an anarchist but he's dead, London is the one missing, and Campbell may just be mixed up in it all," repeated Chief Witherspoon.

"And he may not," said Bernard. "Sir."

The chief narrowed his eyes. "You're not suspended yet. But you will be fired if you don't solve this case and clear Mr. Campbell's name."

"Clear it?" Thomas said. But he snapped his mouth shut again, taking a step back as the chief whirled on him with a glare that would silence a roaring lion.

"Yes," he spat.

"And what if the reporter was right?" Bernard dared to

ask, drawing the chief's attention back on himself. "What if Campbell *is* an anarchist?"

"Clear Campbell's name, or I know where the first cutbacks in the Spokane police force will be."

* * *

As soon as Bernard walked in, Marian knew something terrible had happened. She set down her cup and saucer quickly as he came and squatted before Roslyn.

"Thomas and I are on our way to speak with Mr. Campbell, but we thought we'd stop in and ask for your prayers."

"My prayers?" Roslyn asked.

"Yes," her husband said with a nod. "It is Sunday after all, isn't it? I'm afraid Thomas has been suspended."

"Suspended!" Roslyn repeated.

Marian turned to see Thomas standing, holding his hat in his hands in the doorway, a sheepish look on his face.

"Yes," said Bernard. "He took the blame for what happened with Bach and now we've got to solve this case before we both lose our jobs."

"But, if Thomas is suspended, how can he help you?"

"I don't care what Witherspoon says." Bernard looked at his brother. "I need his help." He stood. "I know you didn't think I should interview people on Sunday, but—"

Roslyn waved her hand. "Never mind me. Go, go. Get to the bottom of this."

Bernard gave her hand a squeeze and kissed her on the forehead.

"I only wish we could help in some way," Roslyn said as her husband headed for the door.

"Perhaps I might come with you and speak with the Campbell household?" Marian suggested. "The maids, even Mrs. Campbell, might be more open with a woman."

Bernard just frowned at the suggestion, so Marian ignored him and turned her supplication to Thomas instead, who surely would be more understanding.

But Thomas looked to Bernard, who was shaking his head "no." Thomas looked back at Marian. "I think, with both our jobs at stake, it might be best if we just take this one on our own," he said uncomfortably.

Marian pressed her lips together.

"What about Marian's photography? Perhaps that might be of some use to you?" Roslyn asked from her chair, and Marian nodded hopefully in agreement.

Again, the brothers exchanged glances.

"I'm sorry, but I don't see how that might be helpful," Bernard said tactfully.

"Or perhaps we could see Mr. Pavoni's personal effects?" Roslyn asked, obviously as interested as Marian. "A woman's eye can sometimes see things a man's misses."

Thomas looked to Bernard and shrugged in a manner that said, "I don't see why not?"

Bernard grunted and nodded. "All right, I suppose we could do that. We won't be needing them at Mr. Campbell's."

"And we really could use the help," said Thomas to Marian, as though trying to assuage his guilt for having said "no" before.

"Thank you," said Marian. "I appreciate the chance."

She gave Thomas a smile to let him know she wasn't upset with him, as she really did understand it was not her place to be involved in police investigations, but she was also incredibly curious.

Perhaps she shouldn't have hung up her Red Rogue trappings just yet... As her Nain would say, "The difficult is done at once, the impossible takes a little longer." After all, she had skills that she knew could be highly beneficial in a legal setting if only she was given the chance.

When her eyes fell on the hotel room key that belonged to Pavoni, she knew immediately which skill she'd be using in this instance. She glanced at Roslyn, whose intelligent eyes were watching her every move, making Marian uneasy about her thoughts.

There would be no sneaking out under her employer's careful watch. She'd have to tell her what she planned to do, and pray she agreed it was a worthwhile idea.

* * *

Bernard's long strides carried him quickly to the nearest streetcar stop and then on to the Campbells' residence. He didn't say anything to Thomas until they were walking the final length, grateful his brother had given him the time and space to think of a proper response to the chief's demands.

A block away from the Campbells' house he stopped and turned. "Thomas, I...I know why you did it, and I...cannot tell you how much I appreciate it." Even after thinking for so long about how to say it, he knew it sounded gruffer than he'd have liked.

"Did it?" Thomas looked at him quizzically.

"Took the blame and got yourself suspended so that I could continue the case and prove we're right so you can get back on the roster."

"Oh," said Thomas, blushing slightly. "That." He glanced over Bernard's shoulder. "Shouldn't we...?"

"Yes, but before we go in there, I just wanted you to know that I appreciate it."

"Thanks."

"And thank you for not letting Miss Kenyon join us."

"Marian?" Thomas's cheeks reddened more this time. "Well, I...to be honest, I didn't want her to get caught in the line of fire. We're already walking a thin line. It would've only made things more difficult if she'd come with us."

"I agree. So thank you for not letting your heart muffle your head."

"'My heart muffle my head?'" Thomas's mouth quirked.

Bernard nearly growled. Why must he make this so difficult? "You know what I'm trying to say."

"I do," said Thomas, giving Bernard's shoulder a pat. "Now, can we get on with this? If we're wrong, I'd like to know now so I can start searching the wanteds."

Bernard nodded grimly and straightened his derby. "Let's do this."

They marched up to the grand oak front door and Bernard rang the bell before they could doubt their actions.

The housemaid answered the door and Bernard and Thomas both removed their hats in greeting.

"Detective Carew and Officer Carew here to speak with Mr. Campbell," Bernard said.

The maid bobbed. "I'm sorry, sir, but Mr. Campbell isn't in at the moment."

Bernard's mustache twitched. "We just wanted to stop by and apologize for the misleading information in the paper this morning. Perhaps we'll catch Mr. Campbell another—"

"I'm sorry, sir, what I meant to say was: you can find him out back with the family. Mr. Gladding is putting on his usual Sunday Circus for Miss Helen. Just around back of the house, sir."

Bernard and Thomas exchanged a look, then nodded and thanked the maid as she closed the door.

Sure enough, as they circled the corner of the house and came into the backyard overlooking the valley carved out by Hangman Creek, they could hear the whinnying of a horse, the yips of a dog, and the cheers and laughter of a small gathering.

"Mr. Campbell's not going to like this intrusion," Thomas muttered.

Bernard knew he was right, but it wasn't like they had much of a choice.

The Campbell family, along with a couple neighbors and friends, all dressed in their Sunday best, were gathered around a small enclosed circle, in the center of which stood the coachman, Gladding. In one hand he held a long whip-switch for encouraging the horse, a Shetland pony, which was on the end of the rope held in his other hand.

"Is that a—," Thomas began.

"Yes, it is," Bernard answered with a shake of his head.

On top of the pony rode a small white dog, who was grinning

from ear-to-ear as he rode the pony around the circle, sometimes at a trot, sometimes at a slow canter, depending on what Gladding was calling out.

"It really is a circus," Thomas said with a low whistle of admiration.

The whistle nabbed the attention of Mr. Campbell, whose happy, carefree face immediately turned gray at the sight of them. He leaned over to his wife and whispered in her ear, and she turned and glared at the two of them. The Carews smiled and waved encouragingly.

Finally, Mr. Campbell excused himself and came to join them, though he didn't say anything until he was close enough to growl low at them.

"You dare come to my house on the Sabbath after accusing me of being the worst possible thing a man can be in this country?" He cursed through gritted teeth beneath his breath. "An anarchist?! I thought I had the measure of you, Detective. I guess I was wrong."

"Detective Carew and I do not share that belief, sir," Thomas interjected. "We wish very much to exonerate your name and prove that the reporter responsible is nothing but a slanderer."

Mr. Campbell rocked back on his heels. "You mean a libeler." He considered Thomas gravely. "And you are?"

"Officer Carew."

"Brothers?"

"Yes, sir," said Thomas and Bernard in unison.

The tips of Mr. Campbell's mouth attempted to rise but he held them in place. "So you do *not* think I am an anarchist?"

The brothers nodded.

"I have an idea that dratted reporter stuck his nose into my safe and misunderstood what he found there," Mr. Campbell said. "My papers were disorganized when I checked on them last night."

"I'm very sorry to hear that, sir," Bernard said. "If you'd like to press charges, we can get him for breaking and entering."

Mr. Campbell shook his head. "He didn't take anything, other than misinformation."

"We would love the opportunity to prove the truth, sir," Bernard said. Or at least, what Bernard very much hoped was the truth.

Mr. Campbell considered a moment, and then waved his hand toward the back door of the house. "Well, then. Let's get started, shall we?"

* * *

Marian pushed Roslyn into the Montvale, keeping her head bowed slightly in deference to her employer as Roslyn put on a remarkable act, berating her about the damage done to her "best hat."

"I'm so sorry, madam," Marian said, keeping her eyes low. "I will try to fix it, madam, as quickly as possible."

"You do that!" Roslyn was dressed in her Sunday best, complete with the most outrageous hat they could find. The imperious tone perfected the role.

The look on the clerk's face from behind the desk at the top of the stairs was one of utter astonishment. His eyes nervously flew from the woman in a wheelchair to the stairs, which were clearly the only way of accessing the Montvale's rooms.

"Madam, I don't think—," he began to call out.

"Young man, come down here immediately. I refuse to hold a conversation with someone by yelling."

The clerk jumped like he'd touched an open flame and then scurried down the stairs. "Madam, I'm afraid—"

"I have no desire to stay in this establishment, I can *assure* you," Roslyn said peremptorily.

The clerk looked extraordinarily grateful to learn this. "How can I help you, madam?"

"Do you know who I *am*?"

"No, madam—"

"I am a cousin of Mr. John Binkley, perhaps you know him?"

"Of-of course, madam. He—"

"He owns the entire Montvale Block. And you?"

"Uh, yes, madam?"

"You are going to let my maid run upstairs so she can fix the damage she's just wrought on my best hat!"

The clerk eyed the hat skeptically. Marian and Roslyn had ensured it was the most hideous hat she owned; they'd also run over it a few times with her chair, just to ensure it played its part most dramatically. The size had also been important, for Marian's box camera was hidden inside it.

"Go on, dear," Roslyn said to Marian. "Johnny assured me there were washrooms in his establishment, so I know you'll be able to find everything you need upstairs."

The clerk looked from Roslyn to Marian to the hat and back to Roslyn.

"Of course, madam. Right this way, miss," he said, motioning to the stairs. "The washrooms are clearly marked on each floor, male and female. I'm afraid I cannot leave my post. I'm the only one on duty Sundays."

Marian bobbed a curtsy before Roslyn, glaring at her hat, shooed her up the stairs. Marian obediently ascended.

"Stay right here, young man," she could hear Roslyn saying to the desk clerk. "I'm not finished with you yet. Are you telling me Johnny hasn't made his hotel accessible to his own cousin?!"

Marian held back her grin until she'd turned the corner and the front desk clerk had no chance of seeing her.

She knew the room was somewhere on the second floor, but neither Thomas nor Bernard had supplied the room number. She was going to have to wing it, hoping that Roslyn could hold down the clerk for a good long while.

Roslyn had taken to the whole scheme rather well, much to Marian's surprise. She'd said she would have suggested the idea herself if Marian hadn't thought of it also. Roslyn was clearly a kindred spirit. It had been a decent mile walk from the Carews' house to the Montvale—over the Monroe Street Bridge and into downtown—but the effort would be worth it if they could help the brothers in their case.

Marian stood in the middle of the atrium lobby so she could see the room doors lining all four sides. The whole area was lit naturally by a skylight that rose above the third-floor ceiling. Square pillars circled the lobby, the balustrade of the stairs she'd come up continuing to the third floor, with a railing lining the mezzanine so residents on that floor could look down upon the second-floor lobby. The overall effect was one of wide open space, something one usually didn't get in a hotel that marketed to the itinerant working class.

There had to be over thirty rooms on this floor alone, not to mention the washroom doors at one end. Roslyn had suggested that she begin to the right of the stairs, as someone like Mr. Pavoni was likely to stay on the north side of the building, with its better views. To the south, tenants would only enjoy views of the Northern Pacific railroad, which ran behind the hotel on its way through downtown.

Marian glanced either direction and then turned to the right, finding that the doors on this side were all evenly numbered: 200, 202, 204, 206, and so on. She began trying the key in every door, continuing north as the numbers ascended. She only had to pause once when a couple exited their room on the far side of the lobby. Then she simply pretended she'd just left her room and locked the door behind her, walking with purpose toward the washroom. The couple bobbed their heads in polite greeting and the gentleman tipped his hat to her as they passed. She smiled innocently in response.

Once they'd gone down the stairs, Marian hurried back to the door she'd just tried: 204. The key slid easily into the door of the next room: the northeast corner room, number 206. Marian slipped softly inside and closed the door behind her, breathing a sigh of relief. She'd never been one for sneaking around in the daytime, but so far things had gone quite smoothly.

The room was deceptively simple to look at. The brothers had no doubt already checked the obvious places, like under the mattress, and they'd definitely searched the dresser, as that was where the infamous handkerchief had been found. Now her expertise as a thief would come into play, for she knew that there were much cleverer hiding places in this room than the ones sons of a policeman would have thought of.

She checked the transom windows first, sliding them open and running her hand along the exterior wooden sashes. Next, her eyes roved along the wallpaper, with its simple black damask on white print, looking for an uneven section. She ran her fingers along the paper as she went, reaching high above her five feet two inches, hoping Pavoni hadn't made a secret nook at a height only a tall man could reach.

She pulled the dresser out from the wall and checked behind it, running her fingers again along the smooth paneling of the back, searching for a latch to a hidden drawer. Then she glanced about, her eyes landing on the armless wooden chair on which the suitcase was sitting.

"I wonder...," she murmured aloud, recalling a rather marvelous contraption Archie had once mentioned.

He'd told her that amongst the many "ingenuous inventions" he'd viewed, he'd once seen a chair that had appeared elegantly simple on the outside, but was really quite devious. After cranking a turnkey under the chair, which had a thickly cushioned seat, the chair would play a music box tune whenever someone sat on it.

Marian doubted this chair would play music, but she wondered if maybe...

She lifted the empty suitcase, double-checked it for hidden pockets inside the inner lining, and set it on the ground. Then she examined the armless chair. Its cushioned seat bulged in a way that intimated comfort. Or...

Marian ran her finger along the lining of the chair, and in the very back she found what she was looking for.

Her nimble fingers pressed the snap and up popped the seat cushion, revealing a very small area in which someone had hidden a flat lockbox. She wondered if all the Montvale rooms had this accoutrement, or if Pavoni had acquired the chair for his personal use. Either way, the fact was, she'd found what both of the Carews had missed.

She took her box camera from inside the hat and snapped photographs of the chair, the hiding place, and the lockbox within. Then she replaced the seat cushion and suitcase and examined the room, preparing to leave. She'd spent enough time searching and Roslyn was surely running out of excuses for her.

She returned to Roslyn with a look of regret pasted on her face, the box and camera hidden within the large, still broken hat.

"I'm sorry, I couldn't—"

"Never mind, girl, never mind," Roslyn said, still imperious. "Enough time has been wasted on frivolities. You can buy me a new one tomorrow when the shops open."

And with that, they made their exit, practically running the mile back to the house to examine Marian's find.

* * *

Thomas found himself once more playing the part of pack animal, but he didn't mind so much this time. He and Bernard were finally working a case together again, and something told him they were close to figuring this one out. All it would take was a little cooperation.

He hoisted the large box full of everything Campbell had given them in relation to the plans for the President's visit. It had been a rather simple matter, really, as Mrs. Campbell had already boxed everything up.

Before giving them the box, however, Campbell had led them to his private basement den, opening a closet door to reveal a large safe, which he quickly unlocked and opened, waving an open palm toward the Carews.

"There you are, gentlemen," he'd said in his booming voice. "I have nothing to hide."

Thomas had been impressed by Campbell's openness, though he knew it was possible he might have hidden anything questionable elsewhere, like in his office downtown where he surely kept more of his private work papers. Once Campbell opened the safe and began leafing through the papers it contained, Thomas saw how Bach, if this was what he'd found, might have come to the conclusions he'd published in *The Spokesman*. Campbell's willingness to reveal his private papers, however, was definitely an exonerating gesture. His cupboards were all bared, it could be said. He had nothing to hide.

"I'm a great friend to the President, knew him in the old days back in Ohio, so the idea that I would plot an assassination or other anarchist demonstration is ludicrous," Campbell had said. "As you can see, Detective Carew, I was collecting notes on the enemy, following the paper trail on the blasted anarchists so I could bring them to trial if they tried to repeat what they did in Wardner. It is not necessary to recount the outrages that have been committed in this country, and there should certainly be some lawful way to stop it. It is a disgrace to our state."

Thomas had quietly leafed through the letters with Bernard as Campbell went on.

"There are only two classes of people that ought to mine. One is the party who has any quantity of money, and can afford to lose any certain amount and not feel it, and the other is the party who has not a cent, and can devote his time. People with limited means should never put a dollar in mining," Campbell had said. "I don't care for violence. I've tried to shield my family from the terrible atrocities in Idaho by moving us here." He'd waved to encompass his home. "I realize the miners have families, too, but rioting is no way to accomplish anything in this country. And it's an ugly thing for my daughter to grow up around."

"I've heard it got pretty bad there for awhile," Bernard had said, looking up from one of the letters, "for both the miners and the mine owners."

Thomas had heard that, too. Miners would spit at the owners as they walked down the street, demanding raises, even throwing rocks at their houses. There were strikes all the time, since it seemed like the only way to get the mine owners' attentions. The strike in '99 had been over the fact that the companies were still paying a measly three dollars a day for miners, and only $2.50 for shovelers and carmen. The union men had dared to ask for $3.50 for miners and "muckers" alike.

A thousand union miners and sympathizers had seized a Northern Pacific train and taken armed possession of Wardner before blowing up the concentrator with sixty-five pound boxes of dynamite. Martial law had been declared and over seven hundred insurrectionists had been imprisoned in a stockade they'd referred to as the "bullpen."

It had only been this past January that they'd finally lifted the permit system, which had required all applicants for employment to obtain a necessary clearance card that declared they were not members of the miners union.

But as far as Thomas knew, they'd gotten their raise to $3.50.

He couldn't imagine Mr. Campbell trying to raise his little girl with a mine owner's target on his back. No wonder he'd moved to Spokane.

"There was the added benefit of moving to a large city, as well," Mr. Campbell had continued. "Better telephone and telegraph access, train access, hotels. From a business standpoint it made sense to move to a city with more resources, more economic and social security."

Mr. Campbell had then answered every question put to him quickly and succinctly, and Thomas believed Bernard had been right in his good opinion of the man.

"Thank you, Mr. Campbell, for your forthrightness," Bernard had said, shaking the man's hand. "It makes matters so much simpler. I think I understand now where Mr. Bach was misled and I apologize once again for the misunderstanding. We'll ensure Mr. Cowles prints a retraction in the evening *Chronicle*."

Now Thomas transferred the weight of the box from his left to his right arm as he disembarked from the streetcar behind Bernard, and walked the remaining distance to their front door.

In the front parlor, they found Roslyn and Marian seated just as they'd left them. As he set down the heavy box, however, Thomas realized his was not the only box on the table.

"What's that?" Bernard asked, glancing at the small lockbox and then at Roslyn with a furrowed brow.

Thomas watched Marian's face instead. She was eyeing him as though uncertain of his reaction.

"Why don't you two have a seat?" Roslyn said, waving to the chairs in their own parlor as though they were guests she'd invited over for tea. "Marian, would you please ensure all the doors are locked this time and that we are quite alone?"

Marian nodded and left the room.

"We wouldn't want another reporter accidentally overhearing our conversation again, now would we?" Roslyn clasped her hands together in her lap as she watched the brothers sit down, Thomas on the couch and Bernard in an armchair.

Bernard leaned forward and grabbed the lockbox.

"Before you open that, please listen to Marian's story," said Roslyn, as Marian returned to her seat.

"Miss Kenyon." Bernard's voice sounded lower and more serious than usual. Thomas worried what he might do if he didn't like the story Marian shared with them.

Marian straightened her skirts and cleared her throat. "After you left, Roslyn and I looked over Mr. Pavoni's effects, as had been suggested. We did not notice anything worthwhile until we saw the hotel key. It was then I had the idea—"

Roslyn interrupted. "You needn't take all the blame yourself," she murmured.

Marian nodded gratefully toward her employer and friend. "*We* had the idea," she said, waving her hand to Roslyn, "of taking another look at the man's room at the Montvale."

Thomas glanced at Bernard. He could hear his jaw grinding.

"You went to Pavoni's hotel room?" Thomas clarified. "How did you know which one it was?"

Marian bit her lip. "I didn't. I tried the key in different doors until I found the correct one."

Thomas smiled, but he could still feel the heat slowly building in the armchair across from him.

"We checked that room from top to bottom," said Thomas, eager to know where they'd missed.

Marian bit her lip. "It was in a secret contrivance in the cushion of the chair."

"Ha!" Thomas slapped his knee.

"You were too busy figuring out that Mr. Pavoni was the victim." Roslyn's steady eyes focused on Bernard. Thomas could almost feel her sending comforting thoughts his way.

"I took some photographs, as well," Marian offered. "Once I've developed them, I'm certain they'll be helpful to you and your investigation, as proof of where these documents were found."

Thomas leaned forward. "What do you say Bernard? Would Marian make an excellent candidate for the first female detective in Washington state?"

Bernard didn't reply straight away. It was clear he was too busy collecting his thoughts before he said something he might regret later. He didn't know Marian like he knew Thomas. He couldn't say to her what he really thought. Roslyn was obviously trying to connect eyes with him, but he didn't want to. He just stared at the lockbox before him.

Thomas cleared his throat. "Well, Bernard? Shall we see what Marian uncovered for us?"

Bernard's eyes went to Thomas, who immediately wished he'd let Bernard continue his staring contest with the box instead.

Suddenly, Bernard's brow relaxed and his eyes cleared. He

turned to Marian and gave her half of a smile from beneath his dark mustache.

"Yes, let's. After all, it appears we're all in on the case now. For better or worse."

* * *

Bernard finally looked at Roslyn, and she could feel the tension release from her shoulders. For a moment, she'd been sure he was going to erupt in volcanic anger. Now she relaxed her hands on the arms of her wheelchair and watched as Bernard joined Thomas on the couch to read through the documents inside the lockbox. Roslyn and Marian had already taken a look, but they weren't about to admit this to Bernard.

"I'll make us some tea," Marian said, and left the room while they read.

As the door closed behind her, Roslyn couldn't contain herself any longer.

"Thank you for not getting upset, Bernard," she said quietly.

He glanced up with a brow furrowed in concentration, but his brow lightened slightly at her smile.

"I'm afraid I almost did, my rose. What she—what you two did cannot happen again. I hope you understand that. It could cost me my job if the chief discovers I let a civilian in on a case."

"But we're already about to lose our jobs if we don't clear Campbell," said Thomas.

"Which is precisely why I realized I didn't need to feel so angry. So I let it go." He looked pointedly at Roslyn. "For now."

He returned his attention to the paper in his hand, which

Roslyn could see was still the top letter. She waited patiently for him to let her in on his reactions, but he was as passive as ever.

Thomas, on the other hand, was easily readable. He almost spoke twice as he read, his eyes growing wide and then narrowing with each line.

She recalled her own reaction as she had clutched the topmost piece of paper, her eyes stuck to the heading which directed it to Chief Witherspoon of the Spokane Police. It was a letter denouncing James London as an anarchist who plotted to assassinate the President by planting himself in the home of Amasa Campbell. Pavoni had apologized for having recommended the miscreant to Mr. Campbell's service and signed off with "Sincere regrets."

She watched the brothers finish reading that same letter now, but they still didn't let her in on their thoughts.

Marian returned with the tea things and she and Roslyn helped themselves while they waited. They'd almost finished the pot before the brothers finished their read-through of all the documents.

Then the brothers sat back on the couch with a collective groan.

* * *

"This is worse than we thought," said Thomas, shaking his head at what the ladies had uncovered. In one small lockbox they'd found enough to bury someone, and he knew who. He wondered if Bernard agreed.

Bernard was looking at Roslyn and Marian. "I assume you two have already taken a gander at these."

The ladies exchanged a look, but they both seemed to realize the game was up.

"Yes," said Roslyn, and Marian nodded her head.

"Well, then, let's hear it," Bernard said with a wave of his hand. "What do you two make of this load of incriminating paperwork?"

Roslyn set down her cup and saucer. "Let's begin with Mr. London. Although the topmost letter makes it sound like he was behind a plot to assassinate the President, the rest of the documents seem to contradict that idea."

Thomas and Bernard nodded in agreement as Roslyn continued. "The President was expected to stay with the Campbells, so it makes perfect sense that someone might try to get an operative in there to provide an inside vantage point of all the plans concerning McKinley. Enter Mr. London on Mr. Pavoni's recommendation, a recommendation Mr. London would not require if Mr. Campbell were in on the plot. This means Mr. Campbell is most likely innocent of all collusion, as there is no indication in this paperwork that Pavoni and London ever meant to include him. Indeed, the documents speak of practicing all possible deceptions on him."

"Thank God for that," said Thomas, saying aloud what he knew they were all thinking. "Perhaps we have a hope of saving our jobs after all."

Roslyn smiled at this.

"It is also clear Mr. Pavoni knew what he was doing when it came to espionage and assassination planning," Thomas said. "As we know from Signora Magro, this was not Pavoni's first attempt at an anarchist plot. It's possible he's gotten away with others that we're unaware of."

Pavoni's plan had been a very simple act of misdirection. In fact, it reminded Thomas more of a thief's heist or a magician's illusion. The idea had been to plant an assassin in line behind London. London, being a rather nervous individual, would appear suspicious, thereby drawing the attention of the police guards and secret service protecting the President. But London was simply the distraction. While the police would be busy hauling him off for questioning, the real assassin would have a clear chance to come up with a gun and shoot President McKinley. They'd most likely both go down for the murder, all the while keeping Pavoni's hands clean from a distance.

"I believe the letter on top was written to cast blame solely on London, just as was done for Signora Magro's brother," said Thomas. "It was meant to be Pavoni's fall-back option. Should the plan fail or London threaten not to do his part, he'd mail that letter to the chief."

"The question is: did Mr. London know he was to play the part of the distraction?" Marian asked. "Or was he merely a pawn to be used?"

"Seeing these documents were all found in Pavoni's possession, I'd lean toward believing Pavoni is the mastermind behind it all, not London," Thomas said. "Pavoni has even kindly left behind step-by-step plans for the assassination plot."

"I wonder he didn't get rid of these plans once the President canceled his trip," Marian remarked.

"He must have been killed before he had a chance to clean up the evidence. Or he simply intended to try the plan in a different location," Bernard said.

"At least we have the name of the anarchist who was to pull the trigger," said Roslyn. "Mr. Daniel Ebner."

"Daniel. Now where have I heard that name before?" Thomas murmured, looking at his brother beside him with a raised brow.

"I know what you're thinking. Peter Bach mentioned a cousin named Daniel," said Bernard, his voice low and full of a growing anger. No doubt he was making firm vows to himself never to let a reporter near his house ever again.

But before they went on another headhunt for damfool reporters, Thomas said, "What I want to know is: how will we convince the chief? We don't have much evidence of anything outside these documents."

"Let's get back to what we do know and go from there," said Bernard, always a man for logical, linear reasoning. He had been looking convinced and skeptical by turns over the course of the conversation, less willing to jump to conclusions, no matter how perfectly they fit together.

He pulled out his notepad and a pencil and began to write as he thought aloud.

"One: Pavoni is the body discovered at the bottom of Hangman Creek. On his body were London's calling cards and spectacles, but everything else was his own.

"Two: Someone was planning to assassinate the President, as per these documents.

"Three: Signora Magro claims Pavoni is an anarchist, and London told Mr. Campbell he was all for McKinley, though Mrs. Campbell seemed uncertain of his political affiliations."

"Four," said Thomas, "London killed Pavoni."

"Perhaps, but that's precisely what we can't tell from these documents," said Bernard, picking up a few and scanning them. "We can't know for sure whether London was being blackmailed into participating or if he was a willing assistant, though I agree that the letter was most likely for Pavoni's benefit should London be caught."

"Which means, in a twisted way, that the letter denouncing London is actually proof of London's innocence," Marian concluded.

"Innocence regarding the assassination plot, perhaps, but not necessarily of the murder of Pavoni," Bernard pointed out.

Roslyn spoke up. "Whether London knew about the assassination plot originally or not, it's possible London discovered Pavoni's plan to shift the blame onto him with that letter. What if London pushed Pavoni down the side of the bluff to silence him?"

"That's conjecture again," Bernard said.

"Who else would switch out Pavoni's calling cards for London's and leave behind London's spectacles to mislead the police?" Marian interjected.

Thomas practically beamed at her. "It is the only logical deduction given the facts."

Bernard grunted. "I suppose. But it feels like conjecture. Even if we've got things clear about the assassination plot—"

"About as clear as mud," Thomas put in.

Bernard gave Thomas a look. "—the murder itself is still a mystery."

"I'd like to point out I conjectured the second body in the forge last time," Thomas said with a grin.

Bernard grunted again.

"If London pointedly made it look like he was dead, rather than Pavoni, it wasn't just to mislead us," Thomas went on. "He must be on the run, and hoping the last couple days were enough of a head start."

"If that's true, then it is enough," said Bernard gruffly. "We don't even know where to begin—"

At that moment, Thomas practically jumped out of his seat.

Someone was banging on the door.

* * *

Archie pushed his glasses up his nose and shifted his satchel on his shoulder nervously. He was finally going to do it. They had to be home since it was Sunday afternoon and he knew Mrs. Carew didn't like any work on the Lord's day. There could be no more delaying. He had to tell the Carews about Jennings.

It took a long time before Marian finally opened the door a crack. When she saw it was Archie, she opened it wider and smiled.

Archie's throat dried up and all the spit went down his windpipe and suddenly he was hacking and gasping for breath.

"Oh my goodness!" Marian cried, pulling him inside and closing the door. She led him into the front parlor and poured him a lukewarm cup of tea.

He took in the scene around him, trying to wet his mouth and catch his breath at the same time.

The Carew brothers were seated on the Chesterfield, with

Mrs. Carew across from them in her wheelchair, all gathered around the central table, which was covered in papers and two boxes, one big and one small.

None of them looked pleased to see him. Except Marian, but even she seemed nervous and was apologetically explaining why she'd let him in, as though she shouldn't have.

"It's quite all right. It is Mr. Prescot, after all," said Roslyn, always the hostess.

But it took Thomas standing and slapping him on the back to lighten the mood. "Forgot to breathe the whole trip down the hill?" he asked.

Archie nodded and smiled weakly. "I suppose I did. I do apologize. It seems I'm interrupting something."

"Just talking through some case notes is all," said Bernard, but he didn't stand to welcome him.

He'd seemed so grateful for his help with the pocket watch before.

Archie nodded again. "I'm afraid I come to you with a new case—or rather...a return to an old one, I suppose."

Thomas waved him toward the armchair next to Marian and rejoined his brother on the couch across from him.

Archie was grateful he wouldn't have to deliver his hypothesis while facing those daring green eyes. "What do you know about Jennings?"

Both brothers sat up straighter and glanced at each other with a questioning look.

"The...butler?" Thomas asked slowly.

"From the Baker case?" Bernard added.

"Yes," said Archie. "Reginald Jennings, who ended up being

something of a question when it came to getting his job with Miss Mitchell."

"We haven't found him yet, if that's what you mean," said Bernard.

"Why?" asked Thomas. "Have you seen him?"

"Yes, as have you," said Archie, feeling his confidence returning as the perfect moment of delivery presented itself.

"Me?" said Thomas, raising an eyebrow and glancing again at Bernard with a shrug that said, "I don't know what he's talking about."

"Jennings was the nun," said Archie, clearly enunciating each word and waiting for the applause.

But it didn't come. Instead, he was met by two reddening faces of men who were trying not to laugh.

"The nun?" came a sweet voice from beside him.

Archie turned to Marian. "You may not remember seeing her—or him—but when you visited the Baker, as you came out, she—or he—went in."

"You think the nun was Jennings?" repeated Thomas. "In disguise?"

Archie took a deep breath. "Yes."

Thomas's mouth twitched.

Bernard ran a finger over his mustache. "Explain," he said, and Archie was grateful he hadn't immediately shot down the idea.

"It was the nose that got me. Jennings had a rather distinctive nose, as you may recall."

"Yeah, quite a beak, you might say," said Thomas unkindly.

"I've heard it called 'aquiline,'" said Archie, proud he'd gotten the word right for once.

"You can't claim the nun was Jennings simply based on the nose," said Bernard.

"No, there was also the way she spoke—always with a slight intake of breath before speaking."

"How could you know Jennings spoke that way when you met him, what, once? With me?" asked Thomas.

"It was Mr. Matsumoto who pointed that out to me," said Archie.

Bernard nodded his head. "He would notice a detail like that. And that's all?"

"No, she also smelled of cigarette smoke." Archie waved to Thomas. "You might not have noticed it because you smoke a pipe."

Thomas's brow furrowed at this.

Archie continued, "I've been talking it over with the others up at the House, and it does make sense that he'd want to get in to speak with Eleanor. After all, he was in love with her."

Marian exhaled beside him. "He was?" she asked.

"Yes," said Archie, turning to her. "I believe he might have even taken on another new identity to stay in town close to her, perhaps to see what he could do to get her freed."

"A new identity?" said Bernard. "And I take it you have an idea what identity that might be?"

"I do," said Archie, again clinging to his growing self-confidence. "Your new boarder: Mr. Peter Bach."

* * *

This time Thomas laughed and both of Bernard's brows rose sardonically, but Marian did not respond. She was considering

Archie's accusation, and it didn't seem too far-fetched. After all, hadn't she been speaking with Roslyn only this morning about a conman's ability to choose a new identity and inhabit it completely?

If this Jennings was a man as capable as someone else she knew in a similar line of work—someone who'd taught her all she knew about how to hide a secret self—then it was absolutely possible he'd taken on multiple chosen identities, even a female one. A nun wouldn't be too hard to hide, since it was really the habit everyone saw first, and it seemed to be a natural male assumption that most nuns were unattractive—they couldn't comprehend why a good-looking woman would take a vow of chastity.

And Mr. Bach, well, the man had made Marian uncomfortable from the start, and had the same attributes Archie had listed for the nun: he had a distinctive nose, he breathed in when he spoke, and he certainly smoked. And he'd seemed oddly obsessed with the Baker case, wanted to know all the details and had tried to turn every conversation back to Eleanor.

She realized this was exactly what Archie was saying at that very moment.

"I don't think the idea is as far-fetched as you seem to believe," Roslyn put in, shaking her head at the two brothers scoffing on the couch.

"If Jennings was Bach, I'd know," said Bernard gruffly. "You can't pull one over on me so easily. Besides, Bach is paler, blonder, and blue-eyed. Jennings was darker, as I recall."

"There are numerous examples where a conman was capable of fooling the people around him by simply changing his demeanor or dying his hair," Marian put in. "Could you really swear to knowing Jennings's hair color when you only met him a couple times?"

Bernard grunted.

"And given what we were discussing earlier about Mr. Bach's cousin..." Marian left the suggestion hanging, not wishing to invite Archie into a conversation into which it was not her place to invite him.

Bernard sat forward, his face serious once again. "I hadn't thought of that."

"His cousin?" Archie asked.

"If his 'cousin' is who we think he is," said Thomas, ignoring Archie and watching Bernard's face, "then it's possible Jennings was hired as Bach to give credence to the 'cousin's' cover story as a reporter for *The Spokesman*."

"And to get in close with us so he'd have the first line on the case." Bernard reached for the papers on the table, searching through them for something in particular.

Thomas was shaking his head. "Whether Bach is or isn't Jennings, and whether or not he's involved in this case, he still should know where Cousin Daniel is."

Bernard dropped the papers and stood. "It's time to go."

Archie, Thomas, and Marian stood with him.

"Thomas, with me," Bernard said, heading for the door.

Thomas turned to Archie and Marian and shrugged. "I'm afraid we're off again. Thanks for the tip, Prescot." Thomas patted Archie's shoulder as they left, tipping his head to Marian with a grin. "And thank you for your help, as well, Marian."

Marian blushed as Archie turned to her questioningly. "Oh,

Roslyn and I helped obtain some information for a case, is all," she said with a wave of her hand.

Archie nodded, but still looked curious. He opened his mouth, most likely to ask what information exactly, when Thomas popped his head back in the parlor.

"Mr. Prescot, would you care to see if your hypothesis is correct?"

* * *

"'Confirmed: Campbell's Anarchist Assassination Plot,'" Peter read aloud. "No, too alliterative. What about, 'Assassination Plot Confirmed: Campbell, Pavoni, London Implicated.'"

Still not good enough. He was missing something. The Carew brothers had said as much. He absently rubbed one of his sore shoulders.

"Miss us?"

Peter whirled in his chair to find the Carews had brought along a third this time: the clockmaker of all people. It suddenly occurred to Peter that maybe he wasn't a large clockmaker, but a boxer, come to squash Peter for good. He certainly looked about ready to pummel Peter into jelly.

Peter raised his hands in surrender. "I'm sorry, really I am. But news is news."

"Whatever could you be referring to?" asked Thomas. "I thought you said you didn't know who wrote that libelous article?"

Peter blanched. That was the trouble with lies. It was difficult to tell when it was one too many.

"We're not here about the article this time," said Bernard. "We're looking for your cousin."

Peter's breath caught before he spoke. "My cousin? Daniel?"

"Yes, Daniel—what did you say his last name was?"

"Ebner—but I don't think I—"

"Where is he?" Bernard looked around, searching for him amongst the mostly empty desks.

"He's not here. I haven't seen him since you threatened me."

"Threatened?" said Thomas, his eyes widening as if in surprise.

Bernard leaned in and placed his large hands over Peter's on the chair arms, pressing down on his wrists so he couldn't move.

"That wasn't a threat," he growled. "*This* is a threat: tell me where your cousin is or I'll take you in for false identification."

"False what?"

"Identification," said Thomas. "He means we're on to you. We know you're not really Peter Bach, if there even is such a man."

"What?!" Peter tried to jump, but Bernard's hands held him in place. His heart thumped in his chest. How had they figured it out?

"We've met before, haven't we?" said Bernard, his voice low. "Jennings."

Peter's heart stilled. "Jennings?" repeated Peter.

"He's got the aquiline nose," Mr. Prescot said from somewhere behind Bernard's hulking form. "And have you noticed the breathing thing before he speaks?"

"That's because I could really use a cigarette about now!" Peter yelled.

Bernard let go, but stood so Peter couldn't get up from his chair. Peter rubbed his wrists like he'd been handcuffed.

He swore. "You really know how to make a man feel welcome. Is it because I'm from out of town?"

"No, it's because you're a liar."

"I'm a reporter." Peter shrugged, trying to appear nonchalant though his mind was racing. "I get paid for a good story."

"And how long have you been a reporter?"

"Um…" Peter considered what would be a good length of time. He'd left his parents' home in Old Tacoma only a year ago, but that wouldn't sound convincing. "Ten years?"

"Is that a question?" Thomas asked.

"No. I meant: ten years," Peter said more firmly.

"I think you mean ten *days*," said Thomas.

Again, Peter tried to catch his breath. "Well, yes, I've been a reporter in Spokane about that long, but back in Tacoma—"

"What paper?" Bernard cut in.

"*The News Tribune*," Peter said.

"How are you related to Daniel?"

"He's my cousin on my mother's side."

"And what was her name?"

"Ruth."

"And your father?"

"Jack."

"And your middle name?"

Peter hesitated.

"Ha! He is Jennings!" Mr. Prescot cried triumphantly.

"N-no," Peter stammered as an idea came to him. "I just don't want to tell you. I hate it." He paused for emphasis. "It's Johann Sebastian."

"Your full name is Peter Johann Sebastian Bach?" Thomas asked with a cocked brow. "That's a bit on the nose, isn't it?"

"Yes," he sighed, holding back a smile. It was so ridiculous it was plausible.

"You're related to the composer?" Mr. Prescot asked.

Peter shrugged. "It's difficult to prove, but it's also difficult to prove we're not."

Bernard glanced at Thomas and the clockmaker, whose brow was furrowed.

"Keep an eye on him. I want to talk with Prescot." He led Mr. Prescot back through the desks and outside, leaving Peter with the friendly twin.

"So," said Thomas, cracking his knuckles, "let's talk. Why'd you sneak in to see the Baker?"

"What?!" Peter exclaimed again. "I never—I would never—"

"Yes, you would and you did. We know you were the nun."

Peter's jaw dropped. What were these Carews on about? And how could he learn more to turn it into a story... "I don't know what you all are talking about and why you seem convinced I am someone I am not." He fumbled in his vest pocket. "Here, take my card."

Thomas grabbed it and looked it over. "Peter Bach, reporter, and you list the Review Building for your address? How'd you come to have calling cards for Spokane already?"

"My cousin made them for me."

"Sure, he did. I bet your cousin doesn't even exist."

"Of course he does!"

"I've never seen him," said Thomas.

"He was with me at Dutch Jake's."

"You were alone at that bar."

"Here," Peter said. He got to his feet, but dropped back into his seat when Thomas didn't move. "Excuse me."

"Where do you think you're going?"

"I'm going to get you proof that my cousin exists."

Thomas seemed to consider this for a moment, and then stood back. "Be my guest."

He followed very closely on Peter's heels as Peter led the way through the maze of desks to where his cousin sat. He pulled open a drawer on the right and shuffled around for a moment before finding a stack of what he wanted in the back.

"Here you go," he said in triumph. "Proof."

Thomas took the calling card and read it over. Then he looked up and grinned at Peter in satisfaction.

"I'll be sure to tell your cousin hello for you," he said.

Then he tipped his hat and left Peter standing with his mouth agape, wondering what the hell he'd gotten himself into.

* * *

"Mohawk Block, third floor, number 532," said Thomas, handing the calling card to Bernard.

"That's above the watch shop where I found out about the pocket watch you gave me," Prescot said.

"And Jennings?" Thomas asked.

Bernard glanced at Prescot. "I think he's telling the truth. I don't think Peter Bach is Jennings, even if he is a liar."

"Buck up, old boy," said Thomas, giving Prescot a friendly pat on the shoulder as they left the Review Building. "There's still the possibility that Jennings was the nun."

Prescot's shoulders slumped beneath his hand. Thomas could feel his disappointment. He'd honestly hoped Prescot would be right about the sniveling reporter.

"How'd you get the cousin's address?" Prescot asked.

Thomas shrugged. "I have my ways."

"Do you think Bach's in league with his cousin?"

"I don't know," Bernard answered for both of them. "Possibly. We'll know more when we talk to the cousin. I'm going to have Hollway put an officer on the Mohawk building to bring him in for questioning."

"What about London? What's our next move?" Thomas asked, and he could tell Bernard appreciated him asking.

"I'll send in a brief article with a description of Mr. London, requesting information."

Thomas shrugged. "It's worth a shot."

"Even if no one comes forward with having seen him, perhaps someone can tell us more about where he came from. We know nothing about his background, not even where he's living."

They slowed as they neared City Hall.

"I think we should visit the Baker," suggested Thomas. "Perhaps we'll be lucky and catch her at a lucid moment when Eleanor will tell us the truth about the nun's visit."

Prescot took a deep breath before nodding in agreement. "I'd like to come with you. I still swear I recognized that nun."

Bernard nodded as well and after he spoke with Hollway at the front desk, they made their way downstairs to the cells. Smith was back on jailer duty, and would be for the foreseeable future with a high-profile criminal in the cells, no matter if it was Sunday. He was snoring loudly, his head leaning against the wall behind his chair, his helmet tipped forward over his high forehead.

"Should we wake him?" Thomas asked. "I've always wanted to try that trick where you stick their fingers in a cup of warm water."

"Thomas," Bernard said, in that tone that was too much like their father's.

"What?" Thomas grinned.

"Let's just go in," said Bernard, leading the way.

The door to the cells closed behind them and they padded down to the last one. The Baker, or Eleanor, was waiting for them.

"Good afternoon, gentlemen, or is it good evening?"

She sounded lucid enough, but you could never tell.

Bernard led the conversation. "Eleanor, we've come to ask you about a visitor you had the other day."

The pale woman with the piercing blue eyes nodded, her hands clasped before her calmly. "Yes, I thought you'd like to know what Marian said to me. I'm afraid I don't always remember when the Baker takes over, so I can't be sure."

Thomas let out the breath he'd been holding. They were talking with Eleanor at the moment. So far so good.

"We were wondering about the visitor who came after Marian. A, um, nun."

Eleanor cocked her head. "You mean Reggie?"

Thomas heard Prescot's quick intake of breath beside him. Well, that confirmed that.

"Yes," said Bernard, his surprise quietly contained, "Reginald Jennings."

"What about him?"

"Why did he visit you dressed as a nun?"

Eleanor rocked back on her heels and crossed her arms defensively across her chest. "He loves me, you know."

Bernard studied the woman before answering slowly, "I know."

"He wanted me to run away with him."

Bernard nodded. "Did he offer to get you out?"

Eleanor cocked her head again. "Get me out? I haven't exactly been let out for walks in the garden, no matter if it is Sunday."

Sunday. Thomas jolted. It was possible a "nun" might have snuck in under the pretense of blessing the prisoner with a prayer and a sermon.

"Have you seen him more than once?" Thomas asked, aware of Bernard glaring at him, angry at his interruption. "Have you seen him today?"

Eleanor's head slowly turned to study Thomas, her blue eyes seeming to see much further inside of him than he cared to allow. She stared at him, but he didn't break eye contact, almost hoping he could see when the moment happened, knowing it was coming.

"Yes," she finally said. Slowly. Almost painfully. Like it had taken some effort to get the word out.

And then it was over.

Her head tipped slowly from side to side, in a rocking motion much like a metronome, and a thin sing-song voice murmured, "Old Mother Hubbard went to the cupboard, to give the poor dog a bone; but when she came there, the cupboard was bare, and so the poor dog had none."

She raised her hands and clasped them behind her head,

swinging her elbows back and forth. "Poor puppy. I have nothing for you today. Nothing to give. No bones. No scraps. None. Nun..."

Four

Monday, May 20, 1901

Spokane, Washington

Archie didn't sleep well that night. He kept imagining what Marian would think when Thomas told her Archie had been wrong about Jennings being Peter. It was no consolation that Eleanor had openly admitted Jennings had, in fact, been the nun.

He still felt convinced Jennings was out there somewhere, hiding under a false identity. He couldn't stay in Spokane for long without someone recognizing him and saying, "Hey, aren't you the butler from the Mitchell house?"

Then again, the House was so far out of town, and Miss Mitchell hadn't entertained often, according to Mrs. Curry, so maybe Jennings could just hide in the sea of faces.

Archie flipped over again, this time onto his left side, crossing and uncrossing his arms, trying to get them into a comfortable position.

It was no use. The dim purple of dawn was peeking through the curtains and it was time to start a new day.

With a huff of reluctant acceptance, he hauled himself up and out of bed, pulling his glasses on as he did so and picking up his pocket watch to wind it and examine the time—5:07.

A knock at his door startled him into greater wakefulness.

"Who's there?"

"It's Mrs. Curry. Are you awake?"

Archie grumbled to himself that he'd been awake all night, but he dutifully pulled on his robe over his striped pajamas and opened the door.

"Read this," said the older woman, thrusting a folded *Spokesman-Review* into his hands.

Archie pushed his glasses up his nose and read the headline Mrs. Curry had pointed to.

"'Pavoni Murdered: Police Cover Truth,'" he read aloud, then looked up with alarm at Mrs. Curry.

She shook her head. "Oh, it gets worse." She tapped the newspaper.

"Witnesses can now confirm that the police have misled the public by reporting that the body found in Hangman Creek on Friday morning belonged to a Mr. James London when it was in fact the body of Antonio Pavoni, the State Labor Commissioner from Tacoma. Should anyone have any information regarding the location of Mr. London, they are encouraged to contact the police immediately.

"London is described as a tall, white male, mid-thirties, dark hair and eyes, with a large, Roman nose. He was last seen wearing round-rimmed spectacles and a gray suit. London is wanted for questioning in regards to the murder of Antonio Pavoni, and should be regarded as dangerous. Any and all information should be brought directly to City Hall."

"Do the Carews know about this?" Mrs. Curry asked, when Archie glanced up and puffed air out of his lips in response.

"They do now."

"Did you read the article beneath the one about Pavoni?"

Archie looked back at the newspaper and moved his thumb, which was covering the article below the first one.

"Information Sought: Police seek information regarding a man of the following description who answers to the name Reginald Jennings, but may be known by another name. Roughly 6'1", broad-shouldered, wide face with an aquiline nose, dark hair and eyes, age about 35. Any information should be brought directly to Detective Bernard Carew at City Hall."

Archie's eyes widened. "Wait a minute, that description sounds just like the one of London."

"I thought you'd be interested. I'm certain the Carews have noticed, as well, seeing as they're intelligent gentlemen like yourself. But it sounds like you were on to something when you said how you thought our Mr. Jennings may have taken on a new identity in order to stay near Eleanor. Seems to me our missing Mr. Jennings may be their missing Mr. London."

"Thank you, Mrs. Curry!" cried Archie, handing the newspaper back to the cook and then leaning forward to give her a quick peck of thanks on the cheek.

He closed the door and dressed as quickly as possible,

eternally grateful the cook could 1) read, and 2) liked to read the newspaper first thing in the morning after starting breakfast.

He was down the drive and on the first streetcar of the morning as his pocket watch dinged to tell him it was six o'clock.

* * *

Thomas shook his head as he read. Nonsense. It couldn't be.

And yet, there it seemed to be in black and white. Mr. Bach had gone and done it again.

"You're *not* going to want to read that," Thomas said, handing the newspaper to his brother and filling his empty hand with another buttery scone. He was grateful the ladies of the house had not risen as early as he and Bernard had, so there would be no need to share all the scones piled high on a plate before him.

Bernard took the paper and his eyes scanned quickly over the news. "That little imp took my description and used it in another libelous article! 'The police have misled the public'—rubbish!"

Before Thomas could reply, someone knocked at the front door.

"Who could that be first thing in the morning?" Bernard grumbled as he wiped his mouth and stood to answer it.

He reappeared quickly with a very tired-looking Prescot.

"Good morning, Prescot, care for a delicious scone?" Thomas offered, finishing off his current scone and reaching for another.

"No, thank you. Have you read the paper this morning?" The clockmaker shifted from foot to foot nervously.

"Yes, we were just discussing it," said Bernard.

"What do you think?"

"If I had the ability, I'd sue that damn reporter for all he's worth."

"No," said Prescot, pushing his glasses up his nose. "I meant about the similarity between the descriptions of London and Jennings."

Both brothers looked at him blankly, then each grabbed for the paper at the same time, wrestling over it a moment before each taking an edge as they read together.

Thomas and Bernard had each sent in an article to *The Spokesman.* Thomas's article described Jennings, since he'd had more interaction with him over the course of their last case. Bernard's article described London, based on the notes he'd gathered from the Campbell household, though they'd been printed along with Peter Bach's very biased thoughts.

Prescot pushed his glasses up his nose. "I think London is Jennings."

"You think everyone is Jennings," Bernard said unkindly.

"Nonsense. Just the shifty ones," said Thomas, before shoving another bite of scone in.

"It can't be a coincidence," said Prescot. "Jennings disappeared a month ago; London began his job a month ago. They both are described as tall, with dark-blonde hair and eyes. How simple would it be for Jennings to add spectacles and a nervous attitude to hide the pompous butler he played before? No one he interacted with would ever have known him as the butler."

"But why would Jennings pretend to be London?" Marian asked, wheeling in Roslyn just in time to complicate the conversation. "Conmen don't con without a motive."

"Yes, I've been considering that my entire ride down," said

Prescot with a blushing glance at Marian. "I really think it comes down to love—love of Eleanor."

Thomas glanced at Marian, too. "What do you think, Marian?"

Her cheeks reddened at being put on the spot, but he could tell she already had an opinion ready to share.

"Well, if Jennings was looking for a way to stick around Spokane until he could figure out a way to get Eleanor out, taking on the role of a temporary personal assistant would be ideal. He'd be able to slip in and out without causing a huge fuss, and no one would be the wiser." She came around to Roslyn's side. "And if he really loves Eleanor, there's always the possibility he thinks she's innocent."

"After talking to the Baker a couple times he must know the truth by now," said Thomas.

Marian frowned unhappily. "Yes, I suppose so. But it's also possible that his love has blinded him."

"He must have known Pavoni, though," said Bernard. "The reference letter given to Mr. Campbell bore a realistic-looking signature from Pavoni, and London was seen speaking with Pavoni on several occasions."

"And there's the fact that London's name is all through the assassination plot documents," added Thomas.

"Assassination plot?!" Prescot cried.

"Anyone else you'd like to let in on all the facts? The cook, perhaps?" Bernard growled.

Thomas shrugged and grabbed another scone.

* * *

The five of them adjourned to the front parlor, where they closed the doors once again against prying ears while Thomas brought Prescot up to speed.

"So," said Bernard, ready to bring the conversation back to where they'd left off, "I think we can conclude that Pavoni wanted Jennings-London to get the job with Campbell in order to give him an inside man to the house plans in regards to the President."

Four heads nodded in agreement around him, though Prescot still had a quite baffled look on his face.

"And Pavoni clearly outlined what London's role would be in the plot," continued Bernard. "The question is: How much did Jennings know about it?"

"I don't think you'll be able to deduce that," put in Roslyn. "You'll have to ask him."

"And how, pray tell, are we to find a man who can shift personality and appearance so well he's gotten past two of us already?" Bernard asked, nodding toward Thomas and Prescot on the couch.

"The same way Prescot worked out he was the nun," said Thomas. "Start with the nose and breathing."

Bernard almost shook his head, but then he stopped himself. He suddenly recalled a hobo with red, watery eyes over a large, Roman nose. The dirt and grime that had covered the face, as well as the incredible stench enveloping the man, had caused Bernard to not pay close attention to the details of the man's features. He'd simply wanted to get the information, verify it, and let the hobo move on to his next manure-filled bed.

He swore.

"Bernard!" Roslyn cried.

Bernard's face warmed. "I apologize, Roslyn, Marian. I just realized Jennings conned me, too. And you, twice," he said, looking at Thomas with a grin that reduced some of the shame filling his chest.

"Who?" Thomas asked.

"The hobo." Bernard laughed. He couldn't help it. The ridiculousness of it all. And yet, it fit. "The hobo that came to me Friday morning to report the body, smelling of the sewer and gin so much so that I never took a good, long look at him. But what I did see included a nose I'd never forget, if placed on a cleaner face." He slapped his knee. "By golly, he's good. I mean, he's really good. When he switches characters he goes all for it. He must've lain in the dirtiest pile of trash in the city for half the night before coming in to see me."

"You mean Jennings has now played a butler, a hobo, a personal assistant, and a nun?" Prescot listed off.

"What can't the man do?" Thomas said, laughing with his brother now and shaking his head.

"Once you two have finished chuckling at the acting capabilities of a criminal," interrupted Roslyn, "we still have a more pressing matter to attend to: namely the murder of Mr. Pavoni."

"Right you are, Roz," said Thomas, straightening his features and his tie.

Bernard nodded. "We need to speak with Jennings. We need to find him."

"You could always wait for him at the jail," Prescot muttered.

"The jail?" Thomas repeated. "You think he'll go back?"

Prescot pushed his glasses up his nose. "I think a man who has risked everything—including somehow getting involved in an anarchist plot—in order to see the incarcerated woman he loves, will not be leaving town without saying goodbye."

Thomas nodded and looked at Bernard. "I'm still suspended, so it's your call, Detective. Do we lie in wait for our criminal?"

Bernard nodded perfunctorily. "I think it's all we can do now to get the answers we require."

* * *

He'd been born Andrew Jackson—a name that wasn't his own from the very beginning, as it had belonged to a President before him. He'd grown up on the streets, a nobody. He'd wanted to make his own name for himself.

So he'd made several.

Now he could be anyone he put his mind to.

Even a nun.

The first time he'd put on the habit, he'd worried he couldn't pull it off, that the jailer would notice his rather obvious masculine features. But if there was one thing he'd learned in his years as a conman, it was that they were called confidence tricksters for a reason.

All it took was confidence.

Confidence he was who he said he was, that he had a past, a present, and a future.

Confidence that he was where he was supposed to be, doing what he was supposed to be doing.

Confidence, or lack of confidence, as the character called for: the greatest acting role any man could ever fill.

But all his confidence had gone out the window the first time he'd laid eyes on Eleanor in that cell. So cold, so lonely. Even in prison brown he'd still thought she looked beautiful.

Until she turned on him.

"Come to pray for my soul?" she'd said, her voice scoffing and cold. "I'm afraid mine's well past its expiration date. There's no use trying to save it any longer."

She'd never spoken to him like that before, but he'd known it was just a mask, like the ones he put on. And so he'd removed his habit and revealed himself, thinking maybe she just didn't recognize him, but that'd only made her comments more personal.

"Reginald Jennings," she'd said, her eyes somehow a more piercing blue. "How kind of you to visit. I hope you didn't come all this way to speak to Eleanor. I'm afraid she's been detained."

A cruel yet pleased smile had spread across Eleanor's face. A smile that practically had fangs it was so unlike his sweet Eleanor's.

And yet he'd still refused to think his dear Eleanor had disappeared completely behind this mask. For it had to be just a mask. Like himself, Eleanor must have once known how to switch out her personalities, and she'd just gotten stuck in one. It sometimes happened even to the best. She obviously had forgotten how to take the mask off.

Only he could save her. Only he, who understood what it meant to be multiple people. To carry the burden of the lies that came with multiple identities.

But when he'd returned on Sunday, she'd only been worse.

She'd spoken in nothing but rhyme with a terrible sing-song swaying of her head back and forth, back and forth.

He hadn't stayed long then.

And now, this morning, after reading *The Spokesman* and realizing it wouldn't be long before the police made the connection, before they realized they were looking for one man instead of two, he'd come.

It was time.

Jackson dropped the spent match, adjusted his habit, and got his heart racing. He told himself the fire in the alley before him was growing larger by the second. He must get help.

He rushed to the nearest door, which just happened to be the entrance to the jail cells.

"Fire!" he cried, letting his voice carry higher than usual. "Fire!" he cried again, widening his eyes in fear.

"Where?" the jailer asked, leaping to his feet.

"Just there, in the alley. Get the firemen!"

The jailer leapt out the door without thinking, no doubt figuring the nun was trustworthy. Jackson lost no time in grabbing the keys he'd left hanging on the wall and entering the back hall lined with cells.

Eleanor was waiting for him.

"What are you doing here?" she asked, her voice her own.

He knew he could count on her.

"I'm getting you out," he said, pulling a second habit from underneath his own and thrusting it to her through the bars. He started trying keys in the cell door.

"You can't save me."

He looked her in the eyes. "Yes, I can," he said confidently.

"We'll go to Colorado Springs. There's great sanitariums there and healing waters. They'll fix you."

She shook her head as the door to her cell swung open.

"They can't. Nothing can fix me." Tears filled her eyes.

Jackson wrapped his hands around her face and pulled her to him, kissing her, passionately, a kiss to heal all ails.

"I love you," he said.

She laughed through her tears. "I know. You're crazier than I am!"

He kissed her again.

Then he helped her into her habit, throwing it over her prison garb easily.

He took her hand.

"Let's go."

They raced down the hall, threw open the first door, and—

"Hey, wasn't there just one nun?" he heard the jailer say.

Standing in the door to the outside, blocking their escape, turning his plan from brilliant to impossible in one stance, were three men.

"Good day, Sister," Detective Carew intoned. "I think it's time you told us about Mr. Jennings."

* * *

Bernard sat across from the defrocked Jennings, or Andrew Jackson as he'd revealed himself to be, and patiently waited with fountain pen and paper to write down his confession.

He wished Thomas could be here for this, but he was still suspended, pending this interview. So he was doing it by the book, bringing the conman upstairs to the small room they used for interviewing suspects. A spot of blood still marked the wall where one of his colleagues had taken his questioning to another level entirely.

But Bernard didn't believe in that kind of police work, though he realized with a grimace he'd come awfully close a couple times with Bach. Maybe he owed the man an apology.

Bernard believed that all he needed to know would be found in evidence, facts, and conversation, much like his beloved Holmes. Bernard hoped the chief would be pleased with whatever this man confessed to him now, enough to pardon his brother and prove Campbell's innocence.

Bernard was surprised by the man who sat before him. He was not the pompous butler he'd first met over a month ago, nor the shameful hobo he'd met second, nor the nervous, bespectacled assistant described to him so often these last few days. He was simply a man. A man who, if he was not mistaken, had finally come to the realization that he'd lost the love of his life forever. And not just behind bars.

Bernard did not say anything. Instead, he waited.

Sure enough, Jackson eventually began his speech, but that was what it sounded like: a practiced speech. It was like he'd been anticipating this moment and preparing for it. Bernard wondered if that meant he shouldn't believe a word of it, but for now he listened.

"I suppose you want to know the truth," Jackson began, "but it's rather difficult for me to tell it, when I've been living lie after lie for years now, so you'll excuse me if I don't make much sense. Perhaps you can make more sense out of it than me.

"I discovered early on that the trick was to inhabit a persona completely," he continued, speaking half to himself, half to Bernard. "To not just tell yourself who you are but to *be* who you are in every thought, opinion, and whim. As Jennings the butler I established an entire background, including being born to a life of service, raised by a lady's maid, brought up amongst the cutlery in the kitchen in an upper-class Seattle home.

"Whereas, as James London, I created a variety of nervous tics, one of which I took from our friend the clockmaker, in fact: the pushing up of the glasses on the nose." He did so now, though his face was bare. "As London I also voted for McKinley, which made Campbell like me right away, since I could spew all the correct jargon to reassure him of my political preference.

"I decided I'd need a real reference for this job after what happened with Jennings. I hadn't time to write false documents and I didn't want to risk being unmasked before I'd established my goal..."

"Which was?" Bernard couldn't help asking in the pause.

"To free Eleanor," Jackson said, in a manner that said this should have been obvious. "I had asked her to go with me, before she was caught, before I knew she'd killed her own husband. At the time, she told me no..."

He shook his head. "When I heard about the arrest, I laughed, glad that she'd taken matters into her own hands and finally killed the brute. But then there was talk of insanity, and I thought...well, I thought I could help her."

Something real cracked his voice then, or at least, something that Jackson seemed to believe was real.

"Help her how?" Bernard asked quietly, his pen pausing.

Andrew Jackson shrugged and scratched his chin. "However I

had to. I thought I'd scout it out, figure out a way to bust her out of the joint and then we'd make a run for it. I thought we'd go to Colorado, get her the healing she needed, and I thought my love...I thought my love would be enough till then." He looked up at Bernard. "She won't get better in there, Detective. You know that as well as I do. She needs help, love, someone who cares about her."

Bernard had to bite his tongue. He had to remember that even now, Jackson was playing a role: that of criminal and lover hoping for pity from the jury.

"How did you get Pavoni to write your reference?" Bernard asked, pushing Jackson back toward talking through his plans rather than dwelling on his love.

Jackson paused a moment before allowing himself to be sidetracked. "I knew Pavoni from my time in Tacoma. He's a man with his fingers in all the right pies, so I knew he could get me a job wherever I asked. I knew he would do for me, so long as I did something for him. He told me he needed someone in the house to report back to him what plans were being made before the Campbells presented them officially to the committee. He said he could get me in easily as an aide to Mr. Campbell, as they were looking to hire an extra set of hands to help prepare for the McKinley visit. Applicants had to be vetted by someone on the committee, and wasn't I lucky Pavoni could get me in."

Jackson scoffed. "I should've known there was more to it. After all, I knew I wasn't the only one 'assisting' with his plans for McKinley. There were others."

"Do you know their names?"

Jackson shook his head.

"Do you know where they were placed?" Bernard asked.

Jackson nodded. "Tony worked the committee. I worked the Campbells, where the President would be staying. He had someone at the newspaper reporting news to him before it appeared in *The Spokesman* or *The Chronicle*. And he had someone in the President's entourage during the entire national tour feeding him information from there. Like I said, he was a man with fingers in many pies."

Bernard scribbled all the information down quickly. He had an inkling he knew the name of the man at the newspaper who'd been working for Pavoni, and hoped to be speaking with Daniel Ebner in this very room soon enough.

"The job with the Campbells was an easy one," Jackson continued. "I'm naturally a very organized, methodical person—you have to be to keep all your identities straight. I chose a quiet, unassuming type for London so he could go about his business without too many questions."

As he spoke, Bernard realized the personality of London was coming out in Jackson's movements. His head lowered and he stopped making eye contact, started fidgeting with his fingers, and Bernard could hear the rhythmic *tap, tap, tap* of his booted heel bouncing on the ground underneath the table.

"One day," Jackson went on, unmindful of the change to his persona, "Tony pulled me aside after joining the Campbells for dinner and told me he had good news: as a person working in the house where McKinley was staying, I'd be allowed to meet McKinley before anyone else. I was flattered. I, as London, was especially thrilled at the news I'd get to shake hands with the man I'd voted for." He paused and smiled like he'd thought of a private joke.

"What's so funny?" Bernard asked.

Jackson looked to the side, then to his hands, which he twisted inside and out, finally saying, "To be honest, I've voted for the man multiple times."

Bernard didn't see what was so funny about that.

"But then, on Thursday night," Jackson said, and Bernard was glad he hadn't lost the flow of his narrative, "Tony met me on my walk home, which goes along the bluff overhanging Hangman Creek. We often met there to join in a smoke and exchange information. Speaking of which, have you got a cigarette I could bum?"

Bernard frowned. "I'm afraid not..."

"No matter. Just remembered I've got one." He patted his vest pocket and pulled out a pack. "Do you mind?"

Bernard worried the man would stop the flow of admission if he denied him a way to relax, so he waved his hand and waited for Jackson to light his cigarette, take a puff, and breathe a heavy sigh of relief.

"Thanks," he said, smiling at Bernard.

Bernard nodded. "So, Thursday night..."

"Right, right," said Jackson, taking another puff before continuing. "So this time, Tony said there'd been a change in plans." Jackson fiddled with the cigarette between his fingers as his brow furrowed at the memory. "He told me McKinley wouldn't be coming to Spokane after all because his wife was too ill, so they'd be headed straight back to Washington.

"Well, I'd just been offered a position to stay on with the

Campbells after McKinley left, and, to be honest, I'd grown to like the family in the month I'd been with them, especially Mr. Campbell. He's an impressive individual. Have you met him?"

Bernard nodded.

"I intended to take the job. Figured I'd have more time then to figure out what to do about Eleanor. So I told Tony I'd had an offer and I'd be staying, and that I was grateful to him for getting me the position in the first place."

Jackson frowned, clenching his jaw. "And then...it all went to hell in a hand basket." He took another long draw, almost finishing the cigarette as his cheeks pulled in. Then he blew it all out through his nose and mouth. Bernard was reminded of a dragon about to emit fire.

"Tony tells me he wants me to follow McKinley, says I've got to join his man on the inside. Says I can meet the President 'accidentally' somewhere else on his route...and pull the trigger myself."

Bernard's pen paused. "Pull the trigger?"

"That's what *I* said," Jackson pointed the butt of his cigarette at Bernard. "I was in shock. I couldn't believe I'd gotten mixed up in murder *again!*" He waved his arms and leaned back in his chair. "I mean, I knew I was working for an anarchist, but assassination?"

"Wait, you knew he was an anarchist from the beginning?"

"Well, yeah, but...everyone's got political beliefs." He shrugged, throwing the cigarette butt on the ground and grinding it beneath his shoe. "To each his own, I say."

Then he leaned forward with both hands on the table, looking Bernard straight in the eye. "But I would never, *ever* shoot the President. No matter which side he fell on. I need you to understand that."

Bernard studied Jackson, but didn't say anything.

"It's really important to me that you believe that I'd never shoot *anyone*, if it came to that, but much less the *President*. Like I said: I voted for the guy!"

Bernard nodded slightly, but still didn't agree out loud. The last thing he needed was the chief saying he'd promised something he couldn't deliver.

"So I told Tony he was nuts if he thought I'd do that," Jackson continued. "Told him squarely that I was staying in Spokane and wouldn't be shooting anybody. But then Tony said, 'You'll do exactly what I say or I'll turn Jennings in to the authorities.'"

Jackson leaned back again and spread his arms. "Well, what was I gonna do? As I said, he's a man of high profile that everyone trusts. No one would believe me if I said he was planning to assassinate the President. The word of a known conman?" He laughed derisively.

"I knew if he told you where I was, that would be the end for me—I'd never get Eleanor out then. I knew if Tony put you on to me you'd arrest me as a confidence man in a second." He snapped his fingers. "And if I had told you the truth about him, he'd probably just tell you that *I* was the crazy anarchist plotting to assassinate the President."

Bernard didn't bother to interrupt to tell him about the letter they'd found in which that was precisely what Pavoni had planned.

"So I got angry," said Jackson, no longer looking at Bernard and lost in the memory of the moment. His large shoulders seemed to broaden as he clenched his fists. "I swear I tried to walk away. For Eleanor. But then Tony grabbed my shoulder and said, 'You're not going anywhere.' And then—"

He stopped.

"And then?" Bernard finally asked.

Jackson took a big breath before looking up at Bernard. "I whirled around and pushed him away and he lost his footing and went tumbling down the side of the bluff."

Bernard heaved a sigh. So that was it.

"I swear I didn't mean to," Jackson entreated, his hands open in a pleading gesture now, watching Bernard's face. "It was an accident."

It was clear Jackson had come to the end of his planned speech.

But before Bernard could respond, Jackson appeared to change his mind.

He ran a hand down the back of his neck, sighed, and waved his hands. "I'm sorry." He shook his head. "It's really hard not to lie." He chuckled lightly. "The truth is: I pushed him on purpose."

"It wasn't an accident?"

"No," Jackson said firmly, looking directly into Bernard's eyes. "No, it was not an accident. I watched him bounce down with satisfaction." He smiled wanly at the thought.

Bernard nodded slowly. "Which is the real truth, Jackson?"

Jackson studied him. "It was murder, plain and simple."

Just like Eleanor, Bernard thought. *He wants to end up in jail with Eleanor. Like some awful Romeo and Juliet. If he can't be with her in life, he'll be with her in death.*

That was the truth behind his entire speech.

"You know," Bernard said slowly, "Eleanor may not hang. There's always the possibility that the courts push for insanity. She may end up in an asylum, may even one day be deemed healthy enough for release."

Jackson brightened. "You think so?"

"Yes." And Bernard meant it. "So which will it be, Jackson?"

The conman drummed his fingers. He didn't answer. Another few minutes passed.

This time, Bernard broke the silence. "How did Tony end up with London's identification?"

Jackson actually blushed and leaned back, rubbing the back of his neck as he avoided Bernard's eyes again.

"Well, I had to check on him, so I went down carefully and realized his face was decently bashed in—must've hit a rock or two as he rolled—and was unrecognizable. It was a sudden thought as I realized our build and hair color were similar enough that without his face..." He shrugged. "So I switched our calling cards, left my spectacles, and disappeared into the night."

"And the hobo?"

Jackson's eyes met Bernard's and widened. "You figured that one out, too? I thought for sure I'd fooled you."

Bernard decided he needn't admit he'd only realized the truth that morning.

Jackson whistled in appreciation. "You're better than I thought. The hobo was a simple matter of stealing some clothes off a wash line, tramping them up by rolling in dirt and oil and grease, messing up my hair and using a bit of tobacco to black out a couple teeth."

Bernard nodded. "I figured as much."

"Of course, normally my cons are for myself. I got the gig at Miss Mitchell's in order to try my hand at the oldest con in the book: landing an heiress. Instead...I met Eleanor..." He drifted off for a moment, his eyes no longer seeing the room in which he sat with Bernard.

Again, for one small moment, Bernard felt he was seeing the truth in Jackson, before he switched back to his story. "This time, it started out as helping a friend so I'd have a reason to stay in town while I figured out a way to spring Eleanor from jail."

"Why'd you go the nun route?"

"I heard they were one of the few outsiders being let in to see her. I couldn't fake a policeman—you guys are too close-ranked. That jailer would've called me out in a second. But a nun?"

Bernard shook his head. "What I meant was: why not a priest?"

"Only nuns were being let in." Jackson shrugged. "Woman to woman, I suppose. Didn't you know that yourself? Since you're the lead detective on her case?"

Bernard ignored the question. "So tell me this then: why didn't you just run after you murdered Pavoni? And don't say Eleanor again." He pointed at Jackson with his pen, stopping the word on his lips. "You could've left and let the heat die down. She's not going anywhere."

Jackson scratched his chin, seriously considering his answer. "I suppose...I suppose it was some form of conscience. I mean, I felt justified. After all, the man was planning to kill the President. I hoped if you thought the body was London you'd think it was just a suicide. And if you figured out Tony's connection, you'd find his hotel room and put two and two together yourself. If *you* figured out his plan, people would believe you."

Bernard nodded. "So you're telling me even a conman can put some faith in the law?"

Jackson smiled slightly and shrugged. "I guess I'm gonna have to."

Epilogue

Thomas stood in his uniform at the entrance to City Hall's first floor police station with his hands behind his back, waiting for the arrival of the newest prisoner. When he'd heard Officer Shannon had caught Daniel Ebner trying to catch a train out of town, he hadn't been surprised. If there was one man who knew how to catch the dirtiest lowdown criminals in town, it was William Shannon.

What *had* surprised him was the news that Jennings—Thomas couldn't help still thinking of the conman by that name—had been offered a full pardon by the President himself for uncovering and foiling the assassination plot on his life. Rather than taking him away in chains to join his lover in the cells, he'd been offered a job with the Secret Service, who'd said they could use a man with the ability to create and maintain multiple identities. Not for the first time, Thomas thought it was a good idea to get someone of Jennings's talent working for the good guys.

But Jennings had waved on the offer, saying he'd rather stay in Spokane, close to Eleanor. So instead, Private Detectives Gemmrig and Stauffer of the Spokane Detective Agency had offered him a job, which he'd snatched up happily.

Thomas shook his head. Some people had all the luck.

He couldn't believe he might end up working alongside someone like Andrew Jackson, aka London, aka Jennings.

At least Thomas had been pardoned and congratulated for his part in the catching of a criminal and the uncovering of an assassination plot. No job offers for him or Bernard, but he was just happy to see Bernard ensuring he didn't steal *all* the spotlight, and was sharing it rather nicely with Thomas this time around.

Of course, Bernard could never admit the assistance of his wife, her companion, or their past lodger, or they'd be back to losing their jobs again.

Thomas smiled and rocked on his heels as he thought of Marian's assistance. He wondered where she'd learned how to search a room so thoroughly...but he'd have plenty of time to learn that in the days to come, as she'd accepted his request to court, making him happier than he'd been in a long time.

It was turning out to be quite a good year for him. A good job, two solved murder cases under his belt, and now a beautiful woman to spend his off-time getting to know better.

Heavy, booted steps warned him of the approach of his brother well before Bernard joined him.

"Waiting for Ebner?" Bernard asked.

"Yeah."

"Did you hear Cousin Peter skipped town more cleanly than he did?"

"Oh, really?"

"Apparently so. No one's seen him since he turned in his last article."

"But we're certain this isn't yet another case of multiple identities?"

Bernard chuckled. "Yeah. Many people at *The Spokesman* swore they'd seen the two together, including Mr. Cowles."

Thomas nodded.

"I've been in communication with McKinley's head of security, George Foster," Bernard continued. "He's figured out who in the entourage was working for Pavoni, and is grateful for the tip-off from Jackson."

"Another point for Jennings."

"Just be grateful the commissioner didn't give *him* your job."

Thomas had to agree. "I hear Eleanor won't be with us for much longer."

Bernard nodded. "The smallpox has left the asylum so they'll be taking her under their care until her trial. The doctors seem quite interested in her case."

"As well they should be."

"Another telegram, Carew," Hollway said, coming up to Bernard and handing over the paper before returning to his desk.

Bernard's eyes scanned the telegram before handing it to Thomas with a friendly clap on the shoulder.

"Don't dawdle too long waiting for the anarchist. I've already got another case for us waiting at my desk."

Thomas grinned. He was finding he actually enjoyed working with his brother, within reason.

He turned to the telegram, which was from George Foster, and read: "Much appreciation Ofcr and Det Carew for assistance STOP Rcvd copy assassination plot via mail STOP Anarchists try again we'll be ready for them STOP."

THE END

TO BE CONTINUED IN *CRAZY MAIDS IN A ROW...*

Historical Notes

I've always loved historical fiction and its ability to breathe life into history, reminding us that these were real people in real places with real problems. I take great pleasure in weaving historical fact with fictional characters and events, so I'd like to share with you a little more about what historical goodies can be found within *Cupboards All Bared.*

Construction of the Great Northern Railroad Depot began on May 8, 1901. All references to the building were taken from articles printed at the time, which can be found on my website. There, I've collected a series of clipped newspaper articles referencing the timeline of the building of the depot and its iconic clock tower, which heavily influenced the events that unfold in the Spokane Clock Tower Mysteries, beginning with the first book, *Butcher, Baker, Candlestick Taker.* The clock tower is the basis for the timeline I've created for the book series in its entirety.

Another historical location would be Browne's Addition, which is known as Spokane's first neighborhood, established in 1883. Many of its homes are listed on the historical register, making it a perfect place to walk through to feel a sense of Spokane's past. Speaking of which: you can actually walk the crime scene as described in *Cupboards All Bared*! The bluff overlooking Hangman Creek lies just a five-minute walk from the Campbell House, both of which you can visit today. In fact, it was a visit to this area, now called Overlook Park, and the way my knees turned to jelly looking out and over the ravine, that inspired the death in this story.

The Campbell House was built in 1898 and was donated to the Eastern Washington State Historical Society in 1924. Because it was only lived in for twenty-six years, it is in fabulous condition, and currently is a living museum, set up in the decor of the house circa 1910, complete with actors playing the family and servants at Christmastime. I tried to incorporate as many visible aspects of the house that you can still view today as possible, like the annunciator call bell system, the confused collection of armor on display above the front door, and the rather pink reception room. The museum has done an excellent job of collecting as many historical artifacts as possible in connection to the Campbells' life in Spokane. The chair Marian discovers in Pavoni's hotel room at the Montvale was inspired by a musical chair that can be viewed at the Campbell House, which they didn't acquire until after their European tour in 1909, but I just had to get it in somewhere!

In 1901, the Campbells had five live-in staff. There were two maids, Matilda Peterson and Caroline "Carrie" Olsen, who were both Swedish, though they'd immigrated at very different times and were a couple years different in age. The three male employees were Edward Nelson, the gardener (who didn't manage to make an appearance in this book), Chung Lee, a Chinese cook who'd immigrated twenty years earlier, and Joseph Gladding, the

Ohio-born coachman who stayed with the Campbells until 1905. The only one of these staff members we have pictures of today is Joseph Gladding.

Amasa (pronounced a-MAY-sah) Campbell and Grace Campbell were as described, as was Helen Campbell, their only child. Descriptions of all three are based on portraits from 1904 that still hang in the Campbell House. After building a fortune in the mines of Idaho, Campbell moved his family to Spokane in 1898, and quickly became a leader and known entity in the city. His friendship with President McKinley was a real thing. According to *The Chronicle*, "Mr. Campbell and family are friends of the McKinleys, have known them for a good many years, and on that account they are the natural hosts of the distinguished travelers" (May 7, 1901). And in a letter Amasa wrote on May 11: "Grace and I are going to have the President with us for two days while he stops in Spokane. This is all arranged, and I guess we can take care of him."

President McKinley's visit to Spokane and all the references to the newspaper articles and facts regarding his visit are true, most of them taken straight out of *The Spokesman*, though the planned assassination attempt in Spokane was only inspired by the real one that would occur in September 1901. The McKinley Reception Committee was formed and headed by Chairman George A. Black. McKinley was supposed to board with the Campbells during his stay, and there was much planned for his visit in the manner of parades and speeches. Unfortunately, due to the health of Mrs. McKinley, he had to cancel his visit to Washington state. For a full outline of the events and to read the original articles as published in *The Spokesman-Review* and *Chronicle*, please visit my website.

Other than the Carew brothers, all the police officers mentioned in the book are real people. Desk Sergeant George Hollway, Jailer William Smith, Officer Walter Lawson, Officer William Lewis, Captain James Coverly, Chief William Witherspoon, Commissioner Henry Lilienthal, and Detectives Dougald McPhee, Alexander MacDonald, John McDermott, and Martin Burns were all active members of the Spokane Police Force in 1901. The private detectives of the Spokane Detective Agency, Richard Gemmrig and William Stauffer, mentioned at the end of the book were also real historical figures.

The governor of Washington in 1901 was John Rankin Rogers, though he died of pneumonia later that year. Dr. Nathan M. Baker was the coroner at this time, his office located in the Hyde Block around the corner from City Hall, which was on Front and Howard in 1901. Dutch Jake's Coeur d'Alene Hotel was a theater, bar, and gambling hall audaciously located across the street from City Hall.

The Montvale Hotel was built in 1899 by Probate Judge John Binkley as one of the first Single Room Occupancy hotels in Spokane. Binkley was praised as an "eminently public-spirited citizen, and one whose influence has been very sensibly felt in the development of the city" (Edwards, *History of Spokane County*). The descriptions of the interior are inspired by articles from the time and photographs taken before it was updated. Today it is a beautiful boutique hotel that can still be visited in its original location, though the entrance and the interior have been greatly changed.

The list of watchmakers Archie visits are taken from the Polk's City Directory from 1901 and are exactly as listed. Dodson's was a real jewelry store that only recently closed its doors after 131 years of business. Otto Kratzer was really the watchmaker at that time and the interior is described based on photographs from the time period.

The Spokesman-Review and *The Chronicle* were the main newspapers of 1901 Spokane. Both were owned by William H. Cowles by 1901, who moved them all into the Review Building, which can still be visited today. Reporters were not given bylines at that time, so I was able to introduce my own creations easily into the staff.

Sacred Heart Hospital still exists today after being founded in 1886 by Mother Joseph, an inspirational woman of incredible strength. According to the Spokane City Directory, the Sister Superior in 1901 was Sister Peter of Alcantara, and the hospital was located at "Front av n w cor Browne."

The Eastern Washington Hospital for the Insane, or "the Medical Lake asylum" as it was referred to in the papers of the time, officially opened in 1891. Per an article in *The Spokesman-Review*, Tuesday, May 7, 1901, they suffered a smallpox outbreak in the north wing of the women's side on May 6, which lasted for a few weeks, and worked perfectly for causing a lag in the Baker's arrival there until the opening of the next book...

The mining boom that occurred in Idaho began in 1883. Just as the Northern Pacific Railroad finished their transcontinental line that crossed through the upper panhandle of Idaho, Andrew Prichard led a prospecting group that discovered gold in a land already boasting silver and lead. People became millionaires overnight by investing in the mining companies, and in the railroads that were required to move the materials and people in and out of the panhandle. I recommend *The Coeur d'Alenes Gold Rush and Its Lasting Legacy* by Tony and Suzanne Bamonte for more information.

The disputes, riots, and unrest were not inspired by current events, but actually did happen, culminating in the creation of the Industrial Workers of the World, or "Wobblies," in 1905, whose fights against labor issues would fill the news well into 1917. Back in 1899, Levi Hutton claimed that he was forced to drive a train of dynamite into the concentrator at Wardner, and the place was put under martial law. According to N.W. Durham's *History of Spokane*, "mine-owners of the Coeur d'Alenes who wished to operate under martial law could do so only on condition that they would not employ members of the miners unions and the mine-owners acquiesced in this requirement." At a meeting which Campbell and Finch attended representing the Standard, Hecla, and Gem mines, "mine-owners decided to cooperate with the state and resume operations as quickly as forces could be organized: $3.50 to be paid at Burke, Gem and Mullan for all men underground; $3.50 for miners at Wardner, and $3 for 'muckers.'" Governor Steunenberg would be assassinated years later in 1905 for declaring that martial law. Campbell's thoughts on the matter, as related in this book, come from letters he wrote at that time, some of the lines verbatim straight out of his pen.

Similarly, Thomas's father's thoughts regarding reporters come from *Etiquette for Americans*, published in 1898. The menus planned and executed by Mrs. Curry and Signora Magro come from cookbooks of the time period. For more on this, visit my website, where you can also find a recipe for the best "Italian Cornbread" or "*Pane di granturco.*"

The books discussed by the characters were all written prior to 1901. Edgar Allan Poe's detective, Auguste Dupin, made his first appearance in "The Murders in the Rue Morgue" in 1841. Anna Katharine Green's debut mystery *The Leavenworth Case*, published in 1878, was a bestseller overnight, and introduced the world to the perceptive Detective Gryce, who would inspire the creation of Sherlock Holmes nine years later.

Robert Louis Stevenson's famous novella *The Strange Case of Dr. Jekyll and Mr. Hyde* was published in 1886, and is said to be inspired by a dream he had, though the dream was most likely inspired by articles published at the time concerning the mysterious cases of Felida and Vivet. The articles Roslyn reads regarding these cases can be found online under the titles listed in the story or via links on my website. Founded in 1874, *The Journal of Nervous and Mental Disease* is "the world's oldest independent scientific monthly in the field of human behavior." *The Scientific American* was established in 1845 and is one of the oldest magazines in the United States. Editions circa 1901 can be found online at archive.org. They make for absolutely fascinating reading.

And finally, the title of this book was inspired by a political cartoon I found from 1897, which can be viewed on my website. Drawn by Victor Gillam, it shows President McKinley as Old Mother Hubbard with a dog wearing the face of Uncle Sam, finding the cupboard, which has an image of the US treasury in deficit, bare.

To learn more about the history behind the book's events,

and to read the actual articles referenced, please visit my website at Patricia-Meredith.com.

Thank you for listening and reading!

Acknowledgements

First, I offer praise and gratitude to my Lord and merciful Savior, Jesus Christ, with whom nothing is impossible, for giving me these words and this story.

To my husband, Andrew Meredith—I love you more than you love me, no changes.

My kids, who enthusiastically ask when they can read Mommy's new book.

My parents and parents-in-law, whose faith, support, and encouragement have brought me to this moment.

Special thanks to Corin Faye, my editor and writing partner whose critiques literally forced me to re-write a third of the book, making it infinitely better for it.

To Rebecca Cook, whose voice has once more brought my story to life. Thank you for taking the time to look up all the foreign language pronunciations I threw at you this time!

Alex Fergus at the Ferris Archives and Ellen Postlewait at the Campbell House—without you two I would have been stuck in an infinite research loop! Thank you for helping me find everything I needed and more to ensure this book was an accurate historical representation of the Campbells and their environs.

Susan Walker, the Spokane Regional Law Enforcement

Museum Secretary-Treasurer, for offering access to hands-on research, as well as answering all my questions about detectives and police officers circa 1901 Spokane. Thank you for your continued enthusiasm for my work!

To the entire Crommelin family, but especially Miff, Mariad, and Patrick Serné, for compiling the letters of Marinus Crommelin into *Dear Mother*, a collection of letters sent home from Spokane in 1901, whose descriptions provided the basis for many of my characters' perceptions of their surroundings.

Special thanks to Jan and Tom Falconer, whose relationship greatly inspired that of Bernard and Roslyn Carew. Especially a big thank you to Jan, whose life in a wheelchair since the age of thirty has breathed heart into Roslyn's character. Jan, you are a gift. God is using you and He loves you even more than I do!

My amazing team of Beta Readers: Ben Armstrong, Jason Armstrong, Noelle Austin, Leslie Bryant, Kathy Buckmaster, Alex Fergus, Rachel Fergus, Anne Fischer, Kim Hammond, Leah Humenuck, William H. Keith, Katie Kessler, Maggie Meredith, Renae Meredith, Scotte Meredith, Su Meredith, Diane Meredith-Gordon, Lydia Pierce, Sarah E. Pounder, Andy Rizzo, Beth Rizzo, Catie Rizzo, Dean Rizzo, Jessie Rizzo, Sue Rizzo, and Carole Waters. All of you made this book better with your input!

And you, dear reader. The next book is coming soon!

Thank you all!

Photo by Angus Meredith

About the Author

Patricia Meredith is an author of historical and cozy mysteries. She currently lives just outside Spokane, Washington on a farm with peacocks, ducks, guinea fowl, chickens, and sheep. When she's not writing, she's playing board games with her husband, creating imaginary worlds with her two children, or out in the garden reading a good book with a cup of tea.

For all the latest updates, you can follow her as @pmeredithauthor on Goodreads, Instagram, and Facebook, and sign up for her newsletter at Patricia-Meredith.com.

www.ingramcontent.com/pod-product-compliance
Lightning Source LLC
Chambersburg PA
CBHW021810110726
47902CB00006B/1722